ROGUE: UNT

Remy placed his hand over mine, looking directly into my eyes. Still holding my gaze, he brought my palm up to his mouth and kissed it, sending tingles down my body.

"Hey! Cut that out." I snatched my hand away. "We're trying to be scientific, here."

"Biology is a science." Remy sank back down onto the stool, shaking his hand as if something had stung it.

I clenched and unclenched my hand, which still felt just like a regular hand. "All right, let's see if this works. What do I do?"

"Try something small. I learned that cards give, how shall I put it? The most bang for the buck." He gestured at my fridge, which was studded with business cards.

"Focus. Try to send your energy into it."

I frowned at the card with its smiling squirrel, focusing. "OK."

"Flick it at me."

I flicked the card, ready for the let-down of it not working, and then – bam! It exploded in the air.

MARVEL HEROINES

ROGUE
UNTOUCHED

ALISA KWITNEY

ACONYTE

FOR MARVEL PUBLISHING

VP Production & Special Projects: Jeff Youngquist
Associate Editor, Special Projects: Caitlin O'Connell
Manager, Licensed Publishing: Jeremy West
VP, Licensed Publishing: Sven Larsen
SVP Print, Sales & Marketing: David Gabriel
Editor in Chief: C B Cebulski

Special Thanks to Jordan D White & Jacque Porte

First published by Aconyte Books in 2021
ISBN 978-1-83908-056-2
Ebook ISBN 978-1-83908-057-9

Cover art by Joey Hi-Fi

Distributed in North America by Simon & Schuster Inc, New York, USA
Printed in the United States of America
9 8 7 6 5 4 3 2 1

ACONYTE BOOKS

An imprint of Asmodee Entertainment Ltd

Mercury House, Shipstones Business Centre
North Gate, Nottingham NG7 7FN, UK
aconytebooks.com // twitter.com/aconytebooks

For Holly Harrison, who keeps coming to my rescue when all is sturm und drang.

PART ONE

GAMBLERS & ROGUES

ONE

I turned the key in the ignition of my pickup truck and said a little prayer to the god of lemons and wrecks and zombie transmissions. The starter made a sound like it was clicking bad-fitting dentures, and then commenced to chattering and shaking like a chicken caught in a storm. Don't do this to me, Willie, I begged. I was already running late for work, on account of a series of unwise decisions earlier in the day. Now I had five minutes to make a fifteen-minute drive. Too bad I didn't have superpowers, like those East Coast mutant kids I followed on Instagram. A pair of big old angel wings would suit me just fine, so I could just fly myself out of this pissant Mississippi town.

I turned the key again, and this time my truck made a gasping wheeze of a sound, rattled and then died. *Damnit.* I'd named my '86 pickup after Willie Nelson, hoping it would prove as indestructible as the singer, but instead it was as temperamental as a boomer.

Just like my boss.

Touching the green Tulane charm hanging from my rearview mirror for luck, I climbed down from Willie's front seat, rolled up my sleeves and unlatched the hood. What the heck could be wrong? I'd only just replaced the dang fuel pump six months ago. After the last breakdown, I had considered letting the ancient pickup die the true death, but I kept bringing him back. I had to – Willie might be a cantankerous old frankentruck, but he was all I had to get me where I was going.

Untwisting the cap, I pressed down the Schrader valve, which instantly shot a jet of fuel up into my face.

Idiot girl. Well, that's what you get for rushing. I had nothing but my sleeve to wipe my eyes, which meant my favorite baby-blue hoodie was stained and ruined.

"What's goin' on, Anna Marie?"

Oh, God, it was Chet. I did not have the patience for him right now. Chet had seen my name on a piece of official mail and now it didn't matter how many times I told him to call me Marie, he insisted on using my full name.

Then it hit me. If I didn't want to call into work with car trouble again, then I was going to have to sweet talk my neighbor.

I pasted a smile on my face. "Oh, hey, sugar. Will you look at the fix I'm in?"

Chet set down the ladder he was carrying and puffed out his skinny chest. "Old Willie giving you a hard time?" He grinned at me, eyes gleaming under the brim of his Mississippi Braves baseball cap. At five foot three, with a hedgehog bristle of hair and a permanent scruff on his chin, Chet always reminded me of a slightly manic monkey. "Want me to take a look?"

"You are a prince," I said, even though Chet knew less about trucks than I knew about ballroom dancing. "But I am running so late already… I just don't know what to do."

Chet considered this, bouncing on the balls of his feet. "Well, I was about to paint over the damp spot in my wall before it rains again, but… oh, the hell with it. Let me put this here ladder away and I'll give you a ride."

"You are saving my life is what you are doing."

"Back in a tick." Chet jogged off to set the ladder near his apartment door. A hundred and fifty odd years ago, Sweetbriar Apartments had been a classic antebellum mansion with big white pillars, a wraparound balcony, and the kind of luxury only human suffering can buy. Now it was a crumbling old ruin subdivided into small apartments. When it rained, the ceiling leaked for a week and everything sprouted mold. Guess that's what you get for living in a place built on misery and unfairness, but hey, the trailer park was full, so it wasn't like I had a choice.

"Chet? That you?" Chet's mother opened the door to their apartment. Chet was in his mid-twenties, around five or six years older than me, but his mother kept him on a short leash.

"Just running an errand, Ma."

Dressed in hot-pink lycra leggings and an old Hello Kitty tee shirt, Scary Anne Billings looked straight from him to me, and I could just about see the mad coming off her. Scary Anne was as wiry and energetic as her son, but life had given her a few too many hard knocks and now she was a rage monkey, pure and simple. "Oh, no you don't. You ain't running off on your chores to go gallivanting with the likes of her."

But Chet was already starting his truck, and I regretted every irritable thought I'd ever had about him. "She needs to get to work, Ma."

"Don't you do it!"

Chet's truck gave a happy rumble, and he reversed out of his parking spot and started down the rut-filled dirt driveway. "She's already late."

"I won't keep him long," I called back over my shoulder as I opened the passenger door and hopped up next to Chet.

"It don't take long," Scary Anne called back. "How long did it take her to put that poor Robbins boy in a coma?"

Chet pretended he hadn't heard. "I'll be back afore you know it."

I waited till we had turned onto the paved road before speaking. "I really do appreciate this, Chet." I meant it. Not only was Chet giving me a ride, but he wasn't trying to put his hands on my thighs or asking questions about what exactly had I done to Caldecott County High's star quarterback. That was two and half years ago, back when I was a senior, and Cody was all better now, but Peck's a small town, and good gossip has to last a while.

Chet made a tsk sound and waved my thanks away. "You'd have done the same for me."

"Yeah, but I would've busted your chops about it."

Chet laughed, sneaking a look at me out of the corner of his eyes. "What you done to your hair?"

I tried to smooth it down in front, without much success. "I had the bright idea bangs might look nice. Forgot my hair is as wayward as I am."

"I think it looks real nice," said Chet, unwrapping a stick of Juicy Fruit gum and popping it in his mouth. I flipped down the visor and checked in the mirror. "It's only curling in five different directions." Least that made the white streak a little less noticeable. I was born with it, which is why at school the kids used to call me the Skunk.

Chet laughed. "You couldn't look bad if you tried, Anna Marie."

That was a barefaced lie. After the hair debacle, the only way I could lift my spirits was to binge watch *Broad City* on my phone while eating cheese crackers and painting my toenails dark purple. By the time I peeled myself off the fake leather couch and realized I had no clean shirt to wear, I was already fifteen minutes late for work.

"Hey, been meaning to tell you about something," said Chet, and started telling me about how a friend of a friend got hold of some tincture of mutant growth hormone and boiled it up in gin with a piece of bear root, and after that he could read minds. The story didn't end there, but Chet's stories tended to have a lot of middle, so I let myself tune him out as I leaned toward the open window and watched the trees going by, their green touched here and there with October bronze and gold and coral. It was a cool, misty day, just beginning to warm up, and as we got closer to town, I caught the smell of diesel left from the big trucks that hurtled through Main Street without stopping. We drove past a boarded-up house – the old stagecoach hotel – two gas stations, a squat redbrick building that was the town hall, a smaller boxy white brick building that was our post office, and Frank's pizza, which had been closed since Frank died some ten years back. Welcome to Peck, Mississippi, population 1,063. It was only a little over two hours from here to New Orleans and Tulane University, less if you drove fast, but a whole other world from here. As soon as I had enough money saved, I was headed for the Big Easy. I figured a waitress there could earn enough in tips to attend college part time, especially if she wasn't too terrible looking.

"So," Chet concluded as he pulled up in front of Karl's Diner, "what do you think, Anna Marie?"

"Sounds interesting," I said, figuring that ought to cover everything from a rock concert to reports of bears breaking into people's kitchens. Really, I needed to learn to half listen to people better. "Thanks again for helping me out."

"Only neighborly thing to do. Here, let me get the door for you." He leaned across me and the little hairs on the back of my neck stood up like a cat's fur rubbed the wrong way.

I grabbed my handbag and lurched away from him, yanking the door open and jumping down. "See you later, Chet!"

"But what about next Saturday? You on for trying out the bear root?" He was fairly jittering with excitement at the prospect. "It's authentic Indian medicine!"

I didn't know where to begin correcting him. Forget the politically incorrect term – or the fact that bear root was a Navajo herb, and we were in Choctaw territory. I'd watched a few documentaries, and all the studies seemed to show that most mutants came into their powers right around the time that girls got their periods and boys turned into idiots. If there had been even the teensiest chance of a potion that could transform me, I'd have been first in line to try it, but hey, I was a realist. I didn't have any special talents, unless you could count the fact that I was bad luck to anyone who got halfway close to me.

"Let's talk about it later, OK, Chet?" I grabbed my handbag and jumped down from the truck. "Hope your mom doesn't give you too hard of a time!"

At the reminder of what waited for him on his return, Chet's smile wobbled. He gave me a quick wave and turned his truck around, hightailing it back home. I wasted a moment watching him go, reflecting that Chet ought to be really careful about what he wished for. If I lived with Scary Anne, the last thing I'd want was the ability to read minds. I mean, seriously, that has got to be the worst mutant power ever. Give me super strength or flight or even ice-zapping fingers, but lord, spare me having to hear what people say in the privacy of their own minds when they're not trying to be polite.

On the other hand, if I could project my thoughts into other folks' heads, I might convince my customers to stop ordering tap water and asking for mayonnaise on the side. From there, it would be a short step to total world domination.

Unfortunately, I was just plain old powerless Anna Marie, and mayonnaise was likely to remain the bane of my existence for the foreseeable future.

I opened the diner door and faced my fate.

TWO

The bells on the diner door jangled as I swung it open. "Thank the lord," said Darnique from behind the counter. "I was running out of excuses, and Karl's in a mood."

I unzipped my oil-stained hoodie. "What is it this time?"

An old-timer lifted his cup, and Darnique grabbed the coffee carafe and poured him a refill. "Tiny never showed so the dishes are all piled up, the supplier brought the wrong ketchup, and those bangs do not suit you."

"Tell me something I don't know," I said, tying my black half-apron around my waist.

"Come by tomorrow and I'll work my magic on it." Darnique wore her own hair natural, usually in a high puff, and she was a master of taming wayward hair without chemicals.

"What about tonight after I get off work?" Usually, I would never push myself on a person, but Darnique had become a really close friend over the past year. Also, she lived conveniently close, in the apartment one flight up from mine, and I really did want her to fix my bangs.

She shook her head. "Sorry, girlfriend. I'm doing my mom's hair tonight."

"I'll just wait my turn, then." I glanced in the mirror over the counter and gave my bangs a quick pat down. "So what have we got goin' on here?"

Darnique grabbed her jacket off the hook and lowered her voice. "The counter folks are all taken care of, your old buddies Puke and Dolt are at table three waiting on a heart attack burger and heartburn fries, and Dolly Parton and her horse are sitting in the back, still decidin'." She zipped up her jacket and walked past the out-of-towners. "I have to head out now, but Anna Marie here will take good care of you."

"I was just about to ask you about the Greek salad." This was from the big-haired blonde. For some reason, folks always get nervous when their waitress goes off shift. You'd think they were switching surgeons mid-operation.

"Anna Marie will be right over."

I grabbed my pad and pen and sized up the newcomers. I started working as a waitress part time in my junior year, and I learned a lot about people. Most folks get a bit snappish when they're hungry, but some turn into toddlers and pitch a fit. The big-haired blonde looked like one of those types to me. She was wearing a lot of carefully applied makeup and some doctor had plumped up her cheeks and lips and probably her bust as well, but she had to be at least fifty. "Y'all ready to order?"

Dolly tapped her cheek with one glossy red nail. "How's the Greek salad?"

"I'm not a big fan of olives myself," I said diplomatically, "but some folks really like it."

"That's a no, Lucretia," said the other woman. Bev had called her a horse, but she wasn't unattractive – just a tall, broad-shouldered woman with a strong jaw, short salt-and-pepper hair and thick-lensed spectacles that made her eyes look huge. "Can you recommend one of the salads?" She had a bit of a foreign accent, maybe Russian or German.

"The cobb salad's my personal favorite." Not that I spent a lot of time eating salads, but when I did I liked my greens with lots of crispy bacon and avocado.

"You know what? Forget the dang salad. Give me a burger with the works," said Lucretia. "And fries." She handed me her menu and the sparkle on her diamond rings nearly blinded me. "Real diamonds, fake hair and boobs," she offered with a wink, and I decided I liked her.

"Since we're revealing trade secrets," I said, "you might as well know that there are more calories and fat in the salad than in the hamburger. As the old saying goes, don't try to order healthy at a diner."

"I will have grilled cheese and tomato," said the other woman, glancing up at me. Behind her thick spectacles, her brown eyes were as big as saucers. They gave me the weirdest feeling, like she could look right through me and see what I was going to do next. "And a coffee with cream."

"Good thing I remembered your lactose pills, Irene," said Lucretia, reaching into her purse.

"Be right back with your drinks." I forced myself to walk past table three, where Puke and Dolt – otherwise known as Duke and Holt – were sniggering over something on Duke's phone. "How y'all doing?"

Duke grinned at me with pure malice in his pale beady eyes. "Doin' just fine, Anna Marie. Picture of health – unlike some less fortunate." I tried not show how much he was bothering me. Duke and Holt had been on Cody's football team, and the two of them had blunt bull terrier faces and matching personalities. Of course they were going to blame me for what happened, even though Cody himself didn't hold any grudges. He was doing just fine now, working for the local sheriff's office. The fact that he never made a professional career out of playing football was not my fault.

"I'll just check on your orders, unless you need anything else?" I brought my pen to my pad, even though I didn't need it. I just wanted any barrier I could get between me and the testosterholes in booth three. Ever since graduation, the boys had switched from football to body building, and I had the suspicion that they were chasing their milkshakes with steroids.

"How about a little taste of your killer bod?" Duke made a kissy face and reached for me with his meaty hand.

I backed away. "Cut it out, Duke."

"Ain't she modest! Lookit them long sleeves," said Holt in a mocking voice.

"Yeah. What's up with that?" Duke leered at me. "You didn't used to cover up so much in school." Trust a bully to zero in on a weak spot. I tended to wear my shirts big so I could cover my hands with the sleeves. Maybe it was a side effect of being a waitress, but I liked to protect myself.

"In my line of work, you touch a lot of nasty things," I said pointedly, turning on my heel.

"And I hear you like nasty things," countered Duke, grabbing at my apron strings and pulling me back. "Ain't that right?"

I longed to punch Duke right in his twice-broken nose, but that was the curse of a service profession – you can't indulge yourself in open confrontations. "Give me a break, Duke. I don't hassle you at your work." Although lord knows he deserved hassle. Duke worked at the local garage, despite a natural-born incompetence around machines. I tried not to feel resentful that they hadn't hired me instead. I know my way around a combustion engine, and I could have learned the newer systems. But I was a girl, and Duke's dad used to work with his boss, and besides, I had never graduated high school. Although why that should matter, I never would understand.

There was a jangle of bells behind me and I turned to see that the new customer was a good-looking stranger in a trenchcoat and sunglasses. "Sit wherever you please," I said, trying not to stare. We don't usually get a lot of out-of-towners in Karl's Diner, and this one could have set off a Geiger counter with pure hotness.

"Thanks, chère." My heart did a little two-step, and Lucretia must have felt the same way, because I heard her say under her breath, "Oh, yummy, a Cajun."

"Please, Lucretia," said the companion, sounding pained.

"Sugar, I ain't tellin' him anything he don't already know," said the unrepentant Lucretia.

The Cajun took this in his stride, giving both women an easy smile as he sauntered over to the booth opposite Duke and Holt. The boys stiffened, bristling like junkyard dogs at this invasion of their territory.

"Here y'go." I handed him a menu, trying to seem casual but wondering what his eyes were like, behind the dark shades. Not that it mattered. Even if his eyes were plain as mud, he would still be delectable from the top of his unruly brown hair to the lean, slouchy grace of his athletic body, showcased in a weathered brown leather trenchcoat that looked like it had its own stories to tell. On another man, that coat would have seemed like an affectation. The Cajun wore it with casual irony, accessorized by the crease of a dimple in his left cheek. As I walked away, I felt like I'd forgotten how to coordinate my lower limbs, and I could hear Duke and Holt muttering rude things that I couldn't quite hear.

On the other side of the kitchen door, I was hit by a wall of steam and the heady smell of cooking burgers and fries. "Well, if it ain't Marie, here at last," said Karl, pointedly checking his watch. "Thank you for gracing us with your presence."

"My car broke down."

"The later you come, later you stay. And you're on dishwasher duty," said Karl, scowling down his beaky nose at me.

"Karl, I can't. I don't even know how I'm getting home tonight."

"Now, Marie. You know what I always say – you won't get anywhere in life if you don't step up and take responsibility for what you do. And what you don't do."

"Fine. I take full responsibility for being too poor to afford a new transmission. You can punish me with a raise."

"That kind of attitude is why you're never going to be anything more than you are right now," said Karl, puffing up like an irate turkey.

I was about to tell Karl that inheriting a greasy spoon was hardly an achievement when the bell dinged behind me. Duke and Holt's burger and pork sliders were plated and waiting on the sideboard. "Thanks, Norville," I told the short-order cook, snatching a fry off Duke's plate. "Give me a Jack Tommy and then burn one, drag it through the garden and pin a rose on it."

"Grilled cheese with tomato and a burger with the works," translated Norville, his long arms already in motion. He was wearing an old Popeye tee-shirt that matched the Olive Oyl and Bluto tattoos on his arms. He had one earphone in and one dangling on his chest, and I could make out the gravelly voice of Clarence Frogman Henry singing, "I ain't got no home."

Balancing the tray on my arm, I stole one last fry before banging the door open with my hip. As I placed Duke and Holt's food down, I was surprised to find them talking companionably with the Cajun.

"There's no way," Holt was saying. "I'd catch it straight away."

The Cajun appeared to consider this. "There's always that possibility." He glanced up at me again and gave me the merest flicker of a wink. He was shuffling a pack of cards with consummate ease. It was mesmerizing – I could barely see his long, nimble fingers touching the cards, which made it look as though they were moving by magic.

Holt salted his pork slider. "Dang, you are good."

Duke took a bite of his burger before responding to his friend. "Don't be such a sucker. This is some kind of trick."

"No trick," said the Cajun. "You play me, you catch me cheating, you win the pot."

I waited with my pen and pad ready until the Cajun turned his attention to me. I gave him a low-wattage version of my professional smile, just to make it clear I wasn't flirting. "Know what you want?"

I couldn't read his expression behind those dark shades. "Just coffee, thanks."

Oh, great, one of those. I left his menu, in case he decided to add something to his measly cup of joe. I went back to the kitchen to check on the ladies' orders and found that Karl had done the impossible – he had riled up Norville. "That's just plain racist, Karl."

Karl folded his arms over his chest. "You know me better than that. I hired you and Darnique, didn't I? You ever hear me say anything derogatory about black folks?"

Norville sighed. "You were being racist about mutants."

"Because they're different from the rest of us."

Oh, good lord, Karl must have been listening to that nutjob on satellite radio again. "Karl," I said sharply, "exactly why are you starting this now? Norville, where's my grilled cheese and burger?"

"Sorry, Marie." Norville turned back to the grill, but Karl wasn't ready to quit talking anytime soon. "Take my word for it, mutants are the reason we need our second amendment rights. How's an ordinary fellow going to defend himself against someone with superpowers if he don't have a gun?" Karl, like many people, judged others based on his own proclivities. If my boss had been born with a mutant ability, he would have used it to bully other people into submission. The idea that a person might not wield power like a cudgel would never have occurred to him.

Norville didn't trust most people around kitchen knives, let alone guns, and Karl was forever trying to convince his line cook of the error of his ways. Karl was yammering on about every man needing a minimum of three firearms when I carried the ladies' orders out to them. The women had spread a bunch of papers over the table, and I balanced the hot plates while the horsey one – Irene – made room for me to set down their food.

"Thanks for waiting," said Lucretia, as though I had a choice.

"No problem," I said, even though inside I was wondering why the hell they had to spread out so damn much when they knew they had food coming.

"You look a little put out," said Irene, surprising me. I was usually better at hiding my feelings.

"Mmm," said Lucretia as I finally managed to set the food down. "That smells delicious." She shook out a napkin and tucked it into her generous cleavage. Just as I was turning to leave, she added, "You know, I couldn't help but notice those good old boys giving you a hard time."

I waved it off. "Oh, I don't pay them no mind."

"Don't you?" The blue eyes behind those fake eyelashes were laser sharp. "Well, maybe you ought to." It struck me that she was the kind of woman who didn't put up with nonsense and that the big hair and the boobs and the honeyed voice were just distractions, like scent laid over a steel-tooth trap. "Here," she said, sticking one of her shiny fliers in my apron pocket. "Take a look at that later, when you have time." I smiled as best I could, wondering if she was selling some flavor of religion or one of them mail order makeup schemes. Either way, I wasn't interested in peddling anyone's product, so I dumped the fliers in the kitchen garbage without looking.

Things were slow enough after that for me to get a load of dishes stacked in the dishwasher, which left me looking hot and sweaty just in time for the early bird contingent, mostly gray hairs, a few with grandchildren in tow. Holt and Duke ordered beers and to my shock, they moved over to the Cajun's booth. Guess the stranger's charm worked in all directions. Duke and Holt played stud poker with the Cajun until Karl told them all to order something else or free the booth for someone who would. Naturally, they left no tip, but the big-haired Lucretia and friend made up for it by leaving me twenty-five percent of their bill, along with a pair of oversized red sunglasses with rhinestone accents. I thought about putting them in the lost and found drawer, but in my experience no out-of-towner ever came back for anything. The gaudy specs weren't my style, but hey, sunglasses always come in handy. I stuffed them in my handbag.

After that it was the usual dinner crowd of single men nursing beers, single mothers asking for more crayons, and couples too tired to talk to each other. I managed to finish another load of dirty dishes, and then it was nine. As I hung up my apron, I considered how I was going to get myself home. Norville didn't have a car, only a bike, because he lived above the diner. I didn't have the patience for any of Karl's late-night rants, so it looked like I was going to have to walk. I hoped my phone's flashlight would hold out for the next hour or so while I dodged the occasional truck rocketing down the road. I was on my way out, carrying a big garbage bag to put in the dumpster out back when I heard a scuffle and thump from the shadowy treeline just outside of the parking lot. Raccoons? A skunk? I turned on my cellphone's flashlight and walked out to check, cursing when I heard the backdoor slam behind me. Now I was locked out. Oh, well. I dumped the trash in the bin, waving my hand at the smell of rotten food and the swarm of midges. I was just about to walk around the building and head for home when I heard another sound, this one a muffled thump, followed by a deep grunt.

I was not alone out here.

THREE

I stood there, listening, and sure enough, someone gave a second grunt, louder than the first. Oh, man, I sure hoped I wasn't about to catch Duke or Holt getting lucky in the old graveyard. Just beyond the single streetlight illuminating Karl's parking lot, there was a patch of trees just losing their leaves, and a few old graves from the Twenties and Thirties, half hidden in the overgrown grass and weeds. Some of the graves were supposed to date back to the war between the states, but they were so worn you couldn't read more than a letter or two.

Turning off my phone's light, I stepped as softly as I could until I could see two shadowy figures, one big, the other smaller. No, I corrected myself, the big shape was actually two figures, one holding onto the other.

"Not so clever now, huh?" That was Duke's voice, followed by another thump, and a pained grunt.

"I'll give you back the money." The voice was the Cajun's, so weak it was barely recognizable.

"This ain't about money." Thump. "It's about not messing with Peck High's offensive line."

Dagnabit. I stood there for a moment, chewing on the inside of my cheek. I did not want to get involved here. Maybe the boys would just give the Cajun one last punch and then leave him, and then I could make sure they were gone before checking to see the stranger was all right.

Thump. Grunt. Thump. Clearly the boys were not ready to stop, even though their victim was no longer able to speak. All right, then. Taking a deep breath, I found Karl's name on my phone. Just my luck, no answer. I tried Norville. The thumps had changed tone and I realized they were kicking the Cajun now.

Without letting myself think about what I was going to do, I turned on my phone's flashlight and marched on over to the graveyard. "Hey! Duke! Holt! You quit hitting on that stranger before you kill him." It wasn't a plan, exactly, but maybe sounding all prim and teacherish would shake them out of the bloodlust crazy that had taken them over.

The boys turned, and for a moment I could have sworn they didn't recognize me. Was it just the spell of the violence, or something else? I forced myself a little closer, and got a good look at their eyes. "What on earth have you boys been doing?"

"MGH," said Holt, sounding almost giddy as he pulled a small dropper out of his pocket. "Mutant growth hormone boiled up in bear root. Bought it off Chet Billings."

Oh, Chet, you monkey-brained homunculus. Next time I saw his mother, I had a mind to tell her about her son's little side business. Trying not to look as nervous as I was feeling, I forced myself to give a little laugh. I had no idea what all was really in the concoction Chet had given Duke and Holt, but chances were it didn't mix well with stupid on steroids. "Come on, now. You paid good money for that nonsense, but you couldn't bother to leave me a tip?"

Duke took a step toward me, and I could feel the wild energy coming off him. "It releases your own untapped powers."

I wondered if that was true, or if it was just some nasty drug that made people rageful and mean. "Duke, use your head. If that junk was real, it would cost a fortune." Out of the corner of my eye, I could see the Cajun, face down on the ground. I felt a spike of fear, and then one of his hands twitched. It was swollen and bloody, but at least he wasn't dead, or at least not yet.

"Oh, it's real, all right." Duke grabbed me under the arms like I weighed nothing. I grabbed for my pocketbook as he lifted me up over his head. "I can feel it working."

"Put me down!"

"Not so tough now, huh?" Duke spun me until I dropped my bag and my phone, which landed with a loud crack. I looked down at Holt's laughing face and felt a cold chill race up my spine. I didn't know what was in that bear-root concoction, but clearly the boys were riding some kind of high. Ordinarily, they just aggravated me, but tonight there was something jumpy and savage in the air. It occurred to me that they might actually do me some harm.

My heart stuttered and kicked in my chest as Duke slid me down so I made contact with the front of his body. *Don't panic, think.* I had to find a way to manage this, because Cody's former teammates felt like wild dogs to me – liable to get worse if I acted scared and tried to run.

"My, my, aren't you strong?" I said, pushing playfully at Duke's chest. "You think that might be your power? Super strength?"

On the ground, my phone pinged, but I ignored it, turning my attention to Holt. "What about you? Can you tell what I'm thinking?"

It could have worked – Holt was frowning, trying to concentrate – but Duke's hands were pulling mine down his chest. "Can you tell what *we're* thinking?"

Holt's laughter sent another icy wash of fear through me. "Don't need to be psychic for that," I said, trying to make it a joke. "But seriously, Duke, what do you think your power might be? Have you tried anything? Like maybe you can fly now!"

Duke's hands clamped around my upper arms. "I'm not dumb. You're trying to trick me." He rubbed my right arm with his thumb, and I shivered at the unwanted contact as well as the unspoken threat. I didn't know if it was psychological on account of what happened with Cody or if I had developed an allergy, but I did not like being touched, even through my clothes.

"I'm not, honest," I said. "There's something different about you tonight."

"Yeah?"

For a moment, I thought I was going to get away with this. I'd charm Duke, and Holt would do whatever his buddy told him to. But suddenly Holt was behind me, his hands pulling at my jacket. "It's a hot night, Marie." He twisted my jacket, trying to pull it off me, and suddenly my arms were trapped behind my back.

"Yeah," said Duke. "Let's cool you off." He cupped my chin in his hand, and I caught a smell of engine oil and rank male sweat, with a faint chemical tang I could not place. From up in a tree, there was a rustling sound, and then an angry caw. We'd disturbed a crow. Too bad I couldn't ask it for a little help.

"You know, you got real pretty eyes," he said, and out of the corner of those eyes I could see the flutter of a large bird. It gave two more angry squawks, as if objecting to Duke's behavior. "I can't tell if they's gray or green," said Duke, bringing his face within a few inches of mine. "Maybe I need to take a closer look." If my stomach hadn't been clenched tight with nerves, I might have found this a little funny, in a pathetic, creepy sort of way. In his addled little brain, Duke thought he could romance me, with his buddy helping out. He was such an idiot – but in this situation, an idiot could be as dangerous as a genius.

Then he touched the curve of my cheek, his thumb brushing the corner of my mouth, and his eyes went wide, like he'd touched a live wire. I should have been scared, but instead I felt a hot rush of mad coursing through me like a wave. Not thinking twice, I head-butted Duke hard, and to my shock he went flying back.

"Sweet jumping Jesus," said Holt as Duke slammed into a gravestone on the way down.

Holt looked down at his unconscious friend, then back at me. "Lordy, Anna Marie, you planning on killing the whole football team?"

"You best not come at me again," I warned, and in that moment I felt so strong and sure of myself that I didn't question the wisdom of challenging an idiot juiced up on steroids and Chet's mystery gunk.

Holt seemed to swell with outrage. "Who the hell do you think you are?"

I looked straight in his eyes, feeling my own outrage sizzling through me. "I'm a ticked-off Southern woman, hoss. Cross me and I'll shuck your Rocky Mountain oysters and stuff them down your throat."

"That's not right," said Holt, and then he came at me. I sprang forward and ran at him like I'd practiced it a hundred times, plowing into him shoulder-first like a linebacker.

Next thing I knew, Holt was on the ground under me. As I got up, the skin of my bare stomach brushed his hand, and Holt's eyes went wide and then blank, like someone had turned off his lights. What the Sam Hill was happening tonight? It felt like my head was buzzing. Was it something in the drug Holt had taken? Duke had hit his head on a gravestone, but that did not explain what had happened to Holt.

There was a low groan from the ground – the Cajun. "Hey," I said, my body still thrumming with adrenaline as I walked over. "Can you hear me? Are you conscious?"

"Unless this is a very bad dream." The Cajun was still lying face down, and I tried to recall my ninth grade first aid course. Don't move the injured person if you suspect a neck injury. But what if he couldn't breathe lying on his stomach?

"Maybe you'd better roll over. If you can," I added.

"I have lost my sunglasses." He made a move with his hands, as if feeling around for them, then grunted in pain.

"Were they very expensive?" The moment the words were out, I regretted them. "Listen, I'll do my best to find them tomorrow, but I think you might need to go to the hospital."

"No hospital." He got himself into a sitting position, his hair in a tangle over his eyes.

"You in trouble?"

He glanced up, then quickly covered his eyes with a banged-up hand. "Let's just say I prefer to keep a low profile." He took a sharp breath. "Damn, but they did a job on me."

"What's hurting?"

"Head. Ribs. Hands." He gave a wry shrug. "Dignity."

"Because you couldn't fight off two ex-football thugs? Sugar, you need to cut yourself some slack."

"Ah, chère, you are a balm to my wounded ego." He started to lower the hand shading his eyes, then brought it back up.

"Your eyes hurt? That could mean a concussion."

He took a moment to consider this before looking up. "They hurt. How do they look?"

His eyes were dark shadows, but I caught a glint of red. Shoot, could his eyes be bleeding? I shivered. "Like you need a doctor to check you out."

He put his hands on the ground and grunted in pain. "There are people looking for me who have connections." He pushed himself up, then turned to vomit onto Hiram Mulaney, Gone to His Maker 1862.

"You renting a room at the B & B in town?" Out-of-towners had the choice of staying at the Historic Earl Van Dorn House bed and breakfast where you could read about how the short and randy confederate general had been shot dead by a jealous husband, the Peck Village Motel, where you could admire the stains left on the bed, wall and floors by previous visitors, or the Holiday Inn outside of town, where you could enjoy the fact that you were halfway outside of town and on your way someplace else.

"Just passing through."

I could feel my lips thin, just like Aunt Carrie's did when she was disapproving. "So what's your plan? Spend the night out here, bleeding?" It might only be mid-October, but the nights could get cool. I didn't think the Cajun would do too well in his current state if he spent the whole night lying on the cold ground with only his trenchcoat to cover him.

"I have a car."

Of course he had a car. What had I been thinking? Our little town wasn't on the Greyhound bus route to anywhere. I glanced over at the Cajun, and was alarmed to see his eyes were shut again. "Stay with me, now. Where's your car?"

"In front… of the diner."

I thought about it. "What's your name?"

He hesitated a moment before responding. "Remy. And who are you, mon ange?"

"Name's Marie." I felt around on the ground for my phone, hoping my fingers wouldn't encounter any dog poop. "Think you're in shape to drive?" My fingers closed on something cool and metallic. Thank you, lord. I turned on the flashlight and started looking for my handbag, noting the way Remy flinched when the light came on.

"I can manage."

I considered what I was about to suggest. In my head, I could hear Darnique telling me not to pick up waifs and strays, and Aunt Carrie telling me that the devil was often as not a voice inside your head. I could also hear my momma, walking up to a coyote in a steel trap and telling eight year-old me that she wouldn't get bit. "You always take a chance when you get close to someone," she had said, "but mostly it's a chance worth taking." That coyote had stared at my mama and I had just known it was going to snap her finger clear off, but when she pressed down on that trap and it sprang open, darned if the coyote didn't lick her wrist before bounding off.

Something about Remy reminded me of that coyote.

My hands closed on the soft leather of my handbag, a sweet

sixteen present from Aunt Carrie back when there was some sweetness between us, and I realized I had made my decision. "Say, Remy, how about you let me drive? I'll take us back to my place."

That surprised him. "Chère, that would be – I would be most grateful to you."

"You'll still sleep in your car," I said, before he got the idea that he'd be spending the night in my apartment. "But I got some first aid type stuff. I'll fix you up as best I can. Fix you a can of soup, if you like."

His eyes met mine, and in the weak and partial moonlight I thought I saw a gleam of red. Lord, he wasn't bleeding into his eyes, was he? Maybe this was all a terrible mistake.

"You are as wise as you are beautiful," said Remy.

"Talk like that, I'll leave you here," I replied. As I got my arm around Remy's waist, I was careful to keep all pressure off his injured ribs. I glanced back at Duke and Holt, who were still out cold, and realized I couldn't just leave them like that.

There was a soft caw, and I looked up to see the raven perched on a low branch. I had the crazy thought that the bird was watching me to see what I would do next.

"Hang on a sec." It was after nine, so the sheriff's office would be closed. I didn't want to call the state police for a local matter, so I texted a number I hadn't used in over a year and a half, and told Cody where to find his old buddies.

Then I half walked, half dragged Remy through the alley and onto the street, and poured him into the passenger side of his car – a Pontiac Firebird Trans Am, painted black with the distinctive flicking tongue phoenix decal on the front. Ordinarily, I would have been smacking my lips at the prospect of driving one of the last American muscle cars. At the moment, though, I was shaking with nerves, and the Firebird was just a means of hauling my tired ass home. I had to feel in his pocket for the keys before buckling him in, and as the engine turned over I saw headlights coming down the road.

I caught a glimpse of Cody's face in the window of the sheriff's car as he slowed down and started lowering his window, but my stress bucket was full to overflowing, and I could not handle talking to him tonight. I gave my erstwhile boyfriend a happy wave and kept on going.

Remy swiveled his neck to look behind us at the sheriff's car. "What are you doing? You cannot just breeze by the police!"

"It's OK, he's my ex."

"And that makes it better?"

Remy had a point. I glanced in the rearview mirror to make sure that no flashing red and blue lights were following me, and breathed again when I saw Cody turning into the parking lot. It was only much later, back in my apartment, that I remembered that I had cut myself bangs earlier in the day. I stared at my own reflection, surprised and unhappy with myself and acutely aware of the stranger asleep on my couch. I should have woken him up and kicked him out, but he looked so banged up it seemed cruel not to let him stay.

Well, I reasoned, as I took one last look at my butchered hair, maybe I needed a visible reminder that quick, impulsive decisions can leave a body with lasting regrets.

FOUR

Darnique was not exactly pleased with me. "You crazy, letting a strange man sleep on your couch?" She had come down the stairs from her apartment in yellow satin shorty pajamas and a purple robe, her hair wrapped in a purple silk turban. My front door opened into my postage-stamp sized kitchen, and she had hoisted her beauty case onto the counter and gotten halfway through a list of things her mother had done to annoy her before I could get a word in about the man asleep on my couch.

"Where's your sense at?" Darnique lifted a dangerously sharp pair of haircutting scissors from her case. "He could be an axe murderer!"

"Can you lower your voice?" My kitchen was divided from my living room by a formica counter and a row of stools, which meant the couch that the axe murderer was sleeping on was less than ten feet away. Luckily, Remy didn't so much as twitch. "I don't think we're in any imminent danger here." I had meant to send him out to his car, honest I had, but the man had just nodded off on the couch, his lips white from clenching his teeth.

It would have taken a stronger woman than I was to wake him up and kick him out.

Darnique toed off her flip flops and then padded over to Remy. "You sure he's not dead?"

Alarmed, I walked over and took a closer look. There was bruising under the stranger's eyes, a cut on his eyebrow and lower lip, and his left hand was swollen up something awful. I couldn't see his right hand, but it hadn't looked any better last night, when I'd bandaged him up and given him Tylenol. Okay, so he was chewed up like an old dog toy, but there was still some play left in him – his chest, bare under my patchwork quilt, was still rising and falling. "Don't scare me. I already have enough of a complex about putting out boys' lights."

Darnique snorted. "Well, I can see that you didn't exactly dress to seduce this boy."

"You kidding? This is my most seductive nightwear," I said, pouting as I performed a little model walk in my Grumpy Bear sleep shirt.

Darnique laughed. "Fair enough. Now make me some coffee and go back to the beginning."

I measured out the coffee grounds while I filled her in on the previous evening's excitement. "So," Darnique said as I poured the coffee into the souvenir dinosaur mug we both liked best, "what kind of trouble you think he's in?" As Darnique took the first sip, the heat of the coffee turned the dinosaur's skin invisible, revealing the skeleton beneath.

"Nothing violent," I replied, taking a sip of my own black coffee. "Duke and Holt really did a number on him, and he barely fought back."

"So how did you convince them to let pretty boy here go?"

"I fought them off."

Darnique lowered her chin and examined me through pretend spectacles. "Uh huh."

"No, really." I took down a box of quick grits and shook it at her.

"Sure, I can always eat. But what are you talking about, you fought them?"

"Duke was getting pretty handsy."

Darnique's eyes got wide. "So, what did you do – slap him?"

I pretended to read the directions on the box of grits, too embarrassed to look her in the eye. "Actually, I managed to knock both of them out."

"You what?"

"I guess it must have been the drug or whatever moonshine they were drinking. Maybe it messed with their balance? It's not like I know any special ninja self-defense moves."

Darnique shook her head. "Well, that's pretty peculiar, I grant you that."

I inspected my block of cheddar cheese, which had sprouted a green stubble of mold. "Guess that drug riles you up and then knocks you out. Bet they would have passed out even if I never came along." I could tell, even without looking, that Darnique wasn't buying this. Heck, I wasn't buying it myself. That wild rush of mad energy I had felt couldn't be explained away by the fact that the boys had taken bear root and mutant growth hormone. After all, I hadn't taken the drug. Since I didn't have an explanation, I tried to change the subject. "Anyways, I called the sheriff's office, and passed Cody on my way out."

"You talk to him?"

"Nah." I located my paring knife and started shaving the mold off the cheese.

"This the first time you seen Cody since that night?"

I nodded. "We did text a few times and we talked over the phone about a year ago, but this is the first time I've run into him in person." In a way, I was grateful that I hadn't bumped into him earlier, when I was still raw with guilt and missing him like crazy.

Darnique gave a low whistle. "You've got more drama going on than Netflix. So," she said, glancing over at the lump of man under the blanket on my couch, "this just some dogood Samaritan deal?"

I shrugged. "He is kind of glorious when he's not all banged up." It wasn't so much his face. It was a nice enough face, lean and foxy and sharp, when it wasn't bruised and swollen. What made him glorious was what my hippie mother would have called his vibe – the electric quality of his attention, combined with the lazy innuendo of his charm. Even when he'd been fighting not to show how much he was hurting last night, I had felt the tug of attraction.

Not that I had any intention of acting on it.

Darnique nodded, as if coming to a momentous decision. "All right, then. Let's fix those bangs of yours."

An hour later, I had adorable wavy bangs. Darnique had also dyed a second stripe of white, so instead of looking like a skunk, I was rocking a modern take on Bride of Frankenstein. Our grits had congealed into a lumpy mess, but we ate them anyway, with lots of milk, a tiny bit of unmoldy grated cheddar and a healthy dash of Crystal hot sauce.

Just as we were finishing, Remy woke up with a start.

"Easy there," I said, walking over with a mug of reheated coffee. "How are you feeling?"

He squinted up at me. "Grateful," he said. "I don't suppose you found my sunglasses last night?"

"Head hurting? I didn't see your shades, but I might have a pair for you." I handed him the coffee and closed the dented blinds to shut out some of the sunlight. Remy lowered his face in the mug, as if he were trying to inhale it rather than drink it. I'd fixed it with cream and sugar, because he'd gone without any dinner last night.

"Keep track of how much he owes you," said Darnique flatly. "Food and board and whatever else he convinces you he needs."

"Remy, meet Darnique," I said as I rummaged around in my junk drawer for a spare pair of aviators. "She's here in case you're an axe murderer."

Remy looked down as he sipped his coffee. "What's the verdict?"

Darnique tapped her cheek with one long nail. "I'm leaning toward con artist."

He put his head down over the mug and inhaled. "You do me wrong. I am an honest thief."

Darnique tilted her head. "You know, I think I believe you. Even if you can't look me in the eye."

"Leave the boy alone. His head hurts." Then I remembered – sunglasses. I fished around in my handbag and handed Remy the red rhinestone-studded pair. "These got left in the diner last night."

Remy held them in his hand, considering. "This will alleviate my pain, but I may hurt your eyes a bit, no?"

"Only when the light hits the rhinestones." I went over to my freezer and found the package of peas I had used on his hands last night. "Here," I said, handing them over. "Let's get that swelling down."

Darnique picked up Remy's empty coffee cup and brought it over to the kitchen sink. "What did Holt and Duke do to you?"

"Stomped on my hands." Remy gingerly bent and unbent his fingers.

Darnique ran water in the dirty dishes. "Lucky they didn't use a two by four. So, what did you do to rile them up? Besides fleecing them?"

"They generously offered to share in a recreational substance. I did not partake." Remy gave a little shrug. "They took offense."

Darnique and I exchanged a look. "They offered you a drug?" I searched my mind for a moment and then remembered what Chet and Duke had called it. "Was it mutant growth hormone?"

Remy nodded. "I prefer to keep a clear head unless I know the setting and my companions very well."

"Wise choice." Darnique packed up the last of her hair dye and scissors in her case. "Well, Anna Marie, I had best be getting back to my mama before she melts down. You take care of yourself, hear?" She looked over at Remy. "And you watch yourself with my girl there."

Remy spread his battered hands. "You do not know me, but I assure you – I would never repay kindness with evil. Besides," he added with a wry smile, "in my current condition, I could hardly offer much of a threat to her."

Darnique paused at the door. "Oh, I'm not worried about Marie. She knows how to take care of herself. I'm telling you to watch yourself, because the last boy who messed with her? He ended up in a coma." It was a great parting line, but unfortunately, Darnique couldn't quite land the exit. My doorknob was loose and Darnique couldn't work it properly while holding her case. I juggled the knob open for her, narrowing my eyes to show her I did not appreciate the whole "killer cooties" warning. I'd heard enough of that in the past eighteen months to last me a lifetime.

"Least your bangs look nice," she said by way of apology, and then I was alone with Remy.

"Don't hurt me," he said, the moment I turned around, and I barked out a surprised laugh.

"Don't pay her any mind. She's just protective."

"Nice to have friends," he said.

"You want more coffee?"

He smiled. "If the coffee is strong, then my answer is always yes. But there's something I need first."

I looked at him blankly. Was he making a move?

"The bathroom?"

God, I was an idiot. "Of course! Sorry. Over there."

He paused, draped in my quilt, and something flashed across his face too quickly for me to read. "Thank you," he said at last, and then, with a flash of humor, he draped the quilt over his shoulder like a toga before walking to my tiny bathroom.

Damn, was there anything embarrassing I might have left out? I had never had a guy over to my place before, and there was something strangely intimate about having a man in the most personal part of your home. I glanced in the mirror over my sink, and saw that some of last night's mascara had collected under my right eye. I scrubbed it off, and wondered if I should put on some lipgloss or something. No, that would look like I was fishing for something. Was I fishing for something? I was pretty sure that I was not. I had a two-year plan for getting myself out of

Peck, Mississippi, and hooking up with attractive strangers was not any part of it.

Still, I ought to feed the man. Darnique and I had finished the grits, but I still had some bread, so I made cheese toast and hoped it wouldn't hurt Remy too much to chew. I was just looking for the hot sauce, in case Remy liked it on everything the way I do, when the doorbell rang. I looked around, trying to find what it was that Darnique had left behind.

"Back so soon?" I had the door open before I realized my mistake. The woman standing on the other side of my door looked at me as though she could see through my skin.

"I swore I would never visit you until you came to me with a full apology," said my Aunt Carrie. I swallowed hard, placing one hand reflexively on the base of my throat. My aunt was one scary customer. At first glance, she looked like an elf, with her short blonde pixie cut and tiny frame. "But as a Christian, I knew I had to make the effort before you fall even further from grace." On a closer look, you noticed the wrinkles that gave her a permanently disapproving look and the baleful left eye that didn't quite track with the right, and you realized she was a malignant elf in a pastel flowered dress, on a mission to sour your milk and ruin your day.

I considered closing the door in her face, but my hand just wouldn't do it. Aunt Carrie had taken me in and saved me from going into the foster care system, and, in the beginning she had been strict but kind. "It's kind of you to drop by," I said carefully, "but I assure you, my soul does not require saving." Even as the words left my mouth, I wondered how she had heard about me taking a stranger home.

"That is not what I hear." Aunt Carrie took a deep breath. "I hear you got into some trouble with more of those football boys."

Oh, lord, that meant she didn't know about Remy. And there he was, in my bathroom. What was this going to look like to her? Not that I should care what it looked like, I reminded myself. "That was all their fault. They were beating up on a customer. I had to step in before they did him some permanent damage."

Aunt Carrie shook her head. "And what made you think that you ought to get involved, Anna Marie?"

"They were likely to kill him!"

"Then why not call the police straight off? Honestly." Aunt Carrie's powder pink mouth compressed into a thin line. "You're just like your mother – bound and determined to sniff out trouble."

My mother and her sister had both been bound and determined to find some greater meaning to life. For my mother, that had meant joining a group of dangerously idealistic hippies. A cult, you might call it. Of the two sisters, I tended to think that my mother had been the saner one. "I thank you for your concern, Aunt Carrie," I said, not trying to inject much warmth in my voice.

Aunt Carrie blinked. She hadn't expected to be dismissed so quickly. The old me would have bitten my tongue, too conscious of what I owed her to say what I felt. Living on my own had made me bolder. "Anna Marie," she said, her voice softer and almost motherly, "tell me something. Do you regret what happened between us? Because I do."

That brought me up short. "You do?"

"I have prayed on it, and I have come to see that maybe I made a mistake. Maybe I needed to spend less time hating the sin and more time helping the sinner." She reached out for my hand, her dry fingers just brushing mine. "Come on home and let me bring you back into the fold."

I felt a rush of prickling heat all up my spine and jerked my hand away. Her eyes sparked with hurt, and I wished I could explain the awful feeling that left me tasting metal in my saliva. "I wish I could," I said. "But there's something wrong with me. I don't think I'm bad the way you think I am, but can't be good the way you want me to be." I could have said more, explained about wanting to go to Tulane and study psychology, but Aunt Carrie thought the city of New Orleans was the devil's playground and psychology was his infernal device for excusing sin. Besides, she hadn't really come here expecting to save me. She just wanted more proof of how unsalvageable I was, so she could tut-tut about me with her church friends. In her mind, I had a streak of wrongness that ran through me like the shock of white in my hair. That was the real reason I had left home after the Cody incident – I couldn't bear the dark version of me I saw reflected in her eyes.

Truth to tell, though, I hadn't managed to shake off the sense that maybe there was something defective in me – something hungry and bad that made me a danger to anyone who dared to get close.

"I would like to leave this with you, Anna Marie." Aunt Carrie fished around in her bright green straw handbag. She pulled out a thin booklet with the title *Leading Lost Lambs Home: A Christian Guide to Reclaiming Virtue.*

"I'll be sure to give it a look," I said, mostly because I was dying to get Aunt Carrie out of there before Remy emerged from the bathroom.

Aunt Carrie turned to leave, then stopped and looked over

her shoulder at me. "I know you blame me, Anna Marie, for not letting you back in my house after the incident with that boy."

Oh, sweet suffering succotash. "This is not the time for discussing this."

"But I felt that I could not in good conscience allow you to flout my rules while you still lived under my…" Aunt Carrie's eyes went wide, and I knew what she was seeing – a whole lot of half-naked Cajun. "Oh my."

I closed my eyes for a moment, as if that could make the whole situation disappear. "Oh, shoot me now."

Aunt Carrie blinked hard. "I did not realize…" She paused, then, with a visible effort, gathered herself. "I should leave." She looked at me like I was an old dog she was going to have put down and said, "I will pray for you, Anna Marie." She gave a stiff nod and turned on her heel. I imagined she would head off to one of her churchy friends, to console herself with tea and peach cobbler and assurances that she had done everything in her power to bring me up right. There would be a veiled reference to my father and bad blood.

By lunchtime, everyone in her church would know what a harlot I had become.

Part of me wanted to run down the hall and yell after her, "I was just being a good Samaritan!" Another, less gracious side of me had the inclination to shout that I had the perfect right to cavort with unwashed Cajuns in my own dang apartment.

"I just mistimed my entrance, I think?"

I closed my front door and summoned a weak smile. Remy was standing bare-chested in faded blue jeans and sunglasses. "It's all right. She was already convinced that I'm a fallen woman."

"And now she has fresh proof, eh?" Even bruised and swollen, the man radiated charm. "I am sorry to be the cause of conflict."

"Fear not, sugar, for you too can be saved!" I held up the booklet, then opened it at random: "Even though your virtue cannot be regained, you can model yourself on the Magdalen, and save your soul."

Remy murmured something in French, then took the booklet in his swollen fingers and tossed it across the room, where it landed perfectly inside my garbage can.

"Nice throw." My French is passable, but mostly I hear trash talk or descriptions of food, so it took me a moment. "Something about the condemnation being more criminal than the crime? I must have missed that bit in Bible school."

"It's not in the Bible. It's Montaigne."

I nodded as though that meant something to me.

"My foster father was a student of philosophy," he added, and I understood that he was revealing this on purpose, because he understood that I didn't have family the way most folks do. I cleared my throat, wanting to ask a question but suddenly aware that Remy was standing awfully close.

Before I could form the words, my cellphone rang. "One sec," I said, wondering if Aunt Carrie had decided to tell me exactly what she thought of me. The name that flashed on my phone was the last one I was expecting to see. Although, on second thought, I suppose I might have predicted this.

I turned my back on Remy. "Hey, Cody," I said softly.

"Hey, Anna Marie." His voice was even and professional, and I felt a funny twist in my stomach. When we were dating, he always used to call me AM, which made me feel like one of the cool kids. "I saw you last night while I was answering a call."

"I know," I said, deciding it was best to come clean. "I was the one that called it in. Sorry, I know I should have stuck around."

"Yes," he said, finally sounding a bit awkward. "About that. Wonder if you could stop by the station to make a statement this morning?"

"This morning?" I glanced over at Remy, who was making a good show of being preoccupied with checking his own messages. "Can't I do it like this? Over the phone?"

"Sorry," said Cody, and briefly, I thought he was going to say something personal.

It took me a moment to process what he actually did say next. "But Duke and Holt are saying that you and this Cajun fellow attacked them. They're wanting to press charges."

FIVE

Despite what my Aunt Carrie and most of the fine churchgoing folks of Peck thought of me, I had never been inside the police station before. I had been in the village courthouse, on a school trip back when I was in eighth grade, though, and the police station had the same 1950s look, with dark, very blocky wood desks and partitions and walls painted a sickly pale green. There was a smell of wood polish and dust, and the hum of some kind of machinery. On a bench in the corner, an old man was telling a female officer that he damn well knew where he lived. He lived in his house.

Somewhere in the back, I knew, there was a cell with bars on it, but I couldn't see it from here. I wondered if there was any chance that I was going to wind up viewing those bars from the inside. I felt a surge of panic at the thought of being locked up with a bunch of prisoners who would sniff out the fear in me and a batch of guards who would look at me with Aunt Carrie's cold-eyed judgment. After that, I could say so long to my job at Karl's Diner, and there would go all my plans for college.

"Hey, Marie."

For a moment, I hardly recognized Cody. The frohawk I remembered was shaved into a buzz cut that went with the short-sleeved beige deputy's uniform and shiny badge. I remembered him saying that the best way to get rid of racism in the police force would be to recruit more black officers, and I hoped he was content with his career and not still dreaming of football.

"I'm sorry about this," he said, and then Sheriff Schutte came up behind him and cleared his throat.

"I'm happy to answer any questions you have, Cody." I could see Schutte's face pinch at that, so I said, "Sorry, I mean, Deputy Robbins."

Cody started to pull up a chair for me, stopped, glanced back at his boss, and then sank back into his own seat. Schutte was plump, bald and freckled, the beige uniform pulled over his belly. Was it just my reputation, or was I doing something wrong already? I had dressed for my interrogation in a dark green wrap dress and low heels, and now I worried that I looked like I was trying to be flirtatious instead of serious.

Cody pressed a button and woke his computer up. Behind him, Schutte made a grunting sound, and Cody reached into a drawer and grabbed a steno pad and a ballpoint pen. "All right, Anna Marie. Now, can you walk me through the events of last night, in your own words?"

I took a breath and started talking. When I got to the part where I reported that two men were unconscious in the cemetery behind Karl's Diner's parking lot, Cody and Sheriff Schutte exchanged glances.

"So, what happened to the other fellow?" Schutte's voice was bland, but his flat gaze made it clear he was just waiting for me to put a foot wrong and perjure myself. "You just leave him there, too?"

I bit the inside of my cheek. Here was the sticky part. I still didn't know whether Holt and Duke had concocted some full-blown crazy pants story or served up some half-baked version of the truth, embellished with nastiness and garnished with spite. Either way, I wasn't sure if I should admit to bringing Remy home. For all I knew, he was long gone – assuming he could see well enough to drive his Buick down the driveway.

I wondered if I had made a mistake, trusting him alone in my place. It wasn't as though I had a lot to steal, but I couldn't afford to lose what little I had. My favorite silver acorn earrings and grandma's gold and pearl brooch. My ancient laptop. The secret stash of tip money I hid under my mattress. That was the first place a thief would look.

Cody cleared his throat. "That wasn't your car you were driving, now, was it?" Schutte made a grunt and looked disgusted. Clearly, he was going to have some words with Cody when all this was over. But I was grateful that Cody had made it clear that if I told anything other than the truth, I was going to get myself in even deeper trouble.

"No," I admitted. "It belonged to the fellow Duke and Holt were beating up."

Cody frowned and glanced down at the pad in front of him. "Were you taking him to the hospital? Was he seen?"

"No, he – I brought him back to my place. To sleep on my couch," I added.

Cody took a quick deep breath in through his nose and let it out slow. I could tell he didn't love my answer. "I see," he said. "Is this fellow – what was his name? Is he still there now?"

"Remy," I said. "I believe so, yes."

Schutte gave a little grunt. "Did you happen to catch his last name?" The way he asked the question made it clear what he thought of me.

My answer didn't exactly help my cause. "No, officer," I said.

Schutte nodded, like this was no more than he expected. "Let me get this straight," he said. "You're saying this here fellow was beat up so bad you feared for his life, so you drove this stranger to your apartment?"

Put like that, it did sound suspicious. "He didn't have health insurance," I said, sounding defensive even to my own ears. I wondered if they had already figured out that Remy had been my ride into town. "The least I could do," he had said, using his bruised hands as little as possible on the steering wheel. "Just text me when you wish to be picked up." To my surprise, Remy hadn't asked me to lie for him or conceal anything. Call me cynical, but I kept wondering if that was part of his conman method: Convince the mark that it's her idea to lie for you.

Lord, I was getting as cynical as Darnique.

"Now, Duke and Holt have a different story about what happened last night." Schutte pulled over a chair and sank down into it. Out of the corner of my eyes, I saw Cody's face go carefully blank, which meant he was annoyed. "The boys say that you and this Remy were out back, fooling around and taking some new drug. They said you offered to sell them some, and when they wouldn't buy, the stranger started putting the hurt on them." Schutte looked utterly relaxed, like a man recounting a hunting story over a beer. I could feel my own stomach twisting, because Duke and Holt's lie sounded more convincing than my truth. "They said they asked you for help," Schutte added, leaning over with a grunt and picking up Cody's pad. Schutte flipped back two pages, read silently, then looked back at me. "They said, and I quote, 'Anna Marie said that she was angry and that we had best watch ourselves.'" Schutte waved the pad like it was proof of something. "You care to comment on that?"

On the other side of the room, a delivery man came in carrying two shopping bags, and the female deputy walked over, counting out bills. The smell of Italian meatballs filled the air, and I felt the saliva in the back of my mouth turn metallic. Was I going to throw up? Then one side of Schutte's mouth lifted, and anger came to my rescue.

"Yes, I would care. First of all, Norville and Karl can attest to the fact that Duke and Holt were playing cards with Remy while I was still working my shift. Karl had to ask the boys to leave. Second of all, why would I have bothered to call y'all up to make sure those boys wasn't hurt too bad if I was just laughing away at their condition?" Schutte had lost his smirk, but I kept on going. "As for any drug taking, well, here is my arm." I rolled up my green dress sleeve and held it out. "Y'all want to test my blood? Go on and test me. And then go ahead and test Duke and Holt. Check how many steroids they been injecting while you're at it."

Cody cleared his throat, and suddenly I was aware of my pale arm, lying on the desk in front of him. I flashed on the night after the big game, my skin so pale next to his, and I wondered if he was remembering it too.

"That won't be necessary," said Cody, sounding so friendly I began to relax. "You've been very helpful, and we're just about done. All you need to do is write down what you told us in your own words." He made it sound like routine paperwork, but I broke a sweat as I penned the statement, even though I was telling the truth – well, most of it. When I was finished, I pushed the paper over to Cody, who read it over and then stuffed it into a manilla envelope.

"Can I leave now? I don't want to be late for work."

Cody glanced across the room at Schutte, who was over by the delivery bags, sniffing one of the wrapped sandwiches. "May I walk you back to your car?"

I hesitated, and then my eyes met Cody's and I realized he wasn't quite so nice as he'd been playing. He must have suspected that my frankentruck was still out of commission, and wondered if I had gotten into town this afternoon the same way I had gotten home last night. He was hoping to run into Remy. "Sure," I said. "Just hang on a sec."

I had learned how to text without looking at my phone back in high school, so I could message friends while the teacher yammered on. Turned out that this was a useful life skill. "Coming out of police now," I texted Remy. "Cop walking me out."

Remy was supposed to pick me up when I texted him, but I had no idea how he would react when he read my warning. Most likely he would hightail it out of town – assuming, of course, that he hadn't done so already, with my silver earrings and my laptop in his backseat.

"Let me just clock out," said Cody. A moment later, we were outside the station, Cody with his hands jammed into his jacket pockets. I felt like I had gone back in time, only sideways. The last time Cody and I had stood this close, I had been fizzing with excitement, barely able to look him in the eye. Now my belly was gurgling with nerves and I had to force myself to look at him so I didn't seem like I was guilty.

Cody paused in front of the station, seeming at peace with the world. A driver speeding past spotted Cody's beige uniform and slowed down with a screech of brakes. Cody made like he hadn't noticed. "How you been, Anna Marie?"

"Doing all right. Workin'. Survivin'." I glanced down the block, trying to catch a glimpse of Remy's Firebird.

"You still fixin' on gettin' yourself to Tulane?"

Surprised, I met Cody's inquisitive look. We all tend to forget how much we have revealed to friends who are no longer close. "I am. Saving my pennies." I smiled at him. "You askin' as a friend? Or as a cop?"

He didn't answer right away, and I wondered if I had offended him. Or, worse though, made him think I was looking to get back together. "I'm not a cop," he said, after the too long pause. "I'm a deputy sheriff. How are you gettin' back home? That Remy fellow picking you up?"

I shook my head. "I don't think so." It wasn't a lie. I had helped a charming gambler out of a fix. I wasn't a betting woman, but the chances that he would stick around to see me right were probably poor at best.

Cody nodded. "Thought as much." He pulled out his keys and clicked a button, and the squad car parked in front of the station gave a little chirp. "Let me drive you on back."

I thought about refusing, but honestly, what else was I going to do? "Appreciate it," I said. On the short drive back to my place, the air was thick with all the things we weren't saying. As I expected, we pulled up to find Remy's Firebird was gone. Chet was out raking leaves, though, while his mama bagged them. They both watched me get out of the squad car with matching frowns on their faces.

"Thank you, sugar," I told Cody, trying to make it clear that I had not been arrested.

Cody looked at me with a little smile on his face, and for a moment I saw the boy I had known and not the uniform. "You take care, AM. As my mama used to say, don't go borrowin' trouble."

Despite everything, there was a bounce in my step, until I heard the name that Chet's mama hissed after me.

"Lady, let me tell you something," I said, rounding back on her. "Instead of worrying about how I might corrupt your baby boy, you might want to see what all your baby boy has been getting up to lately." The moment I said it, I knew my temper had gotten the better of me again. Now both Chet and Scary Anne had reason to be irked with me. I seemed to be racking up enemies at an alarming rate.

I let myself back into my apartment feeling drained and wondering if I had time for a shower and a nap before I had to start my shift. Damn it, how was I even going to get into town? Old Willie was still on the fritz, and Chet was not going to be inclined to offer me any more assistance.

That's what you get for giving in to your temper, I told myself. I unwrapped my best dress, which was sticking to me as though it were August instead of October. I hadn't realized how much I had been sweating from nerves, but I bet that Schutte had smelled the fear on me and drawn his own conclusions. Shoot, maybe Cody had thought the same. I started unbuttoning my dress, then paused to text Darnique the latest installment in my soap opera life.

"Alors," said Remy from the couch, startling a shriek out of me.

SIX

"What the hell?" I ducked behind the kitchen counter and wrapped my dress clumsily around me. "Why are you sneaking around here like that?" When I stood up, Remy was still lying on my couch, a water-damaged paperback propped on his stomach. "When I saw your car was gone, I thought you'd legged it."

"I moved my car around back, chère," said Remy, turning off the lamp by the couch. "I was not thinking last night, but I think we both prefer to keep this discreet."

The suggestion that we both had some dirty little secret to keep made me even madder. I stomped into my bedroom and shut the door, jagged with nerves. I pulled on my black jeans from the previous night and rummaged in my dirty clothes hamper for a white tee. Sometimes I get optimistic about only wearing something once, but the laundromat takes up a lot of time and energy even when my truck is working, so I usually wind up changing my mind. I was putting on the cleanest of my dirty tees when I heard a knock on my door.

"You can drive me to work in ten minutes," I informed the

closed door. "Then you can keep on driving to wherever it is you're going."

I could almost hear him digesting this. "You have to work now?" His tone made it sound as though this was some kind of revelation. Clearly, the man had never worked a steady job in his life.

"Yes," I replied, applying some deodorant before pulling on my old tee shirt. "Some of us do that. Work yesterday. Work today. Work tomorrow." I didn't know who was making me madder, him or my own fool self. Why had I been so naive and figured the sheriff would just ask me one or two questions, leaving me plenty of time to get home? Why hadn't I just brought myself a change of clothes and walked over to the diner from the station?

Because I hadn't felt comfortable leaving a stranger in my apartment all day. The moment I admitted it to myself, I felt better. "Listen," I said, running a brush through my hair, "I am sorry if I'm being short with you. I am hungry and tired and still wired as a lab rat from everything that's happened since I finished my shift last night. But I did not mean to bite your head off."

"I am sorry that I've been the cause of so much stress."

I sighed. "Thanks, but you had best pack up your things now, cause I'm ready to head out in five." This was true, but also I needed to use the bathroom for something besides primping, and I couldn't do it with him standing right outside the door.

Remy sucked in a breath. "Ah," he said. "All right. But if I may ask one question?"

So much for using the bathroom. "Make it quick."

"Certainly. Only… may I see you? I dislike talking to doors."

I turned the knob. Remy was wearing a black tee shirt and

faded jeans and an unexpectedly serious expression. The dark glasses hid his eyes, and I wondered what I would see if he took them off. A calculating gleam? The faintest glimmer of attraction? A hint of desperation? "I have to keep getting ready." I looked down and saw that my semi-clean white tee had a coffee stain.

"I was wondering… you have already been more than kind to me."

"But bless your heart, you want something more." I ran some water on my washcloth and scrubbed at the stain, which remained unmoved by my efforts. Suddenly it was all too much. Nothing in my life was ever easy. My aunt and Sheriff Schutte and Scary Anne Billings all thought I was a voracious man-eating she-devil, but as far as I could tell I was the oldest living virgin in Caldecott County. I fool around with one boy and he winds up in the hospital with a breathing tube down his throat. I do a favor for a good-looking stranger and he starts thinking what else he can winkle out of me.

I might have felt a little better if he'd been putting the moves on me, but a woman knows when a fellow is flirting. Remy was all business. "What more do y'all want from me? Front you some money? Sign my name to your bank loan? Tune up your car?" I realized that his gaze had drifted down to the wet front of my tee shirt. Fed up, I snapped the wet washcloth at Remy's face.

He ducked and held up his hands. "I am not trying to take advantage of you, chère."

"You sure about that? You're not thinking, hey, you put me up for the night, girl, maybe I should stick around a while, eat your food and do my solid best to charm my way into your pants?"

Ooh, that one hit home. "I was wondering if I might impose

for another night or two, yes." He kept himself very still, like a man trying not to provoke an angry dog.

"Huh. So let me get this straight. Last night, you didn't want to go to the hospital because the police might start sniffing around. Well, they're sniffing. So want to explain why you're so all fired eager to stay on my couch?"

Remy spread his battered hands. "I need time to heal."

I applied lipgloss, determined not to fall for this line. "Sugar, we all need things. I need a car that works, a boss that doesn't make me want to spit tacks every time he opens his mouth, and one month solid of decent tips. Correction – make that three months, so I can put Karl's Diner in my rearview mirror." If I remained in my hometown, all I would ever be was the girl who kissed Cody Robbins into a coma. The doctors were all very careful to explain that I hadn't actually caused Cody's condition. They speculated that years of football had left him susceptible to a sudden stroke. It didn't matter. Everyone blamed me, myself included. It wasn't rational, but I could never seem to shake the feeling that there was something fundamentally wrong with me. I was banking on the idea that a few semesters of psychology at Tulane would set me right – but for that to happen, I needed funds and I needed wheels.

Remy smiled, triumphant. "You say you need a car that works? Et voila – I have a car."

That brought me up short. "You're saying I can drive your car while you stay here?"

He nodded. "As much as you like. There is only a quarter tank of gas right now, though."

I chewed on my nail for a moment, considering. This would certainly solve one big problem. Yet there was something gnawing at me. "I need to know what kind of trouble you're in."

"I already told you–" he began, but I held up my hand.

"I don't want some film noir speech about getting mixed up with the wrong people. I want to know what it is you did to hack someone off, and who you did it to."

Remy nodded slowly. "All right, but there is not enough time to tell you everything now, if you have to go to work."

"Later tonight, then. And Remy… ?"

He turned back to me, and I could see my reflection in the lenses of his sunglasses. "When you're filling me in on all the details? I want you to look me in the eye."

That evening, Dolly Parton and her friend came back to the diner at seven. Dolly – I mean, Lucretia – was dressed in a silky blouse with a bow at the neck, and wearing a pair of white plastic reading glasses that sparkled with rhinestones when she moved her head. I felt a pang of guilt over taking her sunglasses. If I had known she was coming back, I would have left them in the lost and found.

"What can I get you ladies tonight? Some coffee or tea to start?"

"I would love some tea," said Irene, without looking at me. She was bundled into a big gray sweater, and the tip of her nose was red. I turned to Lucretia. "And what can I get you today?"

Lucretia considered for a moment. "Well, I am hankerin' for a brew, but I'll just content myself with an iced tea. No good getting tiddly before the interviews."

Interviews? I didn't want to start asking questions – it was close to six and half the tables were already full. I didn't have much time to think after that, because I had two tables of order-changers, a single mom with a screaming toddler and two old-timers with special dinner coupons that they could not locate in the old woman's bag. Every time I went back to the kitchen, I had to fend off Karl's questions about Duke and Holt – lord, how news does travel in a small town – so no one could blame me for not remembering some passing remark about interviews.

It was only when I came out with their orders – a BLT with avocado for Lucretia, and chicken noodle soup for Irene – that I realized what kind of an idiot I was. My old frenemy Karli Klinger was sitting down opposite Lucretia, wearing her job-hunting clothes – which meant the jeans she was wearing were not ripped, and her shirt wasn't tied up to show off her navel.

"… and then I had about a year of nursing school," Karli was saying. "Only it wasn't quite right for me."

I could have saved Karli some time and money. I would bet that most successful nursing students don't gag at the smell of mayonnaise, public bathrooms, wet dogs and cafeteria specials. Not that I blamed her for the mayonnaise. That stuff is just pure evil.

"Nursing's a great profession," said Lucretia, taking off her sparkly reading glasses to look Karli right in the eye, "but it's not for everyone. Oh," she said, turning to me, "our food has arrived!"

I served the two women, acutely aware that Karli wasn't acknowledging that she knew me. "Anything for you?"

Karli barely glanced at me. "Nothing, thanks."

I fought the urge to say something snarky. "Y'all need anything else?"

"Not right now, but check back in?" Lucretia picked up her BLT and held it gingerly between two perfectly manicured hands. "Maybe I'll be weak again and need something sweet for afters." I smiled and promised I would be back soon. As I walked away, I heard Lucretia say, "I do hope you'll excuse us for eating? We just have so many interviews to do and I am not one of those gals that forgets to eat!" She laughed, a girlish gurgle that instantly made everyone within a three-foot radius smile as well.

Remy and Lucretia had a lot in common. Both of them charmers. Only I couldn't picture Lucretia getting beaten up behind a diner. She wasn't kidding about having a lot of interviews to conduct, though. After Karli came a young man with a full beard who I vaguely recalled from freshman year, followed by two sisters who had left sophomore year when their mom got transferred to an army base in Hawaii. The dreadlocked boy that came after looked like he was still in high school, and after he smiled a little nervously at me, I recognized him as Cody's younger brother.

By then I was deeply curious and feeling more than a little grinchdog about serving all my former classmates as they interviewed for some plum position. Clearly, Lucretia and Irene were looking to hire someone, but of course they would never think to inquire if someone like me was interested. "One more to go this evenin'," said Lucretia. "Then I'll have me that beer."

The last interviewee arrived, and I felt like I'd been punched. "Darnique?"

My best friend gave me a small smile before settling into the booth opposite Lucretia and Irene. She was wearing the lemon-yellow blouse I had bought her for her birthday in March, and her lucky horseshoe necklace.

I snapped into professional mode and made my way back into the kitchen, then hightailed it to the ladies' room, holding up a hand to silence Karl before he could start telling me that I could not take a break right now. I took a moment to fix my eye makeup, which was not as waterproof as advertised. Why hadn't Darnique said anything to me about the interview? We always talked about everything. I checked my phone, and sure enough there were two texts from Darnique in the morning, and a phone call from right about when I was sitting with Cody and the sheriff.

I had no right to feel hurt, but for some reason I still felt as though I'd missed the last bus to the amusement park, and had to sit at home while everyone else I knew had an adventure.

I plastered my waitress smile on my face and returned to Lucretia's table just as Darnique was getting up to leave. She made a quick "call me" gesture with her hand, and then added, "stop by after work, OK?"

Lucretia caught all this. "You two are friends?"

"That we are." Darnique gave me a smile over her shoulder, and I added, "Whatever you're lookin' for, I'm sure Darnique's got it."

Lucretia handed over a plate I had forgotten to clear. "What about you? You're not interested in an all-expenses paid internship with room and board included?"

All the French fries I'd been sneaking all evening turned to glue in my belly. "Oh, you're interviewing for internships?"

Irene tilted her head. "You did not read the brochure we gave you yesterday?"

I could have smacked myself upside the head. The brochure! I had completely forgotten that they had given me anything, but the moment Irene reminded me, I could see myself tossing the glossy folder in the garbage. Why the flipping heck had I been so sure the ladies were peddling cosmetics or some such? I tucked my chin down. "I think I must have thrown it out by mistake."

Lucretia's gurgle of a laugh brought my chin back up. "Oh, lordy, the look on your face! Don't worry, Anna Marie, that's why Reeny and I always order extras." She reached into her big fringed white leather bag and plucked out a brochure. "Here y'go, sugar."

I looked at the picture of three smiling and clean-cut college age students, an African American young man, an East Asian young woman, and a brunette who could have been Middle Eastern. In bold black letters, the brochure asked: Are You Living Up to Your Full Potential? Find out what you can really do at the Borger Institute for Creative Achievement! I felt the slick paper getting damp under my palm. "I suppose it's too late to apply now?"

Lucretia looked at me straight, and for a moment, I saw a different, more serious woman within her sparkly eyes. "Not for you."

I drove back to my apartment in a daze, as fizzy and distracted as if I were falling in love. I wasn't exactly sure what "creative achievement" meant when you took it out of the box and shook it. I pictured it a bit like the Caldecott County High Presidential Classroom program, which selected the brainiest, nose-down juniors and seniors and rewarded them for all their hard work by sending them off to a hotel in Virginia where they could tour the FBI training academy at Quantico and mess around with other frisky brainiacs from all over the US of A.

All kidding aside, though, it was the kind of thing that looked amazing on a college application form. You got a plum internship, it was like someone stamped you on the forehead with glowing gold letters: You. Are. Extraordinary.

I had worked my butt off junior year to get that stamp of approval. I took AP history and English, wrote for the school paper, even volunteered to visit the homebound at Aunt Carrie's church, which made Aunt Carrie happy because she thought I was getting religion.

In my spare time, I read lots of psychology books to improve myself – *Predictably Irrational*, *The Power of Habit*, *Emotional Intelligence* and *The Wisdom of the Enneagram: The Complete Guide to Psychological and Spiritual Growth for the Nine Personality Types.*

I scored an eight, the challenger, whatever that's worth. I'm also a Scorpio.

In any case, all my hard work got me was second alternate and my history teacher's encouraging smile. "They mostly pick seniors," she said. "Try again next year."

I might have made it, too, if Cody Robbins hadn't smiled at me and asked me if I wanted to help him with his history essay. After he wound up in a coma, I dropped out of school, too worried and guilty to focus on my schoolwork. I figured I was like Eve, fallen from grace. No one was going to select the local bad girl for any special training opportunities.

Except Lucretia Borger didn't seem to mind that I was a greasy spoon waitress with a bad reputation. "Read the brochure," she had said. "Look us up online. Think up some questions and let's meet up..." she consulted her planner, an old-fashioned notebook, "how about in two days? We could meet in the morning, before you head off to work?"

Two days to prepare for the most important interview of

my life. Suddenly a car honked twice before swerving around me. With a jolt, I realized that I had been driving home from work in such a daze that I had been going ten miles under the posted speed limit. Get it together, I told myself as I turned off the main road and into the Sweetbriar Apartments parking lot. Ordinarily, I would have been racing to get home, but tonight I put the car in park and clicked the dome light on so that I could take a closer look at the brochure in my lap. The first inside page of the brochure blared a boldfaced question: *The Borger Institute for Creative Achievement: Are You Borger Material?*

There was a picture of Lucretia in a jacket so blue it hurt the eyes and extremely high heels, shaking hands with a young woman in a sari, alongside another boldfaced inquiry: *Are You Living Up to Your Full Potential? Find out what you can really do at the Borger Institute for Creative Achievement!*

After this there were a number of bulleted items:

Learn FBI and CIA techniques for reading people's body language and non-verbal cues.

Discover the secret to acquiring quick proficiency in a foreign language in less than a week.

Identify a person's love language – and understand how it fits with your own.

It was all probably a load of sweet-scented bull excrement, but man, did it ever sound appealing. I gave my face a quick check in the rearview mirror – ugh, forehead and nose all greasy from the grill, and was that a pimple forming? Then, just for a moment, I indulged a little fantasy of turning into a sexy super spy, like Avengers' Black Widow. Maybe all the Borger grads went slinking around international airports in leather jackets and dark shades, speaking perfectly accented Russian or Mandarin whenever necessary, taking out the bad guys with expert reflexes and the ability to cause a seizure by pressing a finger to a particular spot on the left thumb.

All nonsense, of course. If I did manage to get accepted, the program would doubtless turn out to involve a tour of some lawyer's workplace, a bunch of lectures, a lot of wilted lettuce and a load of rubbery turkey slice lunches. Still, it was nice to imagine that Lucretia could magically transform me with a wave of her money.

I was so preoccupied that I nearly left the car without the dinner that Norville had bagged up for me. I hadn't wanted to ask for two dinners, since that might lead to questions, but I had told Norville I was starving, and he had given me a double portion. Aside from Darnique, Norville was the only person I was going to miss when I finally showed this town my taillights.

It seemed only decent to feed Remy before turning him out on his ear. As I unlocked my door, I was picturing myself like one of the people in that brochure, all glossy and semi-professional in a blazer and scarf, smiling with perfect dentition, life as tidy and organized as a sitcom teenager's bedroom. I imagined writing "Borger Institute Alumna" on my Tulane application form. Everybody loved hearing that you started out as a waitress or a construction worker, as long as you told them about it in the past tense.

The real problem was Remy. If I had only looked at Lucretia's brochure last night, I would never have brought his kind of trouble home. Now Sheriff Schutte was three quarters convinced that I was involved with illegal drug shenanigans.

All right, then. First things first. Remy was going to have to go. I could make do without a car, and I did not need his kind of complication in my life. "Remy," I said, toeing off my sneakers as I walked in the front door, "I'm afraid this is just not going to work out." I placed the paper bag with tonight's dinner on the kitchen counter. "Remy?" When I didn't hear a response, I walked into the living room, expecting to find him on the couch.

The couch was empty, and the cushions were on the floor. Typical man. I picked them up and put them back, then walked into the hall. Bathroom door was open, so he wasn't in there. Had he gone off for a walk?

I walked into my bedroom, about to pull off my tee shirt, and gasped out loud. My missing houseguest was sprawled out on my bed wearing nothing but playing card boxer shorts. He was also fast asleep.

"Gambling man," I said, "that last laydown was one bad call."

SEVEN

Remy slept on, his well-muscled chest rising and falling in a steady, measured rhythm. As I cleared my throat, I noticed that his hair was spread out damply on my pillow, and I caught the scent of coconuts. The unmitigated gall of the man! He'd used my shampoo and conditioner and laid his wet head down on my side of the bed.

"Yo, Sleeping Beauty. Wake up." He wasn't as pretty now, of course. His left eye was swollen and so was his nose, and the bruise on his temple had darkened to purple. "Remy," I said, "you got to get up." Nothing. He didn't even snort or change his breathing. Irritated, I reached over and shook him. "I said wake up!"

Remy gave a loud grunt, as though he'd been punched, and rolled over and off the bed, landing in a fighter's crouch, hands held in front of his face. Before I could take a second breath, he had grabbed the red ladies' sunglasses from my side table and put them back on. He did not, I notice, seem at all embarrassed about being caught in his baggy boxer shorts. "Sorry," he said, voice a little throaty with sleep. "I must have fallen asleep."

The sight of him, in those ridiculous red rhinestone glasses just made me madder. "In my bed! What were you doing in my bed?"

"The couch has lumps."

"I'll give you lumps! That's my bed. My personal space." I poked him in the chest with my finger, and he backed up. As a kid growing up with the Wood Spirit Alliance, I was always finding strangers in my bed and discovering I had to go to sleep in a pile of blankets on the floor. "The young and whole must be raised to give to the old and injured," my mom explained. "Someday, when you're in need, the universe will return the favor."

The universe owed me bigtime.

"I was going to give you one more night, but this seals it. You're getting out. Now." I pointed at the door.

Remy took a breath. I could see my angry face, still coated with diner grease, reflected in the lenses of his big red women's sunglasses. "I was wrong to go into your bedroom. Very wrong."

"Out!"

Remy flinched. "Please. Do not shriek."

Oh, so now I was being told I was a shrill woman. "Listen, asshat, that wasn't shrieking. You want to hear a shriek?" I took a deep breath. "GET OUT OF MY HOUSE!"

Remy clapped his hands over his ears. "Agh! Fine, I will leave."

I was on a rage roll now. "And take off those sunglasses!" I could hand them back to Lucretia when I had my interview.

"Stop," he said, as I tried to yank them off his face.

"Give them back!" I reached for him again, and this time he dodged sideways and grabbed me by the wrist. He drew in a quick, sharp breath – I guess his hand was still sore – and I took advantage of his distraction and snatched at the sunglasses.

"Stop!" Remy twisted and rolled, taking me with him.

Suddenly I found myself lying on my bed with Remy on top of me. Stunned, I had the briefest of moments to register the sensation of his wiry, hard-muscled body pressing down on me. We both looked at the broken-off piece of the sunglasses in my hand. "Merde," said Remy, as the rest of the glasses went sliding off his nose in slow motion.

I stared up at him in shock. He gazed down at me, looking rueful. "Ah, did I mention I have a little eye condition?"

Eye condition? He had red eyes, like a demon! Last night in the cemetery it had been too dark to see clearly, and I'd thought he'd burst a small blood vessel. Gross, but not alarming. In the light of my bedroom, I could see that his irises were bright laser red.

Maybe they were as dangerous as lasers.

"Gah!" I pushed at his bare chest, wriggling desperately to get out from under him.

"Merde, merde, merde." Remy rolled to his side, freeing me, and I fell to the floor with a thump. Remy was shaking his head like a dog who had run into a tree. "Listen, I know this comes as a bit of a surprise."

I kept my eyes on him as I stumbled back into my dresser, reaching for something to defend myself. My fingers closed on something solid and I held it in front of me like a club. "You keep back!"

Remy looked confused, maybe because I was brandishing a hairbrush. "Aren't you overreacting a bit?" He sounded so reasonable. All those Sunday sermons in Aunt Carrie's church raced through my mind. "Shun the demon, for he will lure you with temptations!" I'd assumed the preacher was using fancy bible talk to scare us into behaving ourselves, but clearly, I had assumed wrong.

"Overreacting? You've got laser eyes!" I shielded my face with my hands.

"Ah, you think I'm like that X-Man, Cyclops? No, my eyes don't shoot death rays."

I peeked through my fingers. "How can I trust that you're telling me the truth?"

"Because I'm looking at you and nothing bad has happened?"

I lowered my hands. He looked back at me, smiling a little. Suddenly, all the fear drained out of me, and a hot rush of fury took its place. "I want you out. Now."

"But I'm not dangerous!"

"Then why did you try to trick me into thinking you were human?"

Expressions flitted across Remy's face, almost too fast for me to catch. He settled on looking pained. "I should have told you. I would have, in a day or so."

I shook my head, because what he said made no kind of sense. "Are you leavin', or do I need to call the cops?"

He closed his eyes for a moment, and looked like a man in pain. Then he opened them again, and he was a demon with scarlet irises set in black. "My head is pounding, chère, I'm as weak as a kitten. I cannot drive like this."

Aunt Carrie always said that a sweet-talking man could gaslight you into thinking you were leading him astray. "Don't you try to trick me into feeling sorry for you!"

"I feel like the morning after a whiskey and tequila mistake."

Lord, forgive me for all the times I snickered at Aunt Carrie for her talk of devils and hellfire. "Shut up. I don't want to hear any more of your lies!"

He pressed his hands to his temples. "Tiens… Not so loud."

My short nails dug into my palms. "Stop trying to act like you're the injured party."

He frowned at me. "What have I done to you, eh? Besides exposed your own nasty little prejudice."

"Prejudice? You're a demon!"

His jaw dropped, and then he threw back his head and howled with laughter. Then he clutched his head again. "Ow. I shouldn't have done that."

Without thinking, I threw the hairbrush at him. Quick as thought, Remy raised his arm to deflect it.

The hairbrush bounced off the corner of my dresser and exploded in midair, and I screamed, cowering down and covering my face and babbling about sin and forgiveness.

When I looked up, I saw Remy examining his hands, a puzzled frown creasing his brows. Picking up a bobby pin, he flung it into the air. I flinched and covered my head, and then I heard the pin drop with a tinny clatter to the floor.

Maybe he needed time to reload. Or recharge. "Please," I said, taking advantage of the respite, and not sure how long it would last. "Don't hurt me."

Remy stared at me with a comical look of amazement. "Me? Hurt you?" He opened his mouth, then closed it. "Because… I am a demon?" I didn't say anything, because it was belatedly occurring to me that Remy's crimson eyes were not necessarily a sign of infernal allegiance. Aside from destroying all my grooming tools, he didn't seem like a fiend on a rampage.

He shook his head. "You feelin' all right, chère? No history of nervous breakdowns?"

By this point, I was beginning to feel embarrassed. Now

that my brain was no longer shouting danger-danger-danger, it sheepishly reminded me that there were other sorts of folks with special abilities and unusual physical attributes. I felt like hitting myself in the head. How had it not occurred to me that Remy was a mutant? Just goes to show you how stupid you get when you panic. Dump a load of stress hormone in your bloodstream, and you just might find yourself acting on some nasty old prejudice you thought you'd overcome. I'd read about this online in a *Psychology Today* piece. Basically, the article said that stress revealed the disgusting leftover beliefs that you thought were gone, but were really just tucked under the cushions of your mind.

"I guess I seemed a little crazy there for a minute," I allowed.

"Just a little." He measured a pinch with his forefinger and thumb.

I felt my cheeks warm. "You got to understand how much I heard about demons when I was growing up."

"I see." Remy leaned back against the wall, either because he was tired or because he was being thoughtful and wanted to leave a lot of space between us. "Well, I promise you not to do anything that will commit either of our souls to the pit." He paused, then gave me a wink and added, "but, for you, chère, I think it would be worth the price of damnation."

Lord, that boy could be about to face a firing squad and he'd still have some flirt left in him. "So, what's the deal?"

"I'm a mutant."

I blew out an exasperated breath, ruffling my bangs. "I got that part. What I don't understand is why you let two thick-necks rearrange your face. Why didn't you explode a hairbrush at them?"

Remy said something under his breath in French, and I caught the word "imbecile."

"I am not an imbecile," I said, feeling my face grow hot. "Pardon me for not calmly reasoning through the events of the past forty-eight hours. Next time I let a stranger into my house and find out he has devil eyes, I'll be prepared with a witty comeback."

Remy choked, and it took me a moment to realize he was laughing again. "Ow," he said. "You have to stop making me laugh – it hurts my poor bruised ribs too much."

"Good." I folded my arms, but his laughter was infectious, and I could feel my anger slipping away.

He wiped his eyes on the back of his forearm. "Oh, lord. And I was not calling you an imbecile, chère. I was talking to myself." He looked down at his bruised and swollen hands as though they had let him down. "I have had some training in self-defense. And I have unusual abilities. My... teacher would be very disappointed in me."

"You mean, like making that hairbrush explode?" I wondered if all mutants had teachers. I had only heard about that one school in New York.

"Ah, I see." His voice was kind now, and so were his eyes, or at least, as kind as red demon eyes could look. "Is that the first time your powers have manifested?"

I blinked. "*My* powers?"

"It was not I who made that hairbrush explode." Remy's smile was wry as he spread his hands wide, like a magician making a big reveal. "It was you."

EIGHT

An hour later, and Remy's words still felt like the second explosion he'd lobbed my way. At first, I had been so stunned I laughed. Then, when I realized he wasn't joking, I had felt jittery and unsettled, as if all my internal organs were vibrating with the aftershock. Of course, nervous and weirded out was my usual reaction to good news. As a kid, I had learned the hard way that it was safer to expect the worst than to hope for the best.

Still, around about the third time Remy had explained why he thought I was a mutant, I began to feel ravenously hungry, which was my version of optimism.

Now we were seated at the kitchen counter, eating the meatloaf and mashed potatoes I'd brought home from the diner. Remy was wearing his jeans and had borrowed one of my oversized white tee shirts so we could wash his black one in the sink. I had changed into my pale green lounge-around pajamas, which Darnique had bought me in case I ever had a houseguest I wanted to impress. Until this evening, they still had their tags on.

"Run it by me again," I said as I slapped the back of the ketchup bottle over my meat.

"You're a mutant, chère. Just like me," said Remy, pouring some more iced tea into his glass. "Some mutants come into their powers before puberty. Some after."

I took a bite of meatloaf. I was not just plain old Anna Marie, neighborhood weirdo. I was a mutant with special mutant powers! In my entire life, I had never won a single prize, and all of a sudden I had hit the jackpot. I wasn't just a high school dropout serving the meatloaf special to my snotty ex-classmates. I was a mutant, with mutant explosive powers. "Do you know other mutants? What about the X-Men? Have you met them?"

Remy nodded as he finished chewing a bite of mashed potato. "I know some other mutants. But you are the first to have the same power as me. Here," he said, tossing me a pea from his plate. "Throw this and concentrate on infusing it with your energy."

The pea was a bit mushy. "And how exactly do I do this? Send it good vibes?" My mother would be all over this, if only she were still around.

"I would not put it like that, but yes. Send the pea good, strong vibrations from your mind."

I concentrated, trying to zap as much force as I could at the mushy pea. "Okay. Now, what?"

"Throw it at the wall."

I made a face. "Who is cleaning it up?"

"Neither of us, if this works as I think it will. The pea will explode."

I threw the pea. It landed with a small splat on the floor. "Maybe we made a mistake," I said, trying to sound neutral as

I cleaned the splodge with my napkin. "Maybe you exploded the hairbrush." I should have known it was too good to be true. No one suddenly discovers they have a hidden mutant power at nineteen.

Remy shook his head. "I am positive it was not me."

I took a swallow of iced tea. "Then how come I can't replicate the result?"

Remy rested his chin on a hand, considering. Then he picked up a pea from his plate.

"You're cleaning up this one."

He tossed it into the air, and this time it exploded with a tiny splat!

"Great." I mashed my potatoes flat with my fork, unable to keep the bitterness out of my voice. "It was you, after all." You would think I'd know not to get my hopes up. Every time I had been fool enough to get excited about something – my mom breaking up with her latest loser boyfriend, the promise of a new kitten, the role of fairy princess in the school play – I wound up disappointed. Mom and the loser always made up. The new kitten was sick and had to go the vet, and never came back. The teacher decided to change the play so there were no princesses, only elves.

Yet somehow, this disappointment felt the harshest. I kept my eyes downcast, so Remy couldn't see I was on the verge of tears.

"Not the hairbrush, chère. I know when I am making things go boom, and that was not me."

I felt a little leap of hope in my chest, and instantly tried to squash it. "So what am I, the weakest mutant in history?"

Remy stretched out his hand. "Touch me?"

I was getting used to his red-on-black eyes. "Listen, I like you and all, but you're leaving here in a day or so and I'm not up for a two-night stand."

"Understood. But this is an experiment. Touch me – very lightly – with one finger."

I touched the back of his hand with my pinky. "Ooh, Remy, you're so hot, this is amaaazing."

"I was thinking – back in your room. I did touch you. Very briefly."

"Did the earth move?"

Remy drew his hand away. "That is enough, I think." He wiped a film of sweat off his forehead and then took a bite of meatloaf. "Now. Try to make the pea explode."

Rolling my eyes, I picked a pea off my plate. "Beware, Oh pea, the force of my pathetic mutant powers!" I tossed it up in the air and frowned dramatically at it.

The pea exploded in my face.

"Oh my God, Remy, it was me, I did do it, I can't believe I actually made it–" I broke off when I realized that Remy had gone very pale and was slipping sideways off his chair. "Are you OK?" I reached out to help him and he held up his hands, stopping me.

"I think, no more touches for now," said Remy with a ghost of his usual cocky smile. "I have a new theory about your powers."

"What is it? What's wrong?" Remy's face seemed strained, as though he were hiding something from me.

"Nothing's wrong, chère. You're a mutant, clearly, and I think you might be a strong one."

"But what? What's the catch?"

"I think your power is activated by touch. So when you touched me, before, you absorbed my power." He leaned back, proud of himself for figuring me out.

I stared at him, aghast. "I'm like a leech?"

He shook his head. "No, no, you're more like, let me think–"

"A leech."

"A conductor."

"A conductor leads an orchestra! How am I a conductor?"

"No, no. Like electricity? A conductor."

I wasn't entirely sure if that was accurate, but then, I hadn't studied electricity since the beginning of ninth grade. Maybe I *was* a conductor. Mollified, I started to clear up the dinner plates. "You want some chocolate peanut butter ice cream?"

Remy opened the freezer. "Oh, full fat – the real thing." He beamed at me approvingly.

"Bowls are up in that cabinet," I said, pointing. "Spoons in that drawer." As I loaded the dirty dinner plates in the dishwasher, I thought how much more confident I felt when I wasn't asking him to explain me to myself. I knew I shouldn't complain, but I felt a little awkward – like the latest of late bloomers. "So," I said, closing the dishwasher door and straightening up, "how unusual is it for a person to develop powers at the age of nineteen?"

Remy handed me a soup bowl filled with half a pint of ice cream. "It is more common to develop powers earlier," he admitted. "Are you certain there were no earlier incidents? Anything from when you were twelve or thirteen?"

I cast my mind back, and found myself thinking about the year I turned eleven. I had been playing with my friend Lenny, dressing up in some of my mother's old things – a length of gold lamé, a stretchy sequined mini dress and a patchwork rabbit fur coat from the Seventies. I was pretending to be a royal sorceress and he was a barbarian mercenary.

Lenny was an amazing artist, and he used to draw comics of

us that we would act out, jumping from the bed (the mountains of Hyrolea) to the throw rug (the sea of Ibruglion) and fighting each other with broom and mop (swords made of Korphilian steel). One day, after practicing our stage combat (clank swords up, clank swords down, Lenny crouches and sweeps the sword at my feet as I jump, I sweep the sword at his head as he ducks) we ended with him on his back, me pointing my sword at his heart. "I have defeated you," I said.

"Then the geas is lifted," he replied, because in the story we had concocted, an evil witch had put a curse on him that he could never touch or be touched with affection until he was bested in fair combat. I threw my sword aside and kissed him. I remember the electric rush of excitement, and something else, something different. I had read about kisses in my mom's old trunk of romance novels, and I knew they could make you lightheaded and warm and tingly. I had never heard that a kiss could make you feel as though you had lightning running through your veins. "Wow," I said.

"Wow," agreed Lenny, wide-eyed.

Without discussing it, we decided to try that again.

Of course, that was the moment my Aunt Carrie chose to enter my room without knocking.

"I wasn't allowed to hang out with Lenny after that," I finished, amazed I was telling a relative stranger some of my most embarrassing secrets. "But for a week afterwards, Lenny was home with a bad cold and I... all of a sudden, I could draw really well." I took another spoonful of ice cream. "But just for a week."

Remy tipped his head to one side. "Tiens. You mean you have not touched anyone from that time? But surely... your aunt must have touched you? Kissed your cheek?"

I shook my head. "Not skin to skin," I said, a little embarrassed to put it so bluntly. Now that I was looking for it, I could remember other clues. The time Mean Morris tackled me in color wars and then had to go home because he fainted. Everyone thought it was the heat, but now I wondered if it had been me. I took a mouthful of ice cream. "This is..." I didn't know how to describe what I was feeling. This was unbelievable? This was incredible? "This is a lot."

Remy smiled, reached out a hand to pat mine comfortingly, and then thought better of it and pulled his hand back. "When I first discovered my powers, I was thirteen. I was alone in my room, throwing a bit of crumpled tissue into the garbage, like so," Remy made a gesture like he was trying to make a basket, "and suddenly, the tissue caught fire."

"Did you freak out?"

"I freaked out."

"You're just saying that to make me feel better."

Remy helped himself to another serving of ice cream from the pint on the counter. "You are always most certain I am lying when I am being completely honest. I wonder what that says about you – and me."

I clapped my hands together. "So what I want to know is, how did Duke and Holt get the jump on you?"

"Mmm." Remy swallowed his ice cream before speaking. "I underestimated them. I thought I would not need my powers to take them on, you see, and that would be safer."

"Safer how? You can explode playing cards!"

"I can explode anything. I prefer playing cards, as they are light and portable and have a certain panache."

"You can explode anything and you let them beat you half to death? What are you, training to be a saint?"

Remy laughed and shook his head.

"Seriously, Remy."

He leaned back from the counter and let out a breath. "I told you there were people looking for me, yes? I was working for a group of businesspeople who operate, shall we say, in the gray areas of the law."

I leaned forward, elbows on the counter. "A crime syndicate?"

Remy acknowledged this with a slight nod. "A thieves' guild. It was not my choice, chère – I was raised in this world, you see?"

"Your foster father?"

"He was the top man – the king, we called him." Remy looked more serious than I had ever seen him. "There was to be an alliance between the thieves and another guild."

This all sounded like the plot to a movie. I figured there was a kernel of truth in there somewhere, but it was smothered in a stew of half-truths and spiced by a few choice lies. "Let me guess. The alliance of robbers? The pickpocket's consortium? Oh, wait, I've got it. The brotherhood of burglars!"

Remy wasn't smiling. "It may seem like a joke to you, but these are dangerous people. You don't want to be on the outs with the Thieves' Guild, but to cross the Assassins' Guild?" Remy shook his head. "We steal objects. They steal lives."

"Wait, wait, wait." The ice cream I had just eaten was now a wet lump of worry in my stomach. "You upset an organized group of assassins?"

Remy looked like he was about to say something, and then reconsidered. "I upset the assassins' and the thieves' guilds. There are mutants who can track other mutants, especially if they use their powers. So I thought to make a little money with the cards, and fight my way out of trouble the old-fashioned way." With a hint of his usual arrogance, he said, "I would have done it, too, you know. I just did not factor in the effect of that drug." He took a deep breath, and I braced myself for what he was going to say next.

"Any more bombshells? Anyone else chasing you down?"

He shook his head. "I was so busy thinking of the obvious danger, that I almost got myself killed another way. If you had not stopped those guys, chère? I do not think they would have stopped themselves."

As much as I liked the idea of myself as heroic defender, I had to set the record straight. "Duke and Holt are bullies and creeps and liars, but they're not killers." At least, I didn't think they were. "Even hopped up on black-market concoctions, I can't see them actually killing anyone."

"Have you ever seen a dog, the first time it catches a squirrel or a rat?"

Aunt Carrie was not a dog person, but I had dim early memories of the dogs that wandered around the compound, scavenging for crumbs of food and, I supposed, affection.

"The first time dogs make a kill, they look amazed," Remy continued. "They are a bit comical, really, like cartoon characters." Remy assumed a look of wide-eyed surprise, which did not quite suit his demon-colored eyes. "Rraugh. How did this happen?"

I laughed, because Remy was a performer, and now I could see him as a Cajun hound. Pleased with my reaction, he scooped up the last bit of ice cream. "Then the dogs start to feel pleased with themselves. They strut about, with the dead rat tail hanging out of their mouths." He moved his shoulders in a canine strut, and I laughed again. "The next time? They know what they have to do to make a kill. And that is how dogs become hunters, and men and women become killers."

I picked up the empty ice cream bowls and brought them over to the sink. In the heat of the moment, I had been scared witless that Duke and Holt were out of control, but now I forced myself to ask the question: Could they really have killed Remy by accident? And if they had, would they have been amazed rather than horrified?

Remy nodded, seeing the moment when I understood just what had been at stake that night. "So you see, I owe you. And even though I do not know you well, I think I understand something of what you might be feeling right now." Remy held my gaze. "When I first learned I was a mutant, I kept it secret, even from my closest friends." I was beginning to get used to looking into his eyes.

"Why? Did you think they would feel differently about you?" Lots of people who considered themselves completely free of prejudice looked at mutants as untrustworthy spies, a fifth column, secretly plotting to take over the world.

His face turned serious. "I knew the moment I told them what I could do, my… family would think about how best to make use of me. I felt it best to learn my own limitations first."

I ran the kitchen tap, rinsing out our ice cream bowls. "I guess I'd better find mine out soon." I couldn't help but think that I had not exactly won the mutant power lottery. Absorbing other people's powers was a bit like having a talent for doing imitations of famous people. It wasn't its own cool thing, like turning water to ice and making frozen bridges across rivers, or blasting lasers from your eyes, or controlling the weather. It wasn't like causing explosions.

Plus, it appeared to have the serious drawback of making guys weak at the knees, and not in a good way.

"Let's start with what we do know." Remy leaned back, making his shirt ride up and giving me a glimpse of spectacularly laddered abs, and then winced and sat forward again. "Your power is in your touch. You absorb the ability of others. Et voilà, you have Duke and Holt's strength. Your friend's artistic ability." He grinned. "My own incendiary talents."

"Sponge-o expulso!" I threw the kitchen sponge up and concentrated hard. The sponge landed moistly on the floor. "Guess I need a recharge."

There was a scrape of the chair across the floor as Remy turned to face me. "I am ready, if you are. I just needed some food to get my blood sugar back up."

"You sure tire easily," I said, with a flirtatious glance back over my shoulder.

"I just needed a little time, chère. You drained me."

Suddenly clumsy, I dropped the wet bowl in my hands. "I drained you?" Dear lord, I *was* a leech.

He stood up, pushing his stool away from the kitchen counter, and walked over until he was standing directly behind me. "I am not drained now. Try me."

"Okay, then." My whole face felt hot, and I regretted ever trying to flirt with a man this experienced. Remy had doubtless been messing around with girls as long as he had been experimenting with his powers, and I was in over my head on both counts. Faking a confidence I did not feel, I turned around and held out my bare hand. "Charge me up, sugah."

Remy placed his hand over mine, looking directly into my eyes. Still holding my gaze, he brought my palm up to his mouth and kissed it, sending tingles down my body.

"Hey! Cut that out." I snatched my hand away. "We're trying to be scientific here."

"Biology is a science." Remy sank back down onto the stool, shaking his hand as if something had stung it. I wondered if, on his end, the tingles had been more like electric shocks.

I clenched and unclenched my hand, which still felt just like a regular hand. "All right, let's see if this works a second time. What do I do?"

"Try something small. A business card. I learned that cards give, how shall I put it? The most bang for the buck." He gestured at my fridge, which was studded with business cards. I collected the cards of carpenters and plumbers and painters who could repair the many broken things in my apartment that the super promised to fix but never did. I never actually called anyone, of course. Outside contractors required money.

I removed a card for Squirrely Sam's Best Pest Control. The mouse that lived under my dishwasher, eluding every catch and release trap, could breathe a little easier tonight. "What now?"

"Focus. Try to send your energy into it."

I frowned at the card with its smiling squirrel, focusing. "Okay."

"Flick it at me."

I flicked the card, ready for the let-down of it not working, and then – bam! It exploded in the air.

Remy grinned like he was my coach and I'd just nailed a double flip. I jumped up, success fizzing in my veins, and squealed with excitement. "It worked!"

"Try it again."

This time I exploded Grand Master Plaster and Handywoman Enterprises, followed by Bill Piper, Plumber, No Job too Small and Matt the Monster Electrician. Unfortunately, my run ended with Septic Stan's card, which gave a sputter and spark before falling to the floor. I picked it up and found only one end slightly singed.

"Huh," I said, making sure the card was not on fire before throwing it into the garbage. "Think I need a top up." With a start, I looked over and realized that Remy had made his way to the stool and fallen asleep sitting up. No – not fallen asleep. His eyes were half open. My heart gave a little lurch of alarm. "Remy?"

Remy came to with a jolt. "What?"

Now that he was alert again, I filled my lungs with air, but my chest still felt tight. "I think you might've passed out."

"Nonsense. I was just resting." He sat up straighter. "How did you do? Do you want to try touching me again?" He waggled his eyebrows suggestively.

"Idiot."

"No, really, all joking aside, go ahead." He held out his hand, resting it on the table. I wasn't sure if he realized that he didn't have the strength to hold it up.

"I think I'm sapping more than your powers. Maybe you need a few more days eating livers and regaining your strength before we try this again."

"Ordinarily, I would be insulted. But since I have gone through a bit of a beating, perhaps we wait a few hours." Remy's smile was reassuring, but I noticed he pulled his arm back in to his body. He had realized I was draining him, but he had made the offer anyway.

Not such a bad guy, after all. And then it hit me.

Cody. We had kissed – well, OK, done a bit more than kissed – and then his eyes had rolled back in his head and it had been EMTs, ambulance, fruitless calls to the hospital for updates that the nurses were not authorized to tell. I only found out he had left the hospital by overhearing some diner gossip. For over a year now, everyone had blamed me, and I had been stung and buoyed up by the unfairness. Now, for the first time, it struck me.

The gossip was right. It was my fault. I had put Cody in a coma. The thought of it tasted bitter on the back of my tongue, like the aftertaste of strong medicine.

Wait, wait, if that had been the case, then I would have absorbed some kind of ability from him. I hadn't turned stronger or faster, or acquired the ability to throw a football into the end zone.

Except that quarterbacks didn't just need good arms and accuracy. They needed to be able to communicate non-verbally with their receivers, think on their feet, and execute complicated game plans. Right after Cody went to the hospital, while the rest of my life had been falling apart, I had turned into a super waitress, able to read Darnique's body language at a glance, handling twice as many tables as before, carrying three times as many plates without dropping a fork.

Karl, set to fire me from my part-time job because I had hobbled Caldecott County's star quarterback, had to change his tune and offer me more hours instead. "What happened to you, kid?" Karl had looked at me in baffled, reluctant admiration. "Guess you found your life calling." Trust Karl to backhand a compliment like he was playing at Insult Wimbledon.

Only, I didn't deserve a compliment. I had kissed a promising young football player and knocked him out for two weeks, not counting rehab. In return, I had become a super waitress. Not exactly what anyone would call a fair trade.

When I looked back at Remy, I found him half dozing again.

"Remy? Maybe you should go lie down." It sounded like concern, but the truth was, all the fun had drained out of this evening. I wanted to take a hot shower. I wanted to sleep. I wanted to be alone.

"But I'm fine, chère. All rested and ready to go another round." He reached for my hand, and I yanked it away.

"Stop! I don't want to put you in a coma, like my last boyfriend." Oh, ugh, that made it sound like I thought we were romantic. I thought about clarifying, then decided to pretend I hadn't said anything weird.

Remy shook his head. "He was human, no? Totally different. Mutant power gives you something to absorb without draining too much life force."

"We don't know how powerful I am, though."

"That's what we are trying to find out. Come on. What are you, chicken?" He stood up and walked toward me, closing the space between us. He was looking at me, our faces so close that all it would have taken was a deep breath and a slight lean to bring us together.

"Remy. I nearly killed the first boy I kissed."

Remy frowned, and I stepped away, turning my back on him. I didn't want to see him getting frightened of me, and I didn't want to see him still willing to kiss me, either. Or, to be perfectly honest, I wanted both of those contradictory things.

His voice made me look back over my shoulder. "You are still guilty about it? Even though it is not your fault."

His words and the expression on his face were completely unjudgmental, and all at once, my eyes prickled with unshed tears. Remy tilted his head to one side and unlike most of the guys my age I knew, he opened his arms, like he wanted to give me a hug. I started to move into him, but stopped myself.

I had never been so drawn to anyone, not even Cody. If I touched Remy a little, I was going to wind up touching him a lot. That could be dangerous to his continued wellbeing. And to yours, said a little voice in my head. *This boy could break your heart.*

"So," I said, turning back to the sink, "what do I do now?" It was finally sinking in: I was a danger to other humans. No – not other humans. To humans. I was a mutant.

Remy gave his left temple a quick scratch. "What you do next, that depends on you, I guess. Are you still kicking me out?"

I inhaled sharply through my nose. Was I kicking him out? There were assassins hunting this man down. I thought of Lucretia Borger's glossy brochure, and my interview the day after tomorrow. I thought of resumé-building internships and paid room and board and a chance to impress the admissions officers at Tulane. Had it all really been earlier today? It felt a million years ago.

I looked in the mutant eyes of the bruised and slightly swollen bad boy sitting next to me in my kitchen. Was I going to send him on his way, to risk meeting up with whoever was chasing him while he was still nursing injuries? Was I going to pretend this evening had never happened and focus all my energy on impressing Lucretia Borger? Could I really spend tomorrow fleshing out my skeleton of a resumé and shopping for an interview outfit?

"I don't know what I'm going to do," I admitted, to myself as much as to him.

"I have an idea." Remy walked stiffly over to his leather duffel bag and pulled out a pack of cards. I half expected a little showman's flourish, like he had done at the diner with Duke and Holt, but instead he just deployed his smile. "How about we let fate decide, eh?"

NINE

Let fate decide, my well-upholstered backside. Remy's hands might have been too bruised for card tricks, but his mind was as dexterous as a six-handed squirrel. A smarter girl would have folded after he won the first hand, but turns out playing cards with a gambler is as exhilarating as driving a souped-up Firebird, and Remy kept me at the card table for hand after hand until I agreed to let him stay for a couple more nights. That hadn't been the only thing I lost, either. Remy suggested we make things more interesting by playing a form of strip poker, only instead of revealing skin, we would reveal little tidbits about ourselves. By the time I called it a night, it was close to one am, and he had learned a great deal more about me than I had intended, while I still knew very little about him.

The next two days seemed to last a lot longer than days usually did. Because Remy was still recovering, we decided not to experiment with any more touches. The more I thought about it, the more I thought my power was probably most concentrated in my hands and lips. Back in biology class, our teacher had shown us a grotesque picture of a person with enormous lips and outsized hands, out of all proportion to the rest of its head and body. Ms Stapylton had explained that the figure was called a cortical homunculus, and it was a representation of where humans have the most nerve endings. She went on to explain that there was more sensory real estate in the brain dedicated to hands and lips and tongue than to arms and legs and elbows. I figured that meant a touch from my elbow wasn't likely to harm anyone, but a handshake could do some serious damage.

As for French kisses, mine should probably be registered as deadly weapons.

Which meant I was likely to die a virgin. I suppose Aunt Carrie would be thrilled, if only she could believe it. On second thought, no. Aunt Carrie's religion was the type that delighted more in condemning sin than in praising virtue.

There had to be some way to control my power, but I had no idea how to turn down my internal dials. Having Remy around didn't make things any easier, because he was always stripping off his shirt and displaying the kind of lean, well-defined musculature that made me think of tracing his external obliques.

There was another small glitch. Sharing a tiny apartment with an attractive man you absolutely positively cannot touch does not get easier over time, and Remy was genuinely good company. He revealed things about himself in tantalizing bits and pieces like when he told me he had grown up belonging to a thieves' guild, and getting into a conflict with a rival gang.

"There is more going on there than he is telling you," Darnique warned. "But I get it. He is charming." She had dropped by for our usual Wednesday over the hump day dinner and movie, and had wound up staying to rewatch an old nineties fantasy mini-series about a waitress who discovers a portal to a fairy kingdom. By the time Darnique tottered groggily to the door, it was one am and we were all giddy from making fun of the fact that all the women in this fantasy world seemed to have Nineties plucked eyebrows while the male lead had a well-moussed mullet.

So Remy got along well with my best friend. It wasn't as though that made either of us trust him. Still, the morning of my interview with Lucretia Borger arrived, and Remy was still staying at my place with no definite end date in sight.

By all rights, I should have been two late-nights exhausted as I drove Remy's car to the address Lucretia Borger had texted me earlier. I wasn't, though. Remy's 78 Bird had a rare sunroof, and now my stripey hair was blowing in the October breeze, making me feel like I was going a hundred miles per hour instead of seventy. I was wearing my best dress, the green wrap number that I had worn to my police interview, hand washed and hung up to dry because I had been perspiring with nerves at the station. I'd paired the dress with a pair of black zip up boots that matched the black blazer that I'd borrowed from Darnique. The jacket sleeves were a little long on me, and they hid the fact that I was wearing green satin gloves. I might come across as a tad formal with the gloves, but I didn't want to shake Lucretia Borger's hand and accidentally cause her to pass out right at the beginning of my interview.

If she asked why I was dressed so formally, I'd say it was my own quirky fashion statement. Besides, Lucretia seemed like the sort of woman who would approve of a little Grace Kelly touch. Suddenly life was filled with adrenaline-pumped possibility, and I felt as geared up as the Firebird.

"Just be careful," Remy had admonished me, one arm behind his head as he watched me grab my bag and keys. "You know what they say about opportunities that sound too good to be true?"

"Says the opportunist who sounds too good to be true," I replied, holding out my hand for the keys to Remy's Firebird. "I'm not so country that I can't smell cow patty when it's on my shoe."

Remy tossed me his keys, making the quilt slip down his naked chest. "Sometimes, when we are on our guard in one direction, we leave ourselves undefended in another. Before you agree to anything, ask yourself what is in it for her."

I tried not to let Remy's words bother me, but they kept tickling the back of my mind. All right, then. Lucretia had asked me to think of some questions. Maybe I could find a nottooobvious way of finding out what Lucretia was really after. In my limited experience with my mother's new-agey group and Aunt Carrie's church, people got involved with charity work for one of three reasons. Either they were trying to rescue their own younger selves, or else they were hoping to convert new members to their religion, or they were trying to mold people into the shape they wanted. If Lucretia wanted to rescue me from Karl's Diner because no one had rescued her at my age, well, I was fine with that. I didn't want to replay my mother's greatest hits and get involved in a personality cult, though. And I would rather pick corned beef hash out of my hair until I turned thirty than allow myself to be brainwashed and manipulated. I hadn't escaped Aunt Carrie only to fall into someone else's trap.

Distracted by my thoughts, I drove past the drive twice before

I spotted it, marked by a county route sign mostly hidden by a thicket of thorny bushes and October-bronzed trees. The driveway was unpaved and rocky, and I took it slow, not wanting to get a flat out here.

For some reason, Lucretia had rented a house that was seriously tucked away from the road and other houses. I was beginning to worry about arriving late when the corridor of trees thinned out, giving me my first glimpse of the property.

My heart flipped like a hooked fish as I recognized the distinctive shape of the roof coming into view. It had been eleven years since I had last been here, but the big house was unforgettable: A rustic luxe log cabin mansion, all stone and timber, with multiple chimneys and intricately carved balconies and huge picture windows, all overlooking a private lake. I hadn't spent much time in the big house – that had been for the big man and his inner circle, and my mom and I had been relegated to the small outer cabins.

I'd never even thought to ask what had happened to the estate after all twenty-three members of the Wood Spirit Alliance disappeared without a trace. Now it seemed obvious: the state had taken over the property, and it had been rented or sold to Miss Lucretia Borger and friend. A freshly painted sign proclaimed that the property's new name was "Raven's Perch." A wooden sculpture of an enormous raven drove the point home.

It felt like an omen of some sort, but I wasn't sure how to read it.

I parked next to a Range Rover with a vanity plate that said "Raven," and an official looking Borger Institute van. There were some landscapers moving dirt and rocks around, but none of them even looked up when I got out of the car. I crunched over the dirt and pebbles in my high heels, carrying my leather pocketbook and a vinyl folder with my GED paperwork and resumé, which basically talked up my high school extracurriculars and tried to make my waitressing job sound like a degree in abnormal psych. Which it was, really.

The big entrance, which had seemed intimidating when I'd been a kid, now looked more like a big resort hotel to me. Clearly, Lucretia Borger's institute had some money backing up its plans.

"You looking for Ms Borger or Ms Adler?"

I turned to see a pretty young ponytailed woman coming toward me, looking like she had been hiking in cut-off denim shorts, Timberland boots and a red bandana. Her features were Asian and her accent was some kind of California, I guessed. "Either or both," I said.

"They're around here somewhere. I'll help you find them."

I fell in step behind her, gazing around at the reception area and trying to remember whether the big rustic earth-toned couches and chairs were new or from my mom's day. The big antler chandelier was the same, of that I was certain.

"I'm Chieko, by the way," said my guide, "but I won't shake hands – I'm covered with sweat and bug spray."

As I struggled to keep up with Chieko's athletic stride in my interview heels, I noticed a bronze plaque on the wall honoring Ms Lucretia Borger for something in print too small to read quickly. Wishing Chieko would slow down, I said, "Are you part of the internship program?"

Chieko smiled over her shoulder. "Yes, indeed. This is my second month. And let me tell you, it would be great to get another girl."

My heels sounded way too loud on the floorboards as we passed a corridor that I recalled led to the kitchen. "How many of you are there in the program so far?"

"Three guys and me. So far."

"Do you know how many more they're looking for?"

I was dying to ask her more, but Chieko was a fast walker and I was fighting back a flood of memories as we walked into a community room with lots of comfortable-looking chairs clustered in small groups, a huge flatscreen TV and a pool table where two guys were so busy playing each other they barely spared us a glance. I vaguely remembered this room as being a dimly lit place where I ran around barefoot and always got splinters in my feet. Now the floor was polished to reveal a lovely parquet pattern in the wood, the walls smelled of fresh paint and there was an ice cream dispenser in one corner. Some serious money was being poured into the old estate.

"Come on, Blob," said the smaller and wirier of the two pool players. "Make your damn shot." He had an Australian accent – I hadn't realized the Borger Institute was looking at an international pool of applicants.

"Don't rush a master, Pyro," said his much taller and stockier companion, in a Texas drawl. He raised one eyebrow, and something about his impish, slightly unhinged look reminded me of the late comedian John Belushi. "I'm calculating angles here."

"Hey, guys," said Chieko. "You seen the ladies?"

"I think Destiny's taking' a sickie," said Pyro, absently flicking a steel Zippo lighter open and closed as he gave me a quick once over. No wondering how he got his nickname. "Said her head was aching."

"What about Ms Borger?" Something in Chieko's tone made this a rebuke. Perhaps "Destiny" was a nickname not to be used among outsiders.

"Miss Borger's in her office," said Blob, "plotting to take over the world." Turning back to his friend, he said, "Ready to lose some money, Pyro?"

Pyro laughed as he rubbed chalk on his cue. "Nice to see such misplaced confidence."

Chieko gave Blob and Pyro a lazy wave as she led us out and up a staircase that looked down on the main reception area. Maybe I was going to fit in here after all – these folks seemed as fond of snarky nicknames as I was. Although, to be fair, I couldn't tell what made any of these folks successful candidates.

Chieko knocked on a door marked "Private" and said, "I have a new prospect here." She looked at me inquisitively.

"Anna Marie," I said. "The waitress from Karl's Diner?"

"Oh, shoot me now, I meant to come downstairs for you!" The door swung open, revealing Lucretia Borger in all her country glam glory, blonde hair curled and teased, face made up for a photoshoot, wearing a showgirl's version of a western dress and cowboy boots. Behind her, a big oak desk was piled high with papers and photographs. On second look, I realized the photos were all of twenty-something prospectives. My stomach sank a bit. Here I was, worrying about whether or not I was ready to trust this woman, when I probably had a runt pig's chance of making an impression.

"I can see how busy you are," I said.

"That I am," said Lucretia. "Come in, come in," she beckoned me inside with a scarlet-nailed hand. "Thanks, Chieko."

Chieko gave a little wave and closed the door behind her.

There was a thump that made the floorboards vibrate and then Chieko said, "Not here, Blob, there's an interview going on!"

"Sorry, Blindspot," Blob replied in a Texas drawl.

Lucretia laughed and gestured to a heavy wooden chair upholstered in earth tones in front of her desk. There was a black shepherd dog asleep in a bed in the corner. The dog raised his head when there was a second thump, this one so strong it made the walls shake. Then he settled down again, as though this were not an uncommon occurrence.

I kept my smile in place and acted as though I hadn't noticed anything out of the ordinary either. If wacky nicknames and concussive thumps were all just part of the program, then I wasn't going to bat an eyelash, even if the plaster in the ceiling started falling on my head.

"So?" Lucretia rested her head on her folded hands. "What do you think so far?"

"Great place. Cute dog." You can never go wrong praising a person's pet.

Lucretia beamed like a proud parent. "Don't let his couch potato attitude fool you. Rowan's a champion Schutzhund protection dog. I am a firm believer in developing the body as well as the mind, and everyone in the program gets some pretty rigorous training." As if on cue, there was another shout from outside, and I looked out the window just in time to see Chieko giving a roundhouse kick to the Australian boy's kidneys. Pyro retaliated by throwing Chieko over his head, and I flinched in sympathy as the windows rattled in their panes.

"I encourage these impromptu bouts," Lucretia added. "They're so good for morale and team building."

Maybe in theory, but I have always disliked all sweaty team-building exercises. If some skinny dude set me sailing ass over teakettle, I was likely to feel a mite cranky afterwards. "Oh," I said, plastering a smile on my face. "That sounds fun." I wondered how banged up I was going to get if I was accepted here. Too bad I didn't have a cool mutant power, like invulnerability. Or super strength.

"Don't lie."

I stared at Lucretia, shocked. Her expression was still pleasant, but her words felt like a slap. "I'm sorry?"

"Don't say things you don't mean. You're not a good liar, so you shouldn't do it in interviews." All of the girlish, flirtatious mannerisms I'd seen Lucretia use in the diner had been replaced by calm stillness.

I stood up, feeling a wave of heat flooding my face. "I'm sorry," I said, eyes stinging as I grabbed my handbag and got up to leave.

"Where are you going?"

I hesitated, then turned to see that Lucretia was smiling fondly at me. "I thought… you just called me a liar. I assumed–"

"That you were rejected for being a lousy liar?" Lucretia laughed. "Lyin's a skill, sweetheart. You just need to work at it. But I'm curious. Say I was makin' up my mind to show you the door. You wouldn't want to try to convince me otherwise?" Her penciled eyebrows lifted. "You wouldn't put up any kind of fight?"

I felt my shame and confusion burning off, leaving me crusty with anger. "You can't change anyone's mind about anything," I said. "That's one thing any waitress knows. There's no use arguing, unless you feel like having a good shout. Otherwise you're better off smiling and spitting in their soup. Besides, I'll bet you just made up your mind the moment I walked in the door, maybe even before. You might give people interviews and make them fill out tests and such, but you're the type who takes a cold read and goes with her gut." I fumbled for the doorknob, but of course I suddenly appeared unable to work doorknobs. The satin gloves didn't help, either.

"Now, that's more like it."

Confused, I turned back. Lucretia was grinning at me like I'd passed a test. "What?"

"Honesty. You can be blunt as a spoon with me, I won't be insulted. Now sit yourself back down." Lucretia waved her two long-nailed hands emphatically at me, and I found myself sitting once more. "You're actually very honest. That's why you're such a poor liar. But you're also someone who goes your own way. You're an independent thinker."

"Thank you." I was having some trouble catching up.

"Now," said Lucretia, "why don't you tell me a bit more about your abilities?"

This was one bass-ackwards interview. "Well," I said, trying to regroup. "I am a hard worker and a team player." I tried to think what other talents I possessed, in addition to hash slinging and dishwashing. "I know a bit about fixing cars," I ventured.

Lucretia made a note on a pad. "What's your greatest strength?"

Lord, I would have been better prepared for this before the whole lying thing. Course, maybe that was the point – throw the candidate off guard, see how quick she can recover. "Flexibility. I can pretty much adapt myself to any circumstance." I wasn't sure if this was true or not, but it sure sounded good.

"What do you need to work on – besides your lying?" Lucretia twinkled to show me she was joking.

I thought about Remy, making chili in my kitchen, and the written statement on Sheriff Schutte's desk that claimed I didn't know where he was. "Maybe I let people influence me a little too much," I admitted, then instantly regretted my candor.

Lucretia leaned forward. "Good that you recognize it. How do you reckon that affects your other abilities?"

Hands hidden in my lap, I tugged at the ragged cuticle on my right pointer. "They say our virtues are also our vices," I offered. "In some ways, it's a strength, the way I let people in." And suck the life force right out of them, but I didn't say that.

"If you become part of our brotherhood – our institute – then you will work on anything that is keeping you from realizing your full power." She folded her hands in front of her. "So, let's see you do something."

Was I meant to deliver an extemporaneous presentation? "Can you be a little more specific?" I said, hoping she wanted me to give an example of something I had accomplished. I had prepared a little story about helping an elderly lady with dementia, just in case.

"I'm askin' you to give me a demonstration." She landed hard on the last word.

It's always a bad sign in an interview when you don't even understand the question. "I don't mean to seem dense," I said, "but I just do not have the foggiest what you are talkin' about."

Lucretia scribbled a note on her pad. "You don't need to be so modest – or so careful. I'm talkin' about your mutant powers."

TEN

I'm talkin' about your mutant powers.

The shock of Lucretia Borger's blunt statement sent ice down my spine. "I… I don't know what you…" I stopped, because Lucretia was lifting one perfectly plucked eyebrow, and I knew she was right. I was a terrible liar. "I only just found out," I concluded, acutely aware of how lame this sounded.

"Oh, my," said Lucretia, her heavy false lashes lifting as she widened her eyes. "This must be very unsettling and new."

Things were beginning to fall into place. The interns' funny nicknames, those teeth-rattling thumps – Lucretia wasn't looking for any old kind of raw talent. She was looking for what the politically correct called differently powered individuals. "So… you suspected I was a mutant? Or you knew?"

Lucretia tapped her nose with one scarlet nail. "Insider secrets, I'm afraid. Now… can you show me what it is you do?"

I shook my head. I was going to fail this interview after all. "Sorry. All I know is, I touch folks, and drain them. If the person has a mutant power, I can tap into that, but if I'm touching a regular person…" I stared down at my gloved hands. I had bought the satin gloves two years ago, thinking I would wear them to my senior prom. Now they felt like a badge of failure. "I don't have any control, you see. It's kind of a craptastic power."

Lucretia looked so pleased, you would have thought she'd won the lottery. "Sweetheart, you may not see it yet, but that's an amazin' ability. You just need to learn how to make the most of it."

"So you've met others like me? With leechy type powers?" I tried to make it sound like a joke, but Lucretia didn't laugh.

"Honey, I haven't just met folks like you. I've got one on my team. That girl you met? Blindspot – Chieko – can absorb memories."

I stared at Lucretia, letting her confidence wash over me. There was hope. She had seen cases like me before, and all I needed was an experienced team to show me how to harness my power. "That's… that's fantastic!" I tried to settle the questions flapping wildly around my head. Did everyone just know that the Borger Institute was really looking for mutant talents? Was "creativity" some kind of codeword, and did mutants have some sort of sixth sense about who was and who wasn't part of the club? Could other mutants just tell, looking at me, that I was a mutant?

Then it struck me that I might be sounding like I was assuming a whole lot more than I intended. "I mean, the program sounds fantastic, and it would be fantastic if I wound up getting accepted." Ugh, that sounded even worse. I decided to try again. "So… everyone you select for this program's got some kind of mutant talent?"

"Yes, indeed. But of course, there's more to it than that. We're looking for the whole package – integrity, creativity, initiative."

Great. I felt myself deflating. All the other interns had probably spent years honing their skills. I was an overgrown kid, beginning ballet when everyone else my age had been twirling in toe shoes for ages.

"Now, now, don't look so glum." Lucretia made a note on what I was sure was my chart. "Do you feel up to telling me just how recent this all is?"

"Brand spanking new." I looked into Lucretia's eyes, and found myself saying something I hadn't planned. "Just the night before last, in fact."

Lucretia gave out a long "hoo" and fanned herself with a brochure. "We need to celebrate." Lucretia swiveled in her chair and rolled over to a sleek silver espresso machine. "Let me see if I remember how Irene said to use this dang thing." She unfastened the machine's filter, cursing under her breath when she bent one of her long nails, and then brought out a gold embossed box. "These beans are Ospina, Premier Grand Cru," she announced, and I nodded like that meant something to me. "Now, I used to think coffee was coffee, and as long as it was hot and fresh, I was happy." Lucretia poured the beans into the machine and then started working various levers. "But then I got rich." The machine made a sound like a sigh and Lucretia poured the coffee into a mug.

A thought occurred to me. "That's not the fancy stuff they make from animal poop?"

Lucretia laughed as she handed me a Borger Institute mug only partially filled with black coffee. "No civet cats were harmed, I swear." Over on his bed, Rowan lifted his head. Lucretia reached into a jeweled bowl on her desk and tossed him a dog biscuit, which he caught on the fly before settling back down.

I inhaled the coffee's rich chocolate and almond aroma, wondering what was going on. Celebrating seemed a bit premature. Sure, I was a card-carrying mutant, for whatever that was worth, but was I what Lucretia wanted? Now that I knew what the Borger Institute was really offering, though, I wanted it, and bad. "Do you know when you'll be making your final decisions about who goes to the next phase of the process?"

Lucretia laughed. "Next phase? Girl, this coffee's $350 a pound. You think I hand it out to everyone?" She clinked my mug. "Here's to the beginning of your real life." She took a sip of her own coffee before offering me her perfectly manicured hand, which showed the signs of aging her professionally plumped and botoxed face did not. "I'm sorry," I said, "but my power works through touch, and I'm not safe for humans."

"Oh, pshaw, don't you worry about me." Lucretia winked one thickly lashed eye. "You could tap me like a maple and I'd still have enough sap to drown your pancakes." Still, I noticed, she retracted her hand and made a little note in my chart. "Oh – and I suppose I ought to give you this, as well." She pushed the paper in front of her across the table. "Here you go. That's your letter of acceptance."

Feeling a bit dazed, I picked up the letter, which said, *Yes! We are delighted to offer you admission to the Borger Institute Young Leadership Program.* In bold, slashing handwriting that did not go with her Vegas showgirl hair and clothes, Lucretia had written in my name, Anna Marie Neiro, and underneath it she had added: Power absorption.

Then it clicked. I was in the program! I felt a rush of pure happiness at being wanted. "But... how did you... what decided you on me?"

"I knew the moment you served us," said Lucretia. "The very first moment." Lucretia winked at me, and it struck me that the last time I had seen her, she had been a blonde, but now her big, elaborately curled and blown-out hair was more of a strawberry blonde shade. "Any other questions?"

I thought about it. "If it's not too personal… I was wondering… do you have any, um, abilities yourself?" It seemed rude, but I was curious. No, more than curious – right or wrong, I would trust Lucretia Borger more if she were also a mutant.

"I sure do," she said. "I can enhance my appearance." She leaned closer and gave me a conspiratorial wink. "My natural appearance is not quite as… voluptuous."

That explained the hair change, I supposed. "Cool power," I said. It would certainly save a lot on hairdressers and makeup.

"And like I said earlier, I got great reserves of energy. Irene always says I'm more like a twenty year-old than a… whoops, there I go, about to confess my real age." Lucretia laughed her infectious gurgle. "Well, what do you think? You in?"

I had to smile. "I'm in."

Lucretia gave a squeal of excitement. "So, what're we waitin' for? Let's drink up!"

I took a sip, too shy to admit I took my coffee with milk. I wasn't sure what I was expecting, but Lucretia's pricey brew tasted like almonds and berries and chocolate and tingled on my tongue like the beginning of a love affair. I was still savoring the taste of a win as I walked back to the Firebird to drive home. Just as I was about to climb in, the back of my neck prickled and I glanced back up at the house. From a balcony on the second floor, Irene Adler was watching me. At least, I thought she was looking in my direction, but she was far enough way that I couldn't be sure. Could she even see me from the second floor, through the thick tinted lenses that obscured her eyes? I waved at her, just in case, and she waved back, and said something I couldn't hear.

Congratulations, I assumed. "Thank you!" I waved again before driving off. In the rearview mirror, I could see that she was still standing on the balcony, watching me until the road twisted sharply left and there was no way she could see me anymore.

ELEVEN

I was riding a wave of giddy optimism all the way home, so it took me a moment to register that something was wrong. I stood in the doorway of my apartment, trying to figure out what was making my nerve endings jangle with alarm.

It was the smell. At first, I thought that Remy must have been on a cleaning bender, because I hadn't smelled that much bleach since the Forbish twins had an accident at the town pool. As I looked around my kitchen, I saw that Remy had left out a few bowls, a frying pan and a carton of eggs.

Strange. You would think a man hell bent on disinfection would want to put away the dishes first.

"Remy?" I covered my nose and mouth with my sleeve as I put the eggs back in the fridge. There was a pat of butter in the frying pan, partially melted, but the burner was off. Okay, color me puzzled. As I turned the corner into the living room, the chlorinated smell of hardcore cleaning products grew even stronger. "Remy? What's with all the bleach? Did something die in here?"

"Not yet," said a deep, mellifluous man's voice. "But the day is still young." The voice was not Remy's, and I froze.

"Why so shy? This is your home, after all," said the stranger, just as someone grabbed me from behind, covering my mouth before I could scream. "Come in, *querida*, come in."

I struggled and tried to shout, but someone's rubber-gloved hand smothered my sounds. I gagged on the intense smell of bleach, trying to kick back at the person holding me. Panic set in as I realized I wasn't getting enough air, and then rubber-glove guy changed grip and suddenly I was seated on the floor, drawing in deep, shaky breaths while tears rolled down my cheeks.

"Calm yourself, my dear. We just want to talk." The voice sounded familiar, and then I placed it: Antonio Banderas, the sexy Spanish actor who had been the voice actor for Puss in Boots in the *Shrek* movies.

I was hauled up like an unwanted cat by the back of my jacket and turned so that I faced into my living room, where it took me a moment to process what I was seeing. A monstrous pig, almost seven feet tall, as thickly muscled as a body builder and improbably dressed in purple silk pajamas. Remy was kneeling on the floor next to him, and someone had opened the cut over his eyebrow, which was bleeding again. A young woman with six arms was deftly binding him in a bright orange rope.

"I take it this is your home? Charming," said the pigman, and I realized with a shock that the melodious, cultured voice I had been hearing, with its seductive Spanish accent, belonged to this misshapen creature. "Part of a plantation, no? So many people have such negative associations with the old trade," said the porcine giant, running his long, surprisingly skinny pointer finger over the top of my wall molding. "Yet the world has hardly become less cruel, and slavery still exists, as it has always existed." He grimaced as he brushed his pointer and thumb together. "Ugh. Dust." Lumbering over to my sink, he rolled up his silk sleeves. Belatedly, I noticed that my spray bottle of bleach cleanser and sponge mop had been left out. "Why do people content themselves to live in filth?"

"Sorry," I said, unable to stop myself. "I wasn't expecting company."

I felt a blow to the back of my head that made spangled stars dance in front of my eyes, just like the cartoons.

"Now, now, Mortimer," said the pig, drying his hands on a white cloth. On his left wrist, he wore a thick platinum watch that glittered where it caught the light. "We must not damage the mercha…the *mujer joven*." With a slight bow, he added, "You may call me Góngora, señorita. And that is Mortimer."

As my vision cleared, I caught a glimpse of the person holding me from behind in the mirror over my couch. Mortimer, as Góngora called him, was a hulking, barrel-chested figure with powerfully muscled legs and pebbly, mottled, toadlike skin. In fact, he looked like a bit like a toad, a toad in a spotless turquoise preppy shirt and beige khakis. "Hello, Mortimer. I'm Anna Marie," I said, because I had read in one of my psych books that if you make your abductor see you as a real person, they will be less inclined to break you apart and sell you for spare parts.

Mortimer looked away, ducking his head like a bashful schoolboy.

"Last but never least, that is the lovely Rita Wayword," said Góngora, pointing at the six-armed woman who was holding on to one end of the rope binding Remy with one hand while stroking his hair with another.

"Did you miss us, Gambit?" Rita was in her early forties, I guessed, with the hard-packed muscles of a serious athlete, the weathered skin of an outdoorswoman, and the short, dyed platinum hair and multiple ear piercings of a new wave fan. She was dressed in a skintight burnt orange shirt, custom made with multiple arms, and olive-green trousers. I wondered if there were special outlets that catered to the specialized needs of mutant physiques, and realized that if there weren't, it would be a damn fine business opportunity.

Remy gave Rita a lopsided grin. "I miss being on the same side as you, chère."

"Then you ought not to have run away. Naughty boy." As one of her hands pinched Remy's cheek, another pulled on the rope, drawing him closer to her. Two of her other arms were clasped loosely behind her back, like a soldier at ease. I wasn't entirely sure where her fifth arm was, but from Remy's little grunt of surprise, I could take an educated guess.

"Rita, I never knew you cared." Remy's tone was wry, even a little flirtatious   a bravura performance, considering the constant movements of Rita's multiple arms. "You were never so handsy when we were working together."

"I was being professional."

Remy made a strangled sound. "And now?"

"I can combine work and pleasure by tormenting you."

"Watch that one, Rita." Góngora walked across the room with surprising grace and inspected my couch for a moment. "His kinetic charge is not his only power. Ugh, when is the last time this couch was properly power steamed? No, never mind. I can tell the answer is never." He snapped his fingers, and Mortimer tied something around my wrists, securing my arms behind my back before leaving my side to attend to his boss.

"Oh, I know all about Gambit's charisma," said Rita, the fingers of one of her hands closing over Gambit's throat. "He used it on me the last time he was our guest."

Now Remy did spare me a look. I wasn't sure exactly what he was trying to communicate, but my best guess was something along the lines of, "Yes, I didn't tell you I had some special mutant sex magic, but don't worry, I didn't use it on you."

"Ah-ah," said Rita, yanking on Remy's rope and jerking him forward. "No telepathic messages to your new girl."

"You know I'm no telepath, chère," said Remy, recovering his balance. "And Anna Marie is nothing more than a waitress."

"Do not be so dismissive of the service professions." Góngora snapped his fingers again, and Mortimer shook out a length of purple silk, then used it to cover the worn fabric of my green and yellow couch. "The blue-collar professions require the ability to problem solve, and in a true crisis, a plumber is often preferable to a scientist. Besides, this girl is lovely. We do not all need mutant powers to be of value." With a little sigh, he eased himself down onto the silk coverlet as Mortimer carefully retucked and arranged the silk so no part of the pigman touched the coarse fabric of my couch.

I eyed the door, wondering if this was my best chance to make a run for it. Out of the corner of my eye, I saw Remy give an almost imperceptible shake of his head: Don't risk it.

"So, little waitress, are you really nothing more than a server of comestibles?" Góngora's piggish little eyes flicked over me, as if searching for something.

"I'm afraid that's about it." Of the people in this room, I trusted Remy more than the other three, and he wanted me to keep my abilities to myself. "No hidden powers here."

"Really?" Góngora gave a little nod, and then Rita left Remy to walk over to me.

"She's lying." Rita passed one of her hands over me, as if feeling for something invisible about a foot from my body. "There is something here." She added another hand, and began making quick, deft gestures in the air, as if speaking in sign language.

Except I knew a little ASL, and Rita was doing something very different. It reminded me of the new age rituals my mom had performed with her hippie commune friends, except when Rita wove her fingers through the air, the air rippled like a stream. Underneath my long green satin gloves, I felt the little hairs on my arms stand on end.

"You are a well," said Rita, as one of her hands scooped into the air, creating a visible indentation. "A sponge." Her fingers combed a rainbow, then erased it. Frowning, Rita moved around me as her hands continued to flick and pluck at the air around my body. "What else are you? A cipher? An empath?"

There was a fresh, ozone scent in the air. I had a flash of an old memory, of my mother tracing a door in the air in front of her, and shaking her head. "I must be doing something wrong," she had said.

That's when it clicked. Rita was using magic. She was using magic to read me, scanning me for potential powers. I had known about mutants, never imagining I might be one. But magic? Real magic, the kind that was useful in a fight?

That was a revelation. How the hell did you fight a six-armed buffed-up sorceress?

Wait, what if I turned it into an interview question. What's your greatest strength? Flexibility. What's your greatest weakness? Maybe I let people influence me too much.

How do you fight a six-armed sorceress?

You are a well. A sponge. A chameleon.

Remy gave me a quick, sideways jerk of the head. We hadn't had time to work out our non-verbal cues, but instinct told me he was saying, might as well go for it. Since my hands were gloved and tied behind my back, I had limited options.

I lunged forward and bit the hand closest to my face.

Rita yelped and drew back before giving a roar of rage and slamming me with an open-faced palm. "You try that again, I'll remove your teeth."

My face numb and then blazing with the impact, I waited for something to happen. I even glanced down at my ribs, wondering if I would start to grow extra arms right away. It occurred to me that my internship interview outfit might not accommodate those extra appendages. Would my new arms rip the seams of my dress? How much would that hurt? That custom mutant clothing line idea seemed even more brilliant now.

"Look at my hand! You drew blood!" Rita looked enraged. "No one tastes my blood and lives."

"Now, Rita," said Góngora. "Don't overreact. I have antiseptic in the medical kit in the van."

Belatedly, I recalled the white van parked in the back of the apartment complex. There were always cars coming and going here – the building catered to short term renters – but I had noticed the white van because of the old rumor that nothing good ever came out of one.

"That's not the point. She's violated the integrity of my energies!"

And yet I didn't feel any different. As Rita and her boss argued, I tried tracing a little mystical shape in the air, to see if I might have absorbed some of her magic, even if I hadn't sprouted additional arms. *Nothing.* Maybe I needed to touch someone with my hands instead of my mouth. Or maybe Rita's mystical powers gave her some protection. Either way, all I'd managed to do was piss the lady off.

Distracted, I didn't notice another one of Rita's hands coming at me until it was too late. She made a two-handed gesture, as if plucking the strings of an invisible cat's cradle, and my ears began to ring. The lights in the room flickered and then started to fade and I felt a surge of panic. I did not want to be unconscious and at Rita's mercy. *Remy.* I didn't know what he could do to help me, but my eyes searched him out all the same.

"The human girl's not worth your time, G. She's nothing special." His voice sounded lazily amused, but I couldn't make out his expression – the room was rippling with dancing shadows.

"*Que lástima*," I heard Góngora say.

"So we just leave her?" This was from Rita, who sounded aggrieved at the prospect of not causing me more harm.

"I do not traffic in humans. My clients consider them – how do you say it in English? Rogue specimens – inferior in quality."

"She could set the police on us," said Mortimer, and I tried to glare in his general direction.

"I agree," said Rita. "I say take her."

"*Que hacer despues*, eh?" The pig pressed his long fingers

together, considering. "It is not my custom, but a pretty little rogue specimen is doubtless worth a little something." The room was almost entirely dark, and I felt as if I were falling down a long tunnel when I heard someone shout. "Mortimer! Don't let her fall and hit her head again! We want her docile, not brain damaged."

For once, the pig and I were in agreement. Unfortunately, I was too far down the tunnel to tell him about it.

PART TWO

REMY, THE PIGMAN & ME

TWELVE

"How much longer are you going to sulk, chère? We're stuck in adjoining prison cells. You can't ignore me forever."

I glared through the wooden bars of the partition dividing us. "Calling this a place a prison is sugarcoating the situation – a prison would have a few more amenities." The swinish Spaniard's base of operations here in Mississippi was a dilapidated horse farm on the outskirts of town, set back from the main road and hidden by thick woods. As a preteen, I had actually come here for a few riding lessons during my brief but passionate horse-girl phase. Now the main house, which had been generously appointed with horse trophies, tartan prints, spider webs and assorted animal fur, had probably been redecorated in gangster modern, and cleaned to the specifications of a massive porcine germophobe.

Góngora wasn't so fussy about housing his prisoners, however. About an hour earlier, Toadface and the six-armed woman had unceremoniously dropped us into the stalls which had once held a few splay-footed, swaybacked ponies. I had caught a fleeting glimpse of a few other faces peering out of the bars, but the guards had discouraged any idle chitchat about who they were and how long they had been held.

"I must admit, you make a good point," said Remy as he attempted to kick some of the filthy straw into a corner. "It is unfortunate that Góngora's aversion to dirt and disorder does not extend to the care and feeding of his captives."

No one had bothered to muck out the stalls before depositing us here, and the acrid tang of equine urine and manure, combined with wet straw and damp cement, was making my gorge rise. "How long do you think they're plannin' on keeping us here?" I asked.

Remy dusted off his hands. "Not long, chère. He's just parking us here temporarily." Remy gestured at his filthy stall with its rubber bucket. "If he meant to hold us for a while, he would have invested in making this better suited for humans."

"Guess he thought his money was better spent elsewhere." I nodded at the alarm system wired into the ceiling, and the cameras stationed at various angles along the rafters. My mind was racing around like a cornered mouse. Was the Pig going to sell us immediately? Transfer us to another facility? Where would I wind up? My head was pounding, and there was a bitter taste on the back of my tongue. *And you thought you were trapped in your dead-end job.* Without warning, the fear in my belly turned back into anger. "Funny how you never mentioned that this slaver dude was looking for you."

Remy looked rueful. "I did not think he would find me."

"You didn't think?" I wanted to punch him. "What a surprise. Any idea what he plans to do with us?"

Remy didn't respond immediately, and fear prickled the

back of my neck. "Or is there no 'us' now that the manure has hit the fan?" Through the wooden bars that separated us, I saw the flicker of guilt cross Remy's face. Of course there's no us, I thought. Remy was the kind of guy who looked all solid and handsome until you brought a bit of pressure to bear. Then he'd crack like cheap particle-board furniture.

"His plans for you are probably not the same as his plans for me."

My heart gave a nervous flip, like a fish on a line. "Terrific. Great."

"Marie. Look at me." Remy was standing right in front of the heavy wood partition, gripping the bars with his bare hands. There was some kind of metal electronic collar around his neck, with a glowing red light in its center. Even with the fresh bruising, he still looked ridiculously handsome, all high cheekbones and determined jaw, his red-on-black demon eyes filled with unvoiced regrets and something else that made me curl my fingers into my palms. I could have reached over and touched him if I wanted.

For a moment, I indulged the thought of pulling off my stained green satin gloves and draining every last drop of his power so I could hurl objects at his head and explode them, one by one.

"Whoa," said Remy, shivering. "That's some look, chère."

"You're pushing your luck."

"Will it help if I apologize?"

I pulled off my glove and pressed my hand over my pounding forehead. "Yes, of course, just say a few words and everything's right with the world." I made a sweeping gesture that was meant to encompass the filthy horse stall that was my prison cell, the bruises I had sustained, and the entire manure-coated essence of the situation.

"You have every right to be angry, chère. I never intended any of my troubles to rain down on you, but they did. So we're in this together now, us." His rueful tone and whiskey and absinthe accent made me warm to him again, until I remembered what I had just learned.

"Stop trying to manipulate me with your charm. I am wise to you now."

"If you think I'm using my powers on you–"

"Oh, so you admit you have some charm power!"

"I'm wearing an inhibitor collar, Marie." He touched the brass-colored metal. "I can't access any of my powers."

So we were well and truly stuck here. "That's supposed to make me feel better?"

"No point sulking."

"I am not sulking," I said, as I sat down on a bale of hay. "I woke up with the mother of all migraines, and I'm trying not to vomit on myself." Something scuttled under the straw covering the cement floor and I jumped up, grateful that I was wearing boots that covered my calves.

"Marie? You OK, chère?" Remy was back at the partition.

"Define 'OK'."

Remy gave me a crooked smile. "Not wanting to kill me?"

"Depends." I didn't try to keep the resentment out of my voice. There were things you told someone before you asked to spend the night. Like, whether or not you had a communicable disease. If you happened to be married. And last but not least, if you had recently pissed off a bunch of organized crime bosses and assassins. As far as I knew, Remy wasn't guilty of either of the first two, but that was cold consolation to me now. Back at my house, Remy had made it sound as though he had offended some minor local gang members. Clearly he had minimized the situation. "You have any idea what your old friend Piggly Wiggly wants us to do about going to the bathroom?"

Remy frowned. "Do you need to–"

"At the moment, I just need to be sick." Maybe sooner than eventually. But even if I needed to pee like a horse, I was not prepared to actually pee like a horse.

"At least we have some light," said Remy, "so we can see what's crawling around in here."

"Light's not a selling point for me at the moment." The fluorescent bulbs along the ceiling gave off a high-pitched whine that made my eyeballs vibrate.

"Shh." Remy held up a hand.

"What?" But now I could hear the footsteps coming down the central corridor, and the jangle of keys as a door was unlocked and slid open. "Please," said someone in a stall further down. A woman or a very young man. "I don't feel well."

"You will be given a thorough medical check," said a flat, northern voice that I recognized as belonging to Rita, the six-armed witch who had introduced me to at least four of her fists. Then the door was slid shut, and there was a squeaking sound, as if someone was being wheeled instead of walked out of their cell.

I had assumed that there was one upside to being taken by a slave trader: We were valuable enough for our jailers to keep us relatively unharmed. Apparently, this was not the case. Remy was still standing by the barred partition, but the daylight that had been streaming in through the windows was fading and it was impossible for me to read his expression.

A moment later, he looked away, toward our closed door, listening as the prisoner and guard moved past us.

We had been lucky, this time.

Suddenly exhausted, I crouched down, and the slight movement made my head pound. I could taste champagne and grits in the back of my throat, and I drew in sharp, deep breaths to keep them there. Hard to believe that just a few short hours ago, I was celebrating the beginning of my new life as a mutant badass-in-training.

Impulsive decisions. How many times had my Aunt Carrie warned me not to borrow trouble? Funny attitude from a woman who carried the Bible around like a club, but from here on in I was taking her advice. No more ill-advised rescue missions.

Easy promise to keep – I was in no shape to rescue anybody at the moment. In fact, if someone didn't rescue me, I was likely to spend the rest of my life giving foot rubs to lecherous, third-rate princes and gargoyle-faced movie execs.

The back of my mouth filled with bile.

Hanging my head, I focused on my breathing, pulling my hair back from my face in case I lost the battle to keep the contents of my stomach down.

"You OK, chère?"

I glanced over to see Remy looking at me through the bars. "Don't watch me puke."

"I won't." He paused. "Spiral must have cast one hell of a spell on you. Mostly, her incantations wear off with no ill effect."

Spiral, I surmised, was his personal nickname for the six-armed, hard-faced witch responsible for my current state of wretchedness. Well, partially responsible. Mortimer, the toad-faced guy, had done his part to rattle my brains, and both Mortimer and Spiral were working for Góngora, the Spaniard who sounded like a kindly aristocrat and looked like a prizewinning Chester White hog.

I had the sense that Rita had a personal grudge against me, possibly because she felt possessive of Remy. Or maybe because I had bitten her hand hard enough to draw blood.

Ultimately, though, the person who had landed me in this abandoned horse stall, waiting to be sold off to the highest bidder? That would be the sweet-talking Cajun with the demon eyes, sitting here beside me.

THIRTEEN

"All right, Rogue Specimen," said Rita, unlocking my stall and waking me from a fitful sleep. "Rise and shine. Time to get clean." Before I had time to react, she had aimed a hose of cold water at me, leaving me drenched and spluttering. "Here," she said, throwing a bucket into a corner. "That's your en suite bathroom." She folded four of her arms, leaving two to hold the keys to my padlock. "Act fast, limited time offer."

I folded my own two arms. "I am not doing my business with you standing here."

Rita shrugged. "Suit yourself. I'm only changing buckets once a day, so that leaves you with going on the floor."

"Fine." Trying to pretend I was camping, I went to the corner of my stall. "Don't suppose anyone has a radio they can put on?"

From a stall somewhere further down the line, I heard the click of a radio, and the sound of a slightly nasal newscaster saying, "I am here with hundreds of people, all gathered together to pay witness to what is perhaps the greatest turkey event in all of Thanksgiving history." Thank you, I thought, wondering how one of the prisoners had managed to smuggle a radio into their stall.

Rita, who had turned her back to give me some modicum of privacy, pointed angrily with one of her hands. "Hey! You! Cut that out."

"Here is the airplane, just coming into sight... that's a vintage World War II Spitfire, if I'm not mistaken – and oh, and I can just see a banner," the newscaster went on, heedless of Rita's wrath.

"Don't make me come in and get you," said Rita, sounding for all the world like an irate parent.

But the newscaster would not be deterred. As I finished my business, he described the dark shapes starting to drop from the plane and then, with increasing horror, related the fact that the turkeys were dropping on the crowd, injuring the onlookers and creating a scene of panic and chaos. In the background, I could hear people screaming and a child crying, interspersed with a few disturbingly wet splatting sounds.

Belatedly, I realized this wasn't an actual news program, but some kind of spoof.

Rita strode over to the cell and unlocked it. "Damnit, Mortimer forgot to put the damper collar on you." An inhibitor collar. So, the cheerfully oblivious newscaster was really a fellow prisoner, thoughtfully creating a smokescreen of sound to give me some privacy. *Thanks, stranger.*

"Come on," said an incongruously cheerful voice. "You can't object to the *WKRP in Cincinnati* turkey drop episode. It's a classic!"

"I don't care if it's Hamlet. Shut up or I'll put you on mute."

"I take requests," said the optimistic prisoner. "Do you have a favorite progra–"

"Silence is my favorite program," said Rita, marching back to my stall. "You done in there?"

I handed her the bucket. Waving three of her hands over it, she muttered something under her breath before handing it to Remy. I felt embarrassed until I realized that she had probably just magically cleaned the bucket. Since I didn't want to listen to Remy answering the call of nature any more than I had wanted him to listen to me, I yelled out, "Hey, mimic person? Just wanted to say thanks."

"I can mute you too," said Rita. To be fair, she did not cast any more spells, and as she walked down the aisles, I saw her unlock one of the stalls.

"Thanks a lot," said the unmuted captive. "I swear, no more TV quotes."

There was a click, and then Rita said, "I don't care what you talk about without me here, but this collar will keep you from getting into any trouble."

After she had left, I heard the mimic say, "As God is my witness, I thought turkeys could fly." It was his own voice, though, with no sound effects.

Before any of us could start talking again, the barn door opened and the toadlike Mortimer came through, wheeling a cart. He passed me an aluminum water bottle and an aluminum bowl filled with what was either tex mex chili or pig slop.

"Say, Remy," I said, sniffing suspiciously at the slop. "Why do you think I didn't absorb Rita's powers?" If touching someone skin to skin was the key, surely a bite should have had an immediate effect.

Remy gestured for me to lower my voice. "Spiral – Rita – has the power to repulse all forms of possession. I suppose what you do is similar."

So magic could protect against mutant powers? The world was a lot stranger than I had realized, and I had been raised by two very strange women. Either way, it appeared that my mama and her sister had not been totally nuts when they talked about "psychic energies" and "demonic forces."

Speaking of demons...

"When I called you a demon," I said, fixing Remy with a fierce glare, "you made out like I'd lost my marbles."

"Spiral isn't a demon. She's a magic user."

"Oh, forgive me for not being politically correct."

"It's not about that. There are demons. She just happens to be a magic user with cybersorcerous modifications."

I had never felt so small town in my life. "We don't get too many of them in Mississippi."

"There aren't too many like Spiral anywhere." Remy took a bite of his chili, made a face, and then took another.

"Huh. You think maybe it's time you tell me how you got mixed up in all this and how it's absolutely not your fault, and by the way, why the hell didn't you warn me I could wind up getting trafficked by a slave-trading pig?"

"You knew the Thieves' Guild and the Guild of Assassins were looking for me."

"Yes, but you said they couldn't find you if you didn't use your powers!"

"I did not say that." Remy went on eating his chili, apparently unperturbed.

"You implied it!" The words came out at top volume, making my temples throb. Lord, the man was infuriating. Did he really think that none of this was his responsibility?

A muscle jumped in Remy's jaw. "I did not think my father – that Jean Luc would involve Góngora. But there is no other explanation. An assassin would take me out, and no one else – it is a point of pride, you see."

"So you had no idea that you were putting me in danger? Seriously?"

"I swear."

There was a rustle and thump in the stall next to ours. "Hey, lovebirds," said the unseen occupant of the other stall. "It's very entertaining listening to you make up and all, but can you shut up a sec and just let me sit here in silence and brood?"

I sat up. "Who are you? How long have you been here?"

Remy was staring at the dividing wall on the other side of his stall, but his surly neighbor must have been sitting down, out of sight. "Do you have powers?"

"Of course I have powers," said the neighbor, who sounded female or young or both. "I can walk through walls, don't you know? I just like being a prisoner because it feeds into my dark romance fantasies."

"I'm Marie," I said, pulling off my blazer and laying it on a hay bale. As I straightened up, I realized that my dress had a rip down the armpit seam that qualified as a wardrobe malfunction. "My friend's name is Remy."

"Some friend. You were yelling at him a moment ago. In my experience, that means you guys are going for it or about to go for it."

"Sorry to disappoint," I said, talking over Remy and preventing him from saying whatever he was going to say. "We're going be like one of them snarky sitcom couples you think will get together, but never do."

"Until they finally do get together and ruin the show?"

Smartass kid. I tried to retie my wrap dress so it covered a bit more of me. "What's your name?"

"Lin. Lin Li."

"Is it all right if I ask how old you are?"

"Twenty."

"Try again."

"Sixteen."

I thought about it. Nope. "You're fourteen."

"How did you know?"

"I didn't," I admitted. "I was just fishing." Even though I kept my tone matter-of-fact, I met Remy's eyes in the shadowy stall. A fourteen year-old! I don't know why I would expect a slave trader to have some moral compass, but for some reason this shocked me. "How long have you been here?"

"I don't know. Couple of days. A week, maybe?"

"You have a power, yes?" Remy was looking out in the direction of the other stall, and for the first time I felt that his charisma wasn't just the kind of charm that made you want to nibble his neck. He could make connections with people – even fourteen year-old kids hiding their fear under a deadpan manner. "Don't worry, I have a power too. I can make things explode."

"I can do little."

"I doubt that very much."

"No, I mean, I can dolittle – like the doctor?"

I still didn't get it. "Doctor do little?" Then I got it. "You talk to animals!"

"No," said Lin, sounding bored and exhausted. "That's what

normal people do. I listen to animals. And I understand." Before I could ask anything further, Lin went on the offensive. "So he can make explosions. What about you? What can you do?"

"Nothing," said Remy, looking at me for a moment before facing Lin. "That's why she don't have the collar."

"Lucky," said Lin. "This weighs a ton. I'm probably going to have neck ache when they finally take it off."

All right, so Remy wanted me to pass myself off as human. That had to mean he was cooking up a plan. Somewhere under all the straw in my stall, a mouse squeaked. Jumping up, I walked over to the partition bars. "So what happens now?" I pitched my voice low so only he could hear.

Remy was looking at me with thinly disguised concern. "Me, they will take to my father. You – they will get you ready for auction."

Crap. I looked down at my gloved arms. Lowering my voice even more, I asked, "Wouldn't it help if they knew I wasn't just a smart mouth waitress?"

"Yes and no." Remy's voice was so quiet that I had to lean in to hear him. "If they realize you have powers, you may be sold to someone who wants you for – less objectionable work."

"So why not tell?" Less objectionable work sounded like a euphemism for not having to massage unguents into some flabby potentate's sloping shoulders.

"Because I have a plan for us to escape."

FOURTEEN

Over the next two days, I got to know some of our fellow prisoners when we were marched into the outdoor ring for daily exercise and inspection. It was a glorious October day, warm but not hot, the sky just beginning to lose its summery haze. It reminded me of that new books and pencils feeling, when the academic year was still fresh and you still felt kind of excited about being in school.

I tried not to think about Lucretia Borger's acceptance letter, and the chance that had seemed just within my grasp before it had been yanked away. I had a mission – use my finely honed waitress skills to figure out as much as I could about each prisoner and guard.

"Most mutants don't have big, flashy battle-worthy powers," Remy had explained. "Part of what Góngora will be doing is figuring out how to market each new captive – and how to match them to the right buyer. We need to figure that out before he does – and get you in a position to absorb as many abilities as possible." I felt a stomach-clenching blend of excitement and anxiety at the idea we were depending on my unproven abilities. For better or worse, though, I was the only prisoner not wearing an inhibitor collar, so I was going to have to quarterback this game.

Remy had managed to lift a scribbled duty roster from one of the guards' pockets, but the shorthand list of names and assignments wasn't much to go on. We would have to do our own due diligence, because making an escape plan out of a hodgepodge of oddly powered mutants was a bit like trying to make the daily special out of whatever was left in the diner fridge the day before delivery. On the bright side, making the best of leftover bits was one thing life had prepared me for.

As Lin and I trudged through the dry earth, our swinish captor observed us from the back of a handsome chestnut gelding that kept stamping its foot and pawing the ground. Góngora had dressed himself in a classic British riding jacket, specially tailored jodhpurs and shining high boots cut to accommodate his trotters. He smiled benignly down at us as we passed, and even gave me a mocking salute with his riding crop.

"You've got to admire his commitment to reenacting *Animal Farm*," said Lin in an undertone. "I'm just surprised he doesn't snap a whip at us." In person, the teenage deadpan snarker was a slender, brown-eyed brunette whose family came from a very small island in the South Pacific that had been downwind of a lot of nuclear testing from the Fifties through the mid-Nineties. Perhaps this explained why Lin had a look of world weariness that would have been impressive in a forty year-old. It certainly helped explain why she had an impressive pair of antlers coming out of her head.

"He's too genteel for a whip," I said, trying to get some of the dust we were raising up off the ground out of my left eye. "I'm surprised he's not eating cucumber sandwiches while Rita whips us."

As we passed, Góngora's high-strung horse gave a shrill whinny.

"Frau Blucher," said Lloyd, catching up to us. Deprived of his mimicry powers by the inhibitor collar, Lloyd compensated by providing constant pop culture and literary references.

Lin raised an eyebrow. "Frau whofer?"

"*Young Frankenstein* reference. Classic Mel Brooks movie? Every time her name is mentioned, the horses panic." Lloyd was a tall and slightly goofy looking music teacher with thick black hair that stuck straight up. At first, I figured Lloyd would be the kind of teacher endlessly pranked and teased by his students, because he was such an earnest, classic nerd, but then I realized there was a sly, stealthy intelligence lurking behind his thick, black-framed eyeglasses. "Don't tell me you don't know who Mel Brooks is!"

Lin gave a derisive snort. "My parents like Mel Brooks. I like the son's zombie books, though."

"Did you read the latest one, about Bigfoot?"

"Not yet, but I was wanting to. Was it good?"

As Lin and Lloyd discussed Bigfoot, we passed an attractive, curvy blonde who used a wheelchair. She had wholesome, corn-fed, girl-next-door looks, and she wore her long hair – natural blonde, or maybe slightly lightened – in two braids. I wasn't sure what her name or power was, because I had only seen her briefly, when the guards moved her out of the horse barn and into a room in the main house. It seemed that Góngora didn't think a person who used a wheelchair needed exercise, because she was kept outside the fenced horse enclosure which had once been used for outdoor lessons. I hoped the insects weren't bothering her. Presumably because she wasn't moving around, she was surrounded by a halo of tiny midges or gnats.

Then there was Axel. He was a true redhead, with a trim beard and pale skin that was already starting to burn under the Mississippi sun, even though it was a fairly cool day. Like Cody, he played football, and he was good-looking enough that Remy kept glancing over at us as we walked the circuit.

Axel did not want to talk about his powers.

"I don't want to talk about it."

"Come on, Axel, how bad can it be?"

"Absolutely worse." We were walking around the outdoor ring under the watchful eyes of Rita and Mortimer, aka Spiral and Toad. Toad was positioned outside the gate, wearing mirrored sunglasses, a navy windbreaker and a glum expression that said he'd rather be assigned somewhere else. Of course, that might just have been the natural downturn of his mouth – resting toad face. Rita was also wearing sunglasses, but she looked like a woman on a mission as she paced around the inside of the fence. Her form-fitting khaki slacks were tucked into high leather boots that made her look like a horse trainer, and showed off the impressive muscles in her thighs.

Like everyone else, I had been given a baggy bright yellow suit, a bit like doctors' scrubs. From a distance, we looked like a bunch of ambulatory bananas. Everyone else was wearing a brass-colored inhibitor collar, the red lights shining as a constant reminder that they were electronically dampening the wearer's mutant abilities.

The others also had little patches on their yellow scrubs, giving a clue as to the special sauce of each wearer. Lin's patch was a pair of antlers, and underneath was the title "Nature Girl." This made Lin indignant. "Why do I have the gendered name? Remy isn't Gambit Guy. Lloyd isn't Parrot Man." Remy's patch was a little explosion, a playing card, and the name, "Gambit." Lloyd's new name was "Parrot," and his symbol was an African Grey.

"I still don't understand why I can't be 'Mimic,'" said Lloyd, fingering his patch. "Parrot makes me sound like someone's neurotic pet."

"There's already a Mimic," said Axel, putting his hands in his pockets and hiking up the legs of his jumpsuit as he walked. "He absorbs other people's powers."

Lloyd pushed his glasses up with one finger. "Then he ought to be called Absorb."

"But if he were female, he would have to be Absorb Girl," said Axel with a smirk.

Lin, walking behind Axel, lowered her head and butted him with her antlers. "And what the hell are you supposed to be, Axel? Acid Lad? Mr Venom? Poison Boy?"

Axel's patch was a bottle filled with green bubbles. "Acid Lad works."

"Wait," I said. "What is your power, anyway? Can you transform one liquid into another?"

Axel sighed. "No. What's it to you?"

I shrugged. "Living vicariously." I didn't have a patch, of course, as I was Góngora's inferior human specimen, thrown into the mix because I had been in the wrong place at the wrong time. "Can you turn yourself into a green ooze?"

"Sorry."

I searched my brain. "How about neutralizing poison? That's a fine power."

Axel made a face. "Let's put it this way," he said, shoving his hands into his pockets. "I learned about my powers when I gave my girlfriend second degree burns on her face and neck."

I winced, sorry I had pressed him so hard. Without thinking, I said, "I know what it's like, hurting someone without intending to." We stopped talking as we passed closer to Rita, who was wearing a skintight shirt that showed off the ripcord lean muscles in her six arms, three of which were folded in front of her while the other three were fisted on her hips.

Rita must have overheard my last comment, though, because she gave me a nasty smirk before calling out, "And how exactly do you know what Axel's feeling? Have you vomited hydrochloric acid on someone, Rogue Specimen?"

So that was Axel's power. No wonder he didn't want to talk about it. It was on the tip of my tongue to confess what had happened with Cody, but from across the yard I saw Remy watching me. "I vomited on my Aunt Carrie the first time I had a drink," I improvised. "It wasn't acid," I added, "but she was plenty upset."

Axel gave me a disgusted look. Clearly, embarrassing yourself in front of your aunt was not at all the same as accidentally disfiguring your girlfriend, and now Axel had me pegged as the kind of idiot who doesn't know the difference between their embarrassment and your major trauma.

Rita shook her head, as if marveling at my stupidity. "Just keep to yourself, Rogue."

I paused. "I'm not good enough to talk to mutants? That's reverse prejudice. Besides, if you think mutants are so terrific, why are you helping Góngora makes slaves out of them?"

Rita grabbed the front of my yellow scrubs with three of her arms and hauled me up so I was dangling. "Góngora's one of us. The rest of these prisoners are going to get trained and employed by the elite guilds. In time, they can earn their freedom. You? You'll be someone's fetch and carry girl – if you're lucky."

I stared down into Rita's hard face and couldn't stop the words from tumbling out of my mouth. "If the job's so all fired terrific, then why aren't they hirin' folks instead of capturin' them?"

Rita lowered me until my nose was level with hers. "Listen, Miss Rogue Specimen, I'm sure your life has been all Southern-fried cotillions and candy-coated racism, but let me clue you in. Góngora didn't invent the mutant slave trade, and he could hardly stop it singlehanded. So he decided that the best way to help mutants was by gaining some real power. If someone was going to make money off mutants, it ought to be a mutant."

I could smell Rita's breath – spearmint gum and the kind of fury that grows over a foundation of guilt. "If you're so sure that you've got the moral high ground here, how come I make you so mad?"

Something flickered in Rita's pale eyes. I had hit a nerve. "You don't understand." She lowered me to the ground. "Góngora helped me out of a very bad situation in Prague. He didn't have to do it, and now I owe him my loyalty."

I straightened my shirt, hoping the baggy yellow prison trousers didn't show a damp spot, because truth to tell, Rita scared the heck out of me. I just didn't know how to shut up when someone was bullying me. "Tell me something, Rita," I said, more softly. "You seem to like Remy, if I'm not mistaken. You really OK with serving him up to the folks who want to kill him?"

She hadn't been expecting that. "I do like Remy," she said. "But we're on opposite sides of this one, and there's nothing I can do about that."

I nodded and walked away, wondering if there was a chance we could turn Rita. Unlike the Toad, she didn't seem to view her boss with pure adulation. On the other hand, she seemed like the kind of person who took her duties seriously – and she was no dummy. Out of the corner of my eye, I saw Rita shaking out her fingers, a look of puzzlement on her tanned face. Shoot. Had I given myself away?

"You be careful, chère," said Remy, when I crossed over to where he was doing stretches against the fence. "If Rita finds out that you're playing her, she'll make you regret it."

"Okay, Gambit," I said, deliberately using Rita's name for him. "So how about you implement some of that Cajun charm on your old friend?"

Remy grinned and whipped off his baggy yellow shirt, revealing his admirable chest and shoulders. "As if I would do such a thing, when my heart belongs to you." With that, he set off at a loose-limbed jog that took him directly past the six-armed sorceress' gaze.

Behind me, I heard a sharp cracking noise, followed by a horse's frightened whinny. There was a startled cry, and as I turned, I saw Góngora topple from his horse in a pink blur. For a split second, the image in front of my eyes flickered, and the slave trader seemed smaller. Then there was a loud thump and a cloud of dust as horse and rider came down. A moment later, the weird flickering was gone, and I dismissed it as a nerve twitch – probably the result of stress.

There was a yelp of dismay from the Toad as he raced over to the massive porcine figure lying on the grass right outside the exercise ring. Góngora's pale riding breeches were ripped and coated with dust and a smear of blood. Off to the side, I saw the blonde watching from her wheelchair with a surprisingly hard look on her wholesome face. It might have been my imagination, but the swarm of insects around her seemed even thicker than before.

"Góngora! Are you hurt?" The Toad's webbed hands fluttered over the pigman's body.

"Don't touch me," said Góngora, and his voice sounded higher and more nasal than usual. He rolled, trying to get up, then let out a startled squeal of pain. "My leg," he said.

"Please, let me help you." Unable to assist Góngora, the Toad was wringing his hands in distress.

"Watch the prisoners!" Góngora heaved himself upright, followed by Rita's voice shouting.

"Stop right there!"

I felt a tug on my arm and whirled around – Remy was grabbing my sleeve as he ran toward the fence, yanking me along. Rita raised three of her hands, and just as I was taking in the fact that Remy had spent precious moments saving my ass, the sorceress rolled her wrists and made a gesture that stopped Lloyd, Lin and Axel in their tracks. They had been trying to slide under the fence to escape the exercise ring – Axel had nearly made it out.

"Come on, come on," said Remy, as if I were dawdling instead of doing my best to catch up to him. I didn't see Rita's hands move again, but I knew what must have happened when I felt my body lock in mid stride. I was bent forward at the waist, right leg bent and left leg behind me, and I should have fallen over when

I froze, but something held me suspended. A few strides in front of me, Remy was caught as he vaulted his legs over the fence. I wondered how the heck Rita was going to let us down without hurting us.

The answer came swiftly – she wasn't. I crashed into the ground, the air rushing out of my lungs. *Air. Breathe.* Suddenly I could move again, and I moved onto my hands and knees, struggling to get my breath back. The pain came a moment later, mostly centered on my left hip, where I had landed.

By the time I had stopped gasping and shaking, the blonde woman in the wheelchair was gone, and Remy was watching me with concern. I must have looked as miserable as I felt.

"Don't worry," Remy said when we were marched back to the horse barn, which seemed a whole lot farther away than it had earlier in the day. "That was never going to work. But we are getting out of here."

I grunted, feeling a lot less sure than I had before we'd attempted the escape.

"Oh, just shut up," said Axel, moving even more stiffly than I was. "The only way we're getting out of here is with a 'sold' stamp on our foreheads."

"Now, now," said Lin, deliberately scuffling along and raising puffs of dirt with each step. "Don't you know you have to humor a dementia patient?" No one laughed. Suddenly the bright blue sky with its perfect clusters of fleecy white clouds seemed a lot darker, as we trudged along the dirt path that led through the lovely green pastures, helpless as any farm animal to alter our fates.

FIFTEEN

The next day, Rita and the Toad were joined by another guard, who had pangolin-style scales, sharp claws, and the improbable name of Sherwood. Clearly, Góngora had a preference for mutants who, like him, were visibly different from typical humans. In a way, it was kind of admirable, since those were the mutants who received the brunt of human prejudice.

At least, it might have seemed admirable if I hadn't been a prisoner about to spend my third night on a heap of old horse blankets and dirty straw. We hadn't seen Góngora or his horse all day, but we had heard a shot from the field behind the barn, and a sound halfway between a roar and a scream. After that, no one did much talking in the exercise ring, and even Lloyd seemed unable to find an appropriate quip. I kept replaying the scene in my mind – the crack, the thump, the odd flicker in my vision – and wondering why the hell I hadn't made a bid for freedom like the others. Had Aunt Carrie's doctrine of submission penetrated my psyche after all? What was wrong with me?

As I did my best to rinse out my mouth and wash my face in fresh water from a bucket, I felt a wave of despair. I had roughed it before, camping out with the girl scouts and coming home filthy with ash and melted marshmallow clinging to my hair. This was different. I was no longer in charge of my own fate, and I couldn't do any of the small rituals that usually made me feel better – soak in a tub, wash my hair, rub lotion into my hands and feet. Worse, though, was the sense that I was failing some kind of test. I hadn't really harbored a fantasy of training with Lucretia's academy and becoming the Southern version of an X-Man, but the thought had danced at the corner of my consciousness. Now I had to face the fact that power or no power, I didn't have the kind of personality a hero needed to succeed.

If I'd been alone, I would have indulged myself with a good cry. As it was, I tried to keep my emotional girdle on, as Aunt Carrie used to say.

"You OK, chère?"

I summoned a smile for Remy, who had repacked the straw in his stall and was now shaking out the horse blanket to cover it. "Okay enough."

"You getting your bed ready?"

"Sure." I forced myself to go through the motions of repacking the straw and shaking out my own horse blanket, but I could feel Remy's eyes on me. He had become alarmingly good at reading my moods, and without waiting for my response, he stretched out by the partition, where there was an inch of space between the floor and the wood divider. This had become our nightly ritual. We didn't touch hands, but we sat with our backs just about touching, pretending that we weren't imagining what we might do if the barrier between us were gone.

Course, there was still the little problem of my uncontrolled power, but having the partition made it possible to pretend. Cushioning my cheek with my hand, I tried to settle by breathing. Something tiny brushed against my cheek – an ant? A fly? Sitting up, I scrubbed at my face with my hand.

"Stop it."

"I can't help it. I hate bugs."

"That's not what I meant. Stop beating yourself up."

I stared at my hands, realizing I had been doing just that. "I froze today. When you all started to make a run for it."

"Yeah. You froze. And I bolted, without even looking back for you." His voice, pitched low so it wouldn't carry to the other stalls, sounded rougher than usual.

I wrapped my arms around my knees, confused and suddenly a little cold. "What are you talking about? You grabbed me. You wasted precious time to help me."

"I turned *back* to grab you. Not my first impulse."

I was silent for a moment. "We both grew up not trustin' much in other people," I said at last. "The fact that you're feeling raw about this now means you're changing."

Remy let out an audible breath. "Maybe." He reached out a hand under the partition. It was a nice hand, long-fingered, a little tanned, the swelling from that fateful first beating almost gone. The urge to twine my fingers with his was so powerful I had to dig my nails into my own palms.

"I can't."

He kept his hand out. "Just for a moment."

I touched him with one finger, lightly. I felt the awareness of him like a current between us.

"You feel anything? The collar disrupts my powers."

Oh, so this was a tactical experiment. Trying not to feel disappointed, I considered whether I had felt anything transfer. "I don't know. Maybe not."

"But there was that jolt."

"Oh," I said, "I assumed that was just…" suddenly conscious of what I was confessing, I left the rest unsaid.

"Good to know it's not just me, then." Voice rough, wry, warm.

"I wish I knew you well enough to tell when you're just flirting like a reflex."

A pause. "Can't you tell?"

"No, I can't tell! I can't even tell what I'm feeling!" I expected him to chuckle and dismiss this with another flirty comment. Instead, he surprised me.

"Then you need to learn yourself better," he said. "Especially with a power like yours, it is no small thing not to know your own heart."

"What d'you mean?" But the implications were already sinking in. "D'you mean I might be absorbing more than just powers?"

"You tell me."

Oh, lord, what if I had to learn how to take a power without soaking up someone else's personality along with it? I had never really thought about it before, but having a mutant power was like having a nice voice, or being coordinated, or having a feel for how to put colors together. You had some native ability, but that didn't make you a singer or an athlete or an artist. You needed to get trained or train yourself. You needed to figure out how to use what you had. Take Lloyd, for example. If you could mimic sounds and voices, that was cool, but in the end it was nothing but a party trick until you figured out what you wanted to achieve and how your ability could help you achieve it. Hell, if I had managed to absorb Rita's powers and sprouted six arms, would I have been able to coordinate those suckers in a fight? Doubtful.

Not to mention that doing something when you're all calm and prepared is a heck of a lot different than doing it when your adrenaline is flowing and your brain is all flight or fighting.

That was the biggest difference between Remy and me. He knew himself. He knew what his powers could do. And that was going to be my biggest challenge, moving forward. I would always be a beginner when it came to my powers, because I would be absorbing someone's gifts without having much time to get to know what they were and how to use them to best effect.

"You're thinking awful hard, chère."

I was going to have to think a whole lot harder. Somehow, I was going to have to do my research and prep myself before I laid my hands on people. Otherwise, I could touch someone and gain their power, but still wind up standing there with my jaw hanging open, frozen in place while opportunity passed me by. "I think today just taught me somethin."

"What?"

I didn't get a chance to respond, because just then there was a bang on the door that made both of us jump.

"All right, everyone. Stay calm and stay quiet." Rita strode down the aisle, while Mortimer checked off names on a clipboard. Sherwood, the pangolin-faced guard, slouched in last, looking between the other two guards before arranging himself with his hands clasped in front of him. Sherwood's scales and inhuman features made it hard to tell, but I'd have laid money on his being both young and inexperienced at this guarding business.

"All accounted for," said the Toad.

Remy, lean and raffish even in his baggy yellow scrubs, leaned against the bars of his stall. "What's the deal? This is later than the usual inspection."

"Nothing to do with you, Gambit." Rita stopped in front of my door, but instead of checking my name off, Toad said, "You got the others?"

"Affirmative." Rita fanned out her six arms, and to my utter astonishment, Mortimer unlocked the padlock securing my door. There was the sound of a metal bolt being slid back and the clank of my wooden door being opened.

"What's happening?" Involuntarily, my eyes sought out Remy's. "Am I being released?"

"Góngora wants to see you," said Toad, as if this were something of an honor. "That's all we know."

I stepped out under the fluorescent light that made everything look more sinister. Rita narrowed her eyes and jerked her chin, and I forced myself to follow the Toad through the barn.

"Come on, Stripey," said Sherwood, pushing ahead of Rita, who bristled. "We don't have all day." He looked as jumpy as I felt.

"Wait a sec. Is she coming back?" Lin's voice was strident, as if she were complaining about a change in her school's detention policy. "Is she in trouble or something?"

"Quiet down," said Sherwood. His voice was belligerent with insecurity, and no one paid much attention to him.

"Stay strong," yelled Axel. He touched his two thumbs together, flashing me a letter 'Z' with his hands. I had no idea what it meant, but it looked heartfelt, so I smiled over my shoulder at him.

"Hang in there, kid," added Lloyd, and I could tell that if the inhibitor collar hadn't been on him, he would have sounded like Humphrey Bogart or some famous Eighties football coach. "And remember – watch your thoughts, they become your words. Watch your words, they become your actions. Watch your–"

"Ass," said Lin, earning a dark look from Lloyd.

I was almost out of the barn when I heard Remy's voice.

"Rita," said Remy. "I know that we've had our differences, but I'm counting on you to–"

"I said shut it!" This time, Sherwood turned and raised his tail – all six feet of it – and lashed it against Remy's cell. Remy shouted, "It's going to be all right, chère." Then the barn door clanged shut, with me on the outside.

SIXTEEN

I had been wrong about the main house. Góngora hadn't just redecorated – he had renovated. A wheelchair accessible ramp had been added to the outside, and a chair lift installed beside the staircase. Where there had once been a solid wall separating the hallway and the main room, there was now a big arched opening, inlaid with more tile. And the old skylight had been enlarged, so the whole house felt brighter and cleaner and more exotic. The tiles and white-washed walls reminded me of pictures I'd seen of Morocco, but maybe there were parts of Spain that looked like that.

Góngora was seated in a big leather reclining chair in front of the fireplace, which had also been decorated with ceramic tiles. There were smaller leather chairs arranged in a semicircle, angled so anyone sitting could admire the oil painting of the swinish master of the house, dressed in his riding clothes astride the chestnut. Presumably, the painting had not been done from life, as it seemed Góngora's riding ability hinged on the horse's ability to remain entirely still.

"Ah, there you are, my little Rogue Specimen." The cultured Spanish baritone was back, but I couldn't erase the memory of that first high-pitched squeal of fright. "That will be all, Rita. Thank you."

Rita glanced at me. "I don't trust this one."

Góngora chuckled. "Ordinarily, I trust your instincts, but I believe in this case you may be allowing a personal grudge to cloud your judgment. In any event, Mortimer is present and perfectly capable of dealing with any irregularities."

Rita glanced back at the Toad, who was lurking between Góngora and a potted palm. She opened her mouth, as if about to object, then closed it and acceded with a curt nod before turning on her heel. Two pairs of her arms were relaxed at her side, but the third pair was jammed into her trouser pockets, giving her the look of a sulky teen as she loped off.

I stood, not sure what to do with my own two arms. I felt acutely conscious of the fact that I had worn the same yellow scrubs for the past three days and nights, unwashed except for that first hosing down. I could smell myself, and it wasn't pleasant. "What did you bring me here for?"

"Nothing terrible, I assure you." He steepled his long fingers. "Forgive me for not offering you a seat, but these chairs are made of a particularly fine leather, impossible to clean except for a light oiling."

Maybe my foul state would afford me some protection. "How about I go home, get washed up and then come back?"

Góngora chuckled, then winced and leaned forward, bringing his feet down. I realized that one of his feet, mostly concealed by his purple silk pajamas and dressing gown, was wrapped in a clean linen bandage. "A rogue in spirit as well as in name, I see." He paused, then looked behind me at the Toad. "Have you prepared the bedroom, my old friend?"

Toad nodded. "Yes, sir. But I must ask, is it truly advisable to trust the girl with such close proximity to your person?"

Bedroom. Proximity. My stomach hollowed out, and I felt suddenly lightheaded with horror. "No," I said, not even thinking. "I can't do that. I won't."

The hard, little piggish eyes met mine. "Calm yourself, human. I have no designs on your person."

I stared back at Góngora, my heart still flinging itself against my ribs – and I believed him. I was still clammy with fear, but I sucked in a deep breath and calmed myself. My captor might look like the quintessential beast, but there was no lechery in his gaze. He wasn't going to bathe me, dress me in a slave girl bikini and leave me chained to his bed. Emboldened, I took a step closer. "What is it you want from me?"

Mortimer stiffened and started to move toward me, but Góngora held up a hand and the Toad slunk back to his corner. "Please – stay where you are. I prefer we keep at least four meters apart." I could see the piggish nostrils flare with alarm, but he kept his manner courteous. So he needed my willing participation – or, at least, he preferred it.

I had no idea what four meters was, but I didn't take a step back, because it felt like that would be showing weakness. "If you're so scared of my cooties, then why did you ask me in here in the first place?"

"Because I require your assistance, my dear."

I could feel myself going all squinty. "Why me? Why not one someone you trust?" My eyes drifted to Mortimer, who looked like he was asking himself the same question.

"Mortimer and Rita have other duties, and you…" Góngora shrugged. "You are of lesser value than the others. Serve me well, Rogue, and perhaps I will keep you in my employ instead of selling you."

In the movies, I'm sure any heroine in my position would have said something witty and disdainful, and maybe even spat on the lovely tile floor. I was smarter than that. Remy had told me to gather as much information as possible so that we could use my powers to effect a jailbreak, and I had just been given the perfect opportunity. The only challenge was looking surly and reluctant enough not to give the game away. "I guess I don't have much of a choice," I said, huffing out a sigh.

"Good, good." Góngora leaned back into his recliner and motioned for Mortimer to take me away. "Mortimer will take you your new quarters to bathe and dress and then you will come attend me."

A bath and new clothes, and the chance to put my mutant hands on the pigmaster and steal his power. I felt downright jaunty as I followed the Toad up the stairs to the living quarters.

It's easy to forget how much a hot bath and clean clothes can improve your state of mind. After days of sleeping rough in the stall and dressing like an overripe banana, it felt insanely decadent to soak in a big clawfoot tub filled with hot water and a cloud of lavender scented bubbles. I felt a little guilty about enjoying myself while the others were worrying about my welfare, but I reassured myself that I was now in a better position to help us break out. I figured there would be plenty of opportunities for me to put my neck on the line and get myself injured in the very near future.

In the meantime, I decided to allow myself to enjoy a little respite from dirt and depression. I even felt recovered enough to be amused at my room's decor. The previous occupant must have been an older woman, because the room's aesthetic was equal parts frilly prudishness and nervous frailty. For a crazy moment, I had the urge to text Darnique a picture of the room with a snarky comment about how there were flowers and birds frolicking on the wallpaper and duvet cover and love seat cushions, while safety bars guarded the bed and the tub and the toilet and the shower. Ironic, right? Like the biggest danger I faced was slipping in the tub.

Well, you don't have a phone, I reminded myself, and if you did, there were more important things to tell Darnique than the fact that the room had a generous but empty closet that smelled of mothballs and, very faintly, of dead mouse. Still, it was comforting to talk to my friend in the privacy of my mind, so I imagined telling her that the bathroom was dated but charming, and that someone had laid out face soap, a toothbrush, toothpaste and a wide tooth comb. There was a connecting door on the other side of the bathroom, and in my head, Darnique told me to lock it just in case, but not to worry about it too much. Just as I was about to get into the tub, I saw a big brown beetle out of the corner of my eye. Now, I have to admit, I'm a little bit squeamish about insects, but three days in a stall had desensitized me. I squashed the bug with some wadded-up toilet paper and sent it to its watery grave.

When I emerged from the tub, hair shampooed and wrapped in a soft mint green towel, I felt stupid with relaxation. Need to remember to pay attention to my surroundings, I thought, which made me glance around the room to see if I could spot a hidden camera somewhere. An initial inspection of the flower and bird lamps and white wicker mirror and dresser didn't reveal any spying devices, and I approached the old-fashioned four poster bed with its high mattress and grandmotherly green and peach patch quilt like a pilgrim arriving at a shrine. A good night's sleep, I thought, and I'd be ready to take on the world. I would be a badass super spy, gathering intel right under Góngora's snout, and then I'd be an actionadventure heroine, racing toward the barn to free Remy and the others, zapping locks and knocking out guards. Okay, so neither Góngora nor either of his two male guards appeared to have any lock zapping powers, but Sherwood had a whip of a tail, exceptional strength and armored skin. I could do a lot with that.

All I needed was a good night's sleep. I glanced at the clock on the wall – eight o'clock, although it felt like midnight. I was exhausted. I dropped the damp towel on the chair and slid under the quilt and sheet, drowsily thinking of Aunt Carrie's disapproval – lazy girl, not hanging up the towel to dry. Immodest, too, flaunting your body like Bathsheba when she thought no one was looking – and how did that end? Betrayal and bloodshed.

My thoughts jumped to the Leonard Cohen song. King David knew a special chord. Her body in the moonlight… all I ever knew of love… what was the next line?

I hadn't turned off the light. Oh, never mind. I was too tired for anything but closing my eyes and drifting off…

SEVENTEEN

"Get up."

I sat up before I could think, blinking stupidly at the woman standing in front of me, dyed blonde hair slicked back, weather-tanned face set in disapproving lines, six arms braced on her hips. "What's happening?" I had a bad taste in my mouth.

"You've got three minutes to get dressed. Góngora doesn't like to be kept waiting." Three of the arms threw garments at me – and I made a reflexive gesture to catch them and missed.

"It's the middle of the night." I scrubbed my eyes, trying to make sense of this new weirdness.

"It's eight thirty. You were supposed to wash yourself off and get dressed, not go to sleep."

Eight thirty? I turned to the clock on the wall – good lord, Rita was right. I had only been asleep for half an hour, but my brain was still swimming up out of the sluggish thickness of dreams I couldn't recall. "I'm sorry," I said, reflexively.

"You will be, if you don't get dressed."

I looked dumbly down at the clothes she had thrown. There

was a white button-down shirt, a black pencil skirt, and a pair of cotton panties and stretchy athletic bra. Everything was some generic brand I'd never heard of, size medium, and still bore store tags. "Can you turn around?"

"Just get dressed."

I changed into the bra and panties.

"Come on, Rogue. We don't have all day."

I ripped the tag off the black skirt. "Admit it. I'm catering staff." I supposed it made sense – as far as Góngora knew, my only talent was waitressing. Maybe I could brush his hand while I was serving him a platter of sausage rolls.

Rita handed me a pair of stretchy black ballet flats. "You'll find out what the boss wants soon enough. And don't forget these." She held out an N-95 mask and a pair of latex gloves. "Góngora won't let anyone closer than six feet without these."

Gloves. That was going to make my mission to absorb powers a whole lot trickier. "What exactly will I be doing for the big man? Dressing him?" That might provide opportunities for a casual touch. I wondered whether I could absorb powers through my wrist. What about my hair? Could brushing my hair against someone's skin do the trick?

"You'll be doing whatever Góngora needs. And don't even think about any funny business. I'll be keeping my third eye on you." I didn't see any visible third eye, so I had no idea if the sorceress was joking or not. Probably not – Rita didn't strike me as a particularly humorous type. She turned on her heel and walked out into the hallway. She stopped at the door next to mine and opened it without knocking. Inside, the wholesome blonde was seated in her wheelchair, staring intently at a fly buzzing on the wall. Guess she hated insects as much as I did.

"We're going downstairs, Tessa," said Rita, grabbing hold of the wheelchair with two of her hands.

Tessa stiffened her shoulders. "I can wheel myself."

Rita nodded, looking slightly uncomfortable. The fly had settled on the wall, and I steeled myself and slammed my palm down on it. The bug dropped to the floor, buzzed weakly, and then went still. Take that, bug phobia. I was toughening up.

Tessa shot me an unfriendly look as she wheeled past me. I tried to think what I could possibly have done to offend her. "What's bugging you?"

Tessa narrowed her eyes at me. "Don't you start."

Rita paused in front of a door at the far end of the hall, and knocked. "*Entrar,*" came the reply, and Rita ushered us into what used to be called the master suite. Of course, in this case, all the old slave owning connotations were spot on.

Góngora was lying in a king-sized bed near a picture window, his grotesquely muscled half-porcine bulk draped in exquisite purple silk sheets, one leg propped higher than the other. Unlike my grannified room, this suite had been repainted white, with cream linen curtains and a beautifully designed leather chair and oak writing desk. There was a strong smell of some expensive, woodsy cologne, and underneath it, a less pleasant odor, of acrid sweat, with a faint metallic undertone – blood.

"Ah, you are both here. Excellent." He pressed a remote control with one spindly-fingered hand, and the back of the bed raised him into more of an upright position. "Come closer, Tessa." He beckoned with one attenuated finger, and Tessa gave me a quick, frightened look before wheeling herself closer to the bedridden slave master.

"You look uneasy," said Góngora, in his smooth, cultured voice. "Perhaps you are uncomfortable with me?"

"You captured me on my way home from college," she said quietly. "Of course I'm uncomfortable."

"But perhaps there is something more that troubles you."

Tessa said nothing, but her hands were clutching the wheels of her chair.

"Remind me of your power?" He sounded interested and supportive, like a prospective employer.

"I don't have any special powers."

"*Basta!*" The word came out so harshly that Tessa and I both flinched. "Do not try my patience. I did not pick you up by chance, because I see your lovely hair or think, oh, this one should be interesting. I did my research. I am only asking you to confirm what I already know. So, I ask again – remind me what is your power?"

Tessa's eyes darted to me, then back to Góngora. "If you already know, then why ask?"

"I tire of this game." Góngora turned to Rita. "Make her understand."

Rita stepped forward on command, "Listen, girl, when Góngora asks you a question–"

"No, no, no." Góngora's voice was still calm and cultured, which made what he said next all the more chilling. "I said *make* her understand."

Rita looked uncomfortable. "I'm not sure–"

"That is disappointing." Góngora sounded like a teacher, talking to his favorite pupil. "I count on you, Rita. If we cannot trust one another, we will never be able to outface our enemies. Still, I understand. Perhaps we are too soft to combat the real evil." The tiny, piggy eyes showed no emotion, but the voice coming from beneath Góngora's snout was shaded with regret and resignation. Then, subtly, he brought a different instrument into the mix, something stronger and more stirring. "But I ask you, my friend, if we cannot be strong enough – if we cannot become powerful enough – what will become of someone like Tessa? Will human traders take a care with her?" Góngora ended, and I was reminded of that last note of *West Side Story*, the baleful tritone that sounds while the rival gangs carry out the dead body of the fallen hero. Góngora, I realized, wasn't just a smooth speaker. He was a virtuoso composer, using his voice the way Bernstein and Lin Manuel Miranda use an orchestra.

He could make people feel things. I wasn't sure if that was charisma or a mutant power, but it explained why he inspired such loyalty in his followers. Would he charm me, I wondered, if he really set his mind to it? I felt a little chill go down my spine. Given a choice between physical pain and psychological manipulation, I was far more comfortable confronting the former.

"As the song says," Góngora went on, "at times, you must be cruel to be kind."

Rita shook her shoulders back, making me think that having three sets of arms must be a bit of a strain. Then she raised one hand and made a gesture, and Tessa gasped. "Tell him what he wants to know," she said, then quickly dropped her hand. Tessa slumped forward.

"Let's try again, shall we?" Góngora stared at Tessa.

"I control insects." She said it to the floor, and for a half second I thought *what's the big deal?* Then I remembered – the horse, rearing up. Had she caused it? Had she sent an insect to bite the horse?

"That is what I was told," said Góngora, and the music of his voice was warm and pleased – except there was a different note playing just beneath it, discordant and alarming.

Tessa looked a little less frightened now. "Wh-why did you need to ask me that now? It's a bit late, isn't it?"

"Not to a Spaniard." Góngora's easy manner was back, but I no longer trusted it. "Now, is it only some kinds of insects that you control?"

"Um, no. I've got a pretty large range." For all her bravado, Tessa wasn't easy around the pigman either.

"What about bacteria? Viruses?"

Tessa looked genuinely puzzled. "Gosh, I'm not sure. I don't think I ever thought about it."

"Foolish, to not ask such basic questions of oneself. Come, then, let us attempt. Come here, to my bedside, and see if you can clear this section of my foot."

"I… I've never tried to communicate with something I can't see."

"Rita." Góngora gestured, and Rita handed Tessa a glasses case. Inside, there was a pair of glasses that reminded me of the devices ophthalmologists use, with lots of different lenses that can click in and out. Tessa put them on, flipped through a few of the lenses, then paused to look intently at the bedridden man's elevated foot. "I think this is… oh, wow, they're listening to me. This is working!"

"Rita, check her work."

Rita waved three of her hands, making the air ripple in front of her. Through the magnified magical circle, I could see a colorful assortment of tubes and spheres, some ridged or furred, some smooth, all rolling away as if driven by an invisible wind. There was a monstrous, fanged and tusked organism as well, scuttling away. I looked at Tessa with new respect, and found that she was grinning. No matter the circumstance, it had to be exhilarating to discover a whole new aspect to your power.

"The area around your leg is clear," said Rita.

"Excellent, excellent." Góngora smiled at Tessa, looking for a moment like a cartoon pig.

Then he turned to me, startling me. "Now, you, human girl. Wash in the sink and put on the gloves." He indicated a lovely, tiled basin sink in the en suite bathroom.

Okay, so this was starting to make sense. Our swinish overlord had brought Tessa in to clear his leg of bacteria and mites and viruses, and I was going to play nurse. I wasn't sure why the big guy trusted me to do such an intimate job when Rita was around with all her many helpful hands, but maybe if I kept my mouth shut, I'd figure it out.

Gloved and masked, I approached the bed, where Góngora had an iPad perched on his stomach. He said something in Spanish – I caught "perdona" and "la hora," and figured he was probably calling someone in Spain.

The response, which sounded like it came from an older man, was also in Spanish.

For a wild moment, as I stood with my gloved hands held up in front of me, I wondered if I should deliberately make them dirty – lick them, perhaps? Or should I get closer, then deliberately injure the pig further so we could all escape? But what to do about Rita, standing sentry?

"You. Rogue. Come here now."

Góngora's sharp summons cleared my brain, and I remembered – idiot, how could I have forgotten – that I had the power to absorb other people's powers. All I needed to do was touch the slaver with my bare hands. Maybe I was still a little fogged with sleep, but my own lapses worried me. "What do you need me to do?"

Góngora didn't seem surprised by my compliant tone. "*Venga aqui,*" he said, then spoke again in Spanish to his friend. "Uncover my leg."

I pulled back the purple silk, revealing an enormous, strangely constructed limb. The thigh appeared to have muscles that human thighs did not, and the bend in the knee was porcine. There was no visible bruising or blood, but when Góngora commanded me to run my hands gently over the leg, he flinched at my touch.

"Rita," said Góngora, teeth clenched. "Cast a spell of privacy over us – visual and audio."

Rita frowned. "But what if she–"

"Do it. But make sure that Tessa continues to clear the area of germs."

Rita nodded, and the air rippled and thickened around us. Suddenly, there was a sense that Góngora and I were in a dome, with all outside noises blocked out.

"Come closer, little human."

Up close, Góngora's ugliness was more pronounced. The coarse hairs on his rough pink skin, the fleshy snout, the unnatural melding of human and swine in his features. "Do you know about the laws of medical privacy? A true doctor or nurse would not be permitted to reveal what they know of a patient's condition. You are not a true medical professional, and you may think you owe me nothing. But serve me well, and I will serve your ends well."

"You'll let me go?" Even as the words left my mouth, I knew he could not afford to risk my going to the authorities. But I wondered whether or not he would lie about it.

"I would do better. I would keep you with me as my personal assistant. You would have great power, and wealth besides. We would travel all over – Europe, the Middle East, Russia." He made a sweeping gesture with his attenuated fingers, and I noticed that up close, his bulky platinum Rolex did not display the time, but had a blank ruby screen. "You would learn the business," Góngora went on. "In time, you might even take on other responsibilities. I offer you a life such as you would never have had in your backward little town."

It was quite an offer. "That sounds…" I searched for the words. "Too good to be true?"

"I swear it, on my mother's life." He was using his voice power again, infusing every syllable with sincerity. Yet I believed him, not because of the exertion of his influence, but because of a feeling in my gut that said this guy has something to hide, and he is going to great lengths to keep it hidden.

"Tell me what you need," I said, trying to put as much conviction in my words as he had in his.

There was a burst of Spanish from the iPad. Clearly, the man on the other end – a doctor, I assumed – was growing impatient with all this delay.

"Run your hands along the… the bones of the leg," said Góngora. "Check for swelling and redness."

"I don't see any redness." I didn't see any swelling, either, but when I touched around Góngora's strangely shaped knee, I felt the roughness of abraded skin, the stickiness of blood, and the softness of inflamed tissue. My patient sucked in a sharp breath. "That's strange." Under my fingertips, the contours of the knee felt different than they looked to my eyes.

"Feel if there is any bone out of place."

Holding Góngora's gaze for a moment before I looked down, I palpated the whole area around the knee and leading down to the bone that runs down the center of the calf. Femur? No, that was the thigh bone. Tibia? Fibula? "I don't think there's anything out of place, but your anatomy is so different, it's hard to–" I broke off, because it was belatedly occurring to me that the anatomy under my fingers was not so different from my own.

Góngora might look like a seven-foot pigman, but he felt completely human. I did a quick mental calculation, trying to picture the height of the man attached to this leg.

Fry me in butter and call me a catfish, Góngora wasn't even a particularly large man. In fact, unless he had the longest torso around, he might not even be as tall as I was.

"I know, my mutant anatomy makes this more difficult," said Góngora, and his eyes were looking intently into mine, as if he could convince me, by the power of his voice and the force of his will, to believe my eyes and not what my tactile senses were telling me. "But just concentrate on the bones under your hand. Think of nothing but the answers to my questions."

Mouth dry, I nodded. The power of illusion. Góngora had the power of illusion. If I could just slip the gloves off... or manage to rip a hole in one... then escape would be as easy as breathing. I could disguise myself as Góngora, or Rita, or one of the guards, march myself into the prison barracks, open the doors.

If the illusion included how people sounded, maybe I could just tie Góngora up, take his place, and order the release of all the prisoners. My hands tingled with excitement, and I struggled to keep my voice calm and steady. "What do I do now?"

More Spanish from the iPad. "Check the entire lower leg for breaks in the bones."

Following instructions, I kept gathering more information. The leg under my fingertips did not feel particularly heavy or thin, and the muscles had a softness that suggested that the real Góngora was no athlete. "You're OK."

Spanish from the iPad, Spanish from Góngora. "A sprain, then. You will need to wrap the lower leg and apply ice. Go, tell Rita to help you."

Of course, there was no way for the bedridden Góngora to tell Rita to drop her privacy spell. I stepped right through the rippling air that surrounded us. Rita looked at me warily. Tessa was sweating with the effort of holding back all the microscopic creepies, but she flashed me a quick look.

"It's OK. It's a sprain. Big G says drop the spell and help conjure up some supplies so I can bandage up his bum leg."

Rita hesitated, then waved her hands. "Góngora," she said, "the human girl says I am to drop the spell?"

"Yes. And please, do not refer to my new assistant that way. What is your name again, girl?"

I tried to keep the smile out of my voice. "Oh, you can just call me Rogue. I think I'm starting to like it."

EIGHTEEN

Góngora was a terrible patient. The first day he called me in a half dozen times, fretting about the possibility of infection. It came as no surprise that the man was a raving hypochondriac as well as a germophobe, but it was wildly inconvenient.

Each time he called me to check his leg, he inspected me to see that I was properly masked and gloved, even though Tessa was present to help disperse any potential disease-causing microbes. Touching him was not the problem – touching him so there was skin to skin transfer, on the other hand, was going to require some ingenuity.

"Is the leg bothering you? Does it feel warm?"

Góngora winced as I unwrapped the bandage, revealing a porcine limb that was red and swollen. "I can't tell. I think so." I probed the skin as gently as I could. It was hard to tell, but I thought there was less swelling under my hand than appeared to my eye. "You know," I said carefully, "it might be easier for me to tell what I'm feeling if I could remove my gloves. I could wash and disinfect thoroughly, but my bare fingertips would be much more–"

Góngora's snout wrinkled in alarm. "Absolutely not. I am very susceptible to small infections!"

Great. I smiled and asked if I could sniff the wound for any odor. He nodded, so I leaned over, lifting my mask from my nose.

"Stop that! Do not remove your mask. What are you trying to do, kill me?"

Two strikes. I applied betadine to the affected area and replaced the bandage. The following day, instead of calming down, Góngora grew more anxious that infection was setting in. Every time his leg itched, he diagnosed himself with sepsis. After the third time he called me in, the pigman decided that I might as well just remain in the room, so I could check on the leg every hour or so. As the wall clock's minute hand moved slowly toward four, my stomach began to growl. I am one of those people who does not forget to eat, and in the late afternoon my body requires either caffeine or chocolate. I glanced at Tessa, who was sitting beside me with exquisite self-possession.

"How do you do that?" I kept my voice whisper-soft.

"Do what?"

"Just sit there."

Tessa glanced up. Góngora flipped another page of a report and scowled.

"I mentally walk through places I've visited in the past," she said, pitching her voice even softer than mine. "I especially like the American Museum of Natural History in New York City. My grandmother's kitchen. The rolling hills behind my house, where I used to explore."

I nodded, taking this in. "But how do you remember exactly how everything look–"

Góngora threw a pillow, which bounced onto the floor, and then winced in pain at the exertion. "Will you two please stop whispering! It is poor manners. And it distracts me." After that, I just sat and stared out of the window a lot.

At first, it was unbearably boring. Góngora continued reading papers, then clicked through documents on his laptop. He made the occasional phone call in a language I couldn't understand. My thoughts wandered, and I thought about Darnique, and how she was doing, and if she was mad at me for dropping out of contact. Last month she had broken up with her boyfriend when he became obsessed with starting a family and said he didn't believe in using birth control. Afterwards, he was all contrite, explaining he was scared she would leave him to go off to college.

"Damn right," was all she said. Still, they remained in touch, and she refused to speak badly about him. Without me there, what would happen if Del called her up and asked her to get back together? Darnique was smart in almost everything, but from my brief contact with Cody and Remy, I could see that desire could make any woman stupid.

As the afternoon wore on, the phone calls increased in frequency. My patient usually conversed in rapid Spanish, but occasionally he lapsed into other languages – one lush and heavy sounding, like thick velvet unrolling itself, the other silken and melodious in a way that made me think of traditional flutes and drums. Russian and Arabic? I had already figured out that there was some kind of deadline approaching, and I was fairly certain that the potential buyers were going to be arriving here.

"I think you wrapped the bandage too tightly," he said, brow knitted. "How will I know if infection is setting in?"

"Want me to check and rebandage it?" I knew he would refuse – he didn't let me touch anything sharp, so Rita was always the one to cut the bandage and supply the small metal tab that fastened it together.

"No." I went to sit back down. "Wait." I turned around. "I'm so warm. Do you think I am running a temperature?"

"May I feel the back of your neck?" I was sure he would tell me no, go get a thermometer, but hypochondria had made Góngora increasingly pliable. When he nodded, I placed my hand on the back of his neck. Instantly, Góngora flinched, crying out.

"What was that? You shocked me!"

The Toad ran into the room a moment later, his sticky, long tongue shooting out and wrapping itself around my throat. "What is it? Did she hurt you?"

"It must have been static electricity. I was just feeling for fever," I gasped as Mortimer's prehensile tongue tightened over my throat.

"Check her hands and the floor for any concealed device," said Góngora.

The Toad spun me out and made me hold out my gloved hands. He turned them this way and that, looking for some concealed weapon. "Numphng."

Góngora touched the back of his neck, then looked at his long, thin fingers. "Do you see any injury there?"

The Toad unraveled his tongue more so he could check. "Hyu sheem awigh."

"*Bueno,*" Góngora said, tapping the injured area again. "It is no longer painful. It must be as she said then, static electricity."

Tessa gave me the very slightest of smiles, as if she knew I had just gotten away with something, even if she did not know exactly what.

I was beginning to think that Góngora was not exactly the sharpest tool in the shed. He hadn't connected the dots about Tessa causing his horse to rear up, and he hadn't entertained the possibility that I might have an undisclosed power. Or maybe that was unfair. Lots of people don't see what they aren't expecting. Most people, even. Darnique always said that the more authority people wielded, the less they really paid attention to the folks they considered beneath them. Or maybe Góngora didn't consider Tessa a threat because she used a wheelchair, and he discounted me because he'd already put me in the box labeled "powerless".

The Toad unrolled his tongue, and I took a moment to steady myself. "I am sorry," I said. "Believe me, I had no intention of causing you any pain. I must have picked up a charge from the carpet. But on the bright side, you don't have a fever."

"Are you sure?" Now that he was reassured about the shock, he was back to worrying about his leg again. "I feel hot."

"I'm sure. Would it be OK if I go to the bathroom?"

Góngora considered this. His own bathroom was a few feet away, but I knew he didn't want to share the facilities. "Be quick about it."

Tessa squirmed. "Can I go, too? I really have to go." She looked at me. "Rogue can help me."

Mortimer opened the door for us. "Don't tarry," he said. "And don't try anything funny."

"We won't be a tick," I assured him, and then hurried out the door, Tessa right behind me.

•••

"What's going on?" Tessa said, after we had both used the bathroom. It really had been hours.

"I managed to touch him. I'm new to all this, so I don't know how long I have before something happens." The nervous excitement in my belly twisted. It felt dangerous and surreal, saying the words out loud. I glanced at myself in Tessa's mirror to see if I had started to change – nope, still me, with my bangs going a bit wild.

"You're not making any sense."

I drew in a breath, realizing I needed to slow down and explain. Tessa might look like a wholesome blonde farmer's daughter, but she was nobody's pushover, and she wasn't going to just go along with me on blind faith. In fact, her tone reminded me of Darnique when we had first met. "I'm a mutant, but Góngora doesn't realize it. I used the back of my earring to prick a few holes in my glove."

"You stealthed him?"

"I know, it seems wrong, but–"

"Are you kidding? That's fantastic! So, wait, what's your power?"

I explained.

"So, what happens now, you turn into a giant pig?"

I shook my head. "When I touched him, his leg felt like an ordinary human's – I don't even think he's very tall. His power must be to cast an illusion."

Tessa laughed out loud. "That's fantastic."

"I know." I glanced in the mirror again. "But nothing's happening. Maybe it wasn't enough of a contact?"

Tessa considered this. "You're not expecting to just transform into a pigly double, are you? Cause if that's an illusion, you have to, I don't know, cast it."

Of course it wouldn't be easy. "You're right. I thought maybe I'd just take on the last illusion he cast, but…" I looked at Tessa, confounded. "How do I do this?"

Tessa tapped her cheek with one finger. "Well… maybe it's like drawing. You start with the broad strokes – you're huge, you're intimidating, you take up space. Then you start working on the details – the snout, the ears, those weird-ass long fingers. What's with those, anyway? Not piggish at all."

I visualized what she was describing, tracing my fingers over my forehead to see if it was flattening out, sliding down my nose as if I could mold it into a snout. "I can see it," I said, opening my eyes. "I just can't seem to do it."

Tessa's mouth skewed to one side. "I was going to start shading in skin texture and those nasty little bristles…"

"Not sure if there's a point." I stared at myself in the mirror. Ugh, I was getting a zit, right on my forehead. I gave a low groan and collapsed backward into an overstuffed chair. "It's not happening."

"You sure you have this power?" There was sympathy in her voice.

I stared unhappily at the ceiling, where a spider was spinning a web. "I am."

She turned her chair, rolling it closer to me. "Maybe it just didn't cross some threshold of sufficient contact?"

"I guess. Or maybe I have more of an affinity for some powers than others." I thought about the mutants I knew of, from the news and entertainment programs. Telekinesis and telepathy often seemed to come in a paired set. Some mutants had enhanced strength or agility, and some had physical differences they could use, like wings or a tail. Some had an extra special something thrown in, like teleportation. Could there be some connection between your mutant power and the way your brain was wired? Did powers impact personality, or the other way around?

"You'll just have to try again, with more contact over a longer period of time."

I groaned. "There's so much I don't understand. I thought havin' powers was like goin' through puberty – you just figured it out as you went along."

"Maybe it would be, if we weren't prisoners," said Tessa. "But right now, we are going to have to accelerate the learning curve."

If only it were that easy. "And by we, you mean me. You already know how to work *your* powers."

Tessa grabbed my hand and a jolt went up my arm. "So, let's start with teaching you what *I* know."

Tessa, as it happened, knew quite a lot.

NINETEEN

I woke to the insistent bleating sound of a large truck, backing up. After a moment of mindless, luxurious stretching – Góngora certainly chose comfortable mattresses for his non-prisoner guests – I sat bolt upright.

The plaintive bleat of reverse was now punctuated by muffled shouts of wait, stop, OK, back it up. Grabbing the white shirt hanging over a chair, I padded over to the window in bare feet, looked down and saw a truck that read Coco Construction and Home Improvement. Three men wearing tee-shirts and carpenters' jeans were moving a large wooden crate out of the truck, while a woman in overalls was unfolding a hand truck, extending the bed to its maximum width. The crate was marked "fragile" in two places, but either the workmen didn't read English or they didn't care.

Góngora's renovation, it seemed, was still a work in progress. As I watched, one of the workers opened the sloped, steel doors leading down to the cellar. He had a bony, open face and hair so blond and short you could see his skull. He looked like the kind of guy who would walk into Karl's Diner, order off the menu and leave a decent tip. I tapped on the glass, trying to get his attention, mouthing the word "help," but my window was too far up, and he was too preoccupied with maneuvering the heavy box.

Maybe I could write a note and throw it down? I was looking around for something to write with when my door swung open.

"Get away from the window," said Rita in a bored monotone.

"But I'm wearing a shirt," I replied, deliberately misunderstanding her. "I'm decent." Actually, that was debatable – the shirt was unbuttoned, and only came to the top of my thighs.

"Aren't you cute?" Rita's tone suggested that this was akin to being the human equivalent of slime mold. "Get dressed."

"I have to use the bathroom first," I complained. When I came out, toothbrush in mouth, Rita looked like she was about to blow a gasket. "What's the new project? Home theater? Home gym?" I removed the toothbrush. "Home torture chamber?"

"What a fine idea." Rita threw my skirt at me. "Clothes. Now."

A few minutes later, I followed Rita into Góngora's room, which smelled like menthol and chamomile. Tessa was in a corner, gazing into the middle distance. Maybe she was taking a mental trip to New Orleans, drinking chicory coffee at a café and digging into plate of fried green tomatoes.

"Hey," I said to Rita, "don't we get breakfast today?"

Rita hushed me.

The pigman, who was holding his phone to his ear, acknowledged our presence by raising one finger, and then continued arguing with the person on the other end of the call. "No, I did not. No. Look it up on your computer – yes, I have the account number right here." He waited. "At last! Can you send the correct one – it's back ordered? I want to speak to your supervisor. Now." He stared at his phone, waiting for someone else to come on the line.

It was impossible to tell from the unwrinkled pig face, or the illusion of a pigface, but it occurred to me that Góngora was probably middle aged or older – a younger person would have used headphones or earbuds.

"Boss, I brought the human here," Rita said, in a much softer tone than she ever used with me. "Is this a good time for her to check on your leg?"

Góngora, distracted, frowned, then waved the suggestion away. "No, no, get the girls out of here. I need to speak to Dr Lorenzo."

Rita nodded. "Lock them in their rooms?"

Góngora shrugged, holding the phone up to his ear again. "Disconnected! *Cosa de mala leche.*" He began dialing another number.

Rita started making a round 'em up herding motion.

"Hang on a sec," I said. "What about fresh air and exercise? Can't you just take us out with the other prisoners to walk around the ring?"

"Where the devil is Lorenzo?" Góngora said, putting his phone down. "Yes? What's the issue? Why are you all still here?"

"She wants to go out."

"So let her go out! Rita, this is not brain surgery. Get rid of them and get back here." Góngora was back on the phone again, berating someone in Spanish.

Turning to me, Rita said, "You know how Góngora requested that you follow the laws of patient privacy?"

"Of course I do." I tried to look like a person who had been too thoroughly influenced to even think of betraying that trust.

"You are hereby gagged from speaking of any personal information you have gleaned from examining his person." She made a series of hand gestures as she spoke, and suddenly, when I thought about talking to Remy about the fact that Góngora wasn't a huge pig person, my throat seized up. I grabbed my throat, appalled. The sensation of being unable to speak the words in my head was deeply unsettling. It felt like my own brain was betraying me. Tessa looked at me, equally miserable.

"Come on, ladies," said Rita. "Let's get moving."

As I followed the six-armed sorceress out of the room, my stomach growled, reminding me I still hadn't eaten. "Hey," I said, testing my vocal cords, "what about breakfast?" At least the spell hadn't completely robbed me of the power of speech.

Rita made a gesture with two of her hands, grabbing something out of thin air before lobbing it at my stomach. I deflected it, then reached down and picked up a hard apple from the floor. Brushing it off, I handed it to Tessa. I was showing off a little, trying to appear unfazed by the spell. "Can I ask for one more?" Rita rolled her eyes, then hurled another apple my way. I caught this on the fly and took a bite – not the sweetest, but not awful, either.

I decided not to push my luck and mention coffee.

It had rained overnight, brightening the grass and making everything smell fresh. Now the sky was clear and the day was warming up. Sherwood the guard was busy watching the yellow-suited prisoners inside the exercise pen, and didn't turn around as we drew nearer.

"This is so aggravating," said Tessa, when we were out of earshot. "I was dying to tell you about–" She broke off abruptly, her face clamping down with irritation as she wheeled herself forward with easy strength. It occurred to me that she could probably beat me hands down in an arm-wrestling match.

"It just feels so weird," I said. "Not being in charge of your own body."

For an awful moment I thought I'd offended her, but Tessa just said, "Tell me about it."

The sky was painfully blue, with picture perfect clouds scudding by and a light breeze lifting and scattering yellow leaves onto the ground. As we drew closer, I could see the others watching us. Remy's red-on-black eyes lit up and he clapped Lloyd on the shoulder. Lloyd began waving his hand excitedly until Lin elbowed him to make him stop. Axel flashed me the thumb-to-thumb "z" signal. I was going to have to ask him what that meant.

"Hey guys," I said, feeling unaccountably shy.

"Oh my god, Marie!" For an unguarded moment, Lin looked genuinely excited before she caught herself and tamped down her enthusiasm. "Your wardrobe got an upgrade," she said. "Lucky you."

Lloyd felt no compunction about showing his delight. "You doing OK, kid?"

"Words cannot express how I am doing," I said carefully.

Axel frowned. "Have you been mistreated?"

"No, no, I'm doing OK." I looked at Tessa, who had attracted a dragonfly, which was perched on the arm of her wheelchair. "I even made a friend."

"Hey," shouted Sherwood, stomping over. "No clumping together! You're supposed to be getting exercise!"

Obediently, we all began a slow march around the ring, with Remy positioning himself right by my side. "You really OK, chère?" His eyes flicked over my white and black outfit, and a nerve jumped in the side of his jaw. "I been thinking 'bout you night and day."

"I'm all right," I said, experimenting with how much I could say before the spell shut off my larynx. "I've been working on our plan."

"You have?"

"Yes. There's a lot I have to tell you, but..." I gestured at my throat. "I can't."

"Did they surgically modify you?" Lin sounded carefully bland, as if she were asking about the weather, but her eyes betrayed her concern.

"Yikes, no," I said, pausing as we walked closer to where Sherwood was standing. Once we were past the scaled guard's earshot, I said, "Actually, I've been treated pretty well. Góngora thinks he's co-opted me with travel perks and health insurance."

"So he trusts you?" Axel's pale skin was a little sunburnt, and he scratched his peeling nose.

"That's overstating it a bit," I admitted.

Tessa made a sound, and I knew the spell was censoring her from saying what she wanted to say.

"Okay, but you must have learned something about the Pig," said Lin, looking at me expectantly.

I opened my mouth. Nothing came out.

"Nice," said Axel. "Guess the Pig did bring you over to the dark side."

"Careful," said Lin, lowering her chin so her antlers stuck straight out. "Maybe she's here to spy on us."

"Stop it, all of you." Remy was standing just behind me, and I turned to see that he was flat out furious. "Marie didn't choose to go to the big house! They dragged her there. She is a prisoner, like us, with no damn choice in what happens. And she is trying to help us get the hell out of here. So what do you do? You attack her!"

There was a moment of shocked silence. Then, from Lin: "Did you really just say the big house? Like, whoa, dude, Marie went to the 'Big House.'" She made air quotes with her hands and lowered her voice.

Lloyd laughed first, and then laughter just kind of rippled through the group, me included. It ended when Sherwood yelled out for all of us to quit standing around and get to exercising.

"So," said Remy, as we walked briskly around the pen, "I'm guessing there's a cat that's got your tongue… and that cat's probably named Rita."

I nodded, relieved.

"Anything you *can* tell me, chère?"

I thought hard. As we walked, I caught a distant smell of diesel oil on the wind. *Bingo.* I could talk about that. "They're building something in the cellar," I said, glancing up to make sure we were still far enough from Sherwood's ears – assuming the young guard had ears hidden among his scales. "I don't know what, but I think it has something to do with that Doctor Lorenzo he has coming."

Remy cursed in French.

Lin quickened her step to catch up, her antlers bobbing. "What? What's the problem?"

Remy glanced at her briefly, then turned back to me. "I met the Pig a year or so ago. My cousin Etienne and I had some business to do with him."

"Shoot, no wonder you like her," said Lin. "You're both sellouts."

"When I found out what the Pig required, Etienne and I ran away." Remy was looking off into the distance, remembering something. "We got into big trouble, us. My father punished us. But not so bad as what the Pig wanted to do."

Lin and I waited.

"This doctor, he conducts experiments… he has a way of activating your latent genes. If the Pig is building him a laboratory…" Remy's voice trailed off.

"Great." Lin gave me an unreadable look. "Maybe this your big chance to become a mutant."

Time to come clean. "I already am."

That got a startled glance from Lin. "You're what?"

"Góngora thinks I'm human, but I'm not."

Lin stopped walking and stared at me, chin thrust out. "So, you lied to me?"

Remy drew in a breath, clearly about to add a lot of spin and context, but I saw no point in beating around the bush. "Yes," I said. "I was trying to play my cards close to my chest. But I'm telling you the truth now."

"Oh, yippee." Lin trudged along, then said, "You really think it might be a lab, Remy? What do you think they're going to do to us?"

Lloyd stepped closer to Lin. "We're going to get out of here," he said to Lin. "You're going to get to make the choices about who you are and how you live your life."

Lin's expression flickered, the sullen, impassive mask slipping for a moment. "Yeah, sure."

Lloyd turned to me. "Did you find out anything else, Rogue?"

I realized that Rita's spell did not prevent me from telling about the potential buyers coming to the horse farm, so I filled them in on that front. "I took French in high school, not Spanish," I admitted, "so I can't be completely sure that I'm translating what I heard correctly. But it sure sounded like they're all coming here."

"Lovely, a dinner party slave auction," said Lin. It was hard to tell, but underneath the flat sarcasm I thought there might be a note of fear.

"Makes sense," said Axel, surprising us all. He was so quiet most of the time I had hardly noticed him walking just behind us. "Góngora is a showman."

"That's good," said Remy. "Understanding the opponent is the first step to conning them."

"Conning them?" Axel fell silent as we passed closer to Sherwood, who was eyeing us all with suspicion. Axel waited till we were farther from Sherwood before continuing. "I thought we were planning a break."

"In order to make the break, we have to build and run a successful con," said Remy, sounding almost jaunty. He likes this, I realized. "The Guild of Thieves will be there, yes?" Remy appeared to take my silence as agreement. "I wonder if they will send my father, or just a delegate." Some of his enthusiasm seemed to drain. "It's going to be difficult to know exactly how to play this with so little information."

"What we need," said Tessa as she rolled her chair alongside, "is someone who speaks Spanish, so we can learn all the details."

"I do," said Lloyd. "But what good will that do? They're not going to invite me in."

"You don't need to get in," said Tessa. "You just need to touch her hand. Then she'll be able to understand Spanish, too, at least for a little while. You take on powers and abilities, right?"

I shook my head. "I don't think it's going to work. Those inhibitor collars tamp your powers down. I don't know if I can absorb anything that quickly when you're wearing them." I sneaked a look at Remy.

"Maybe you just need more absorption time when we're wearing the collars," said Lloyd. "Let's try a little experiment."

TWENTY

Maybe I had overdone it.

When Lloyd's eyes had rolled back in his head, I'd thought at first that I'd killed him. We told Sherwood that it was the heat, even though the day was the coolest we'd had so far, but the young guard had seemed almost comically flustered and didn't question anything. In the end, it had been Axel and Drew who helped Lloyd back to the horse barn to recover.

On the bright side, it turned out that I could absorb powers despite the dampening effect of the inhibitor collar. I just needed to hold on for at least five minutes. Now I had Lloyd's powers of mimicry, at least for a little while. Another bonus: I understood Spanish, because Lloyd did. And I understood a lot more about Lloyd, too. Poor man. I felt guilty, knowing some of his most embarrassing secrets. I felt even guiltier, knowing that I wasn't about to admit to anyone that when I absorbed powers, I also picked up memories. Maybe Lin and Axel would let me touch them anyway, but I wasn't about to put it to the test when so much was riding on the answer being yes.

Shoot. Was I thinking like a villain? If so, I would have to worry about it later.

Back in Góngora's room, I wondered how long I could hold onto my newly acquired abilities. Glancing at the clock, I saw that forty-five minutes had passed since I had let go of Lloyd's hand, and Góngora had neither made nor received a single call.

I was going to need to make my own luck, as Remy might say.

And I probably needed to act fast. With no time to practice, I just had to wing it and hope for the best. Duplicating the sound of Góngora's cellphone ring was no problem. I worried that I wouldn't be able to throw my voice so it sounded like it was coming from somewhere other than where I was sitting by the window, but Lloyd had that bit down to an art. He had also practiced using his powers so he didn't need to move his lips, like a master ventriloquist, and I had received that muscle memory as a bonus gift.

"Hello?" Góngora frowned at his phone. "Why don't I see a number for you? And how did you get this number?"

"Mortimer," I improvised, using the Toad's real name and assuming a woman's Russian accent. With Lloyd's ability to mimic, I added a slightly muffled quality so it would sound as though I were calling from far away. In retrospect, I was probably trying to channel the Black Widow. "My name is Maryasha, and you do not see a number because we have sophisticated blocking technologies." Góngora looked suitably impressed. "I work for a client who is very interested in your product." I added a momentary freeze at the end of the sentence, to add to the cellphone illusion. Damn, I was kind of good at this. A natural.

"Mortimer? When did you meet him?" From his bed, Góngora cast me a suspicious look, and I took pains to examine my ragged cuticles. My hands were getting a bit dried out from all the hand washing. Tending a hypochondriac had its challenges.

"We met," I began, and then, to fill in the time while I tried to think of an answer, I made garbled cellphone breaking up noises.

"What? Can you repeat that? The connection is not good." Now Góngora was properly focused on the phone and not on li'l old me, just sitting in my chair, all prim and proper in my black and white uniform.

Where did we meet? Lord, I had no idea where Mortimer had or hadn't been in recent months. Then I thought of Remy, telling us that this was a con game. So maybe what I needed to do was act like a politician, and ignore the questions I couldn't answer while diverting folks by answering the questions I wish I'd been asked.

"...because, like Mortimer, I have, shall we say, visible differences," I said, as if continuing a sentence. "My boss believes, like you, in hiring those of us who cannot blend in. He is very eager to purchase your product and give them the chance to earn their freedom." That should stroke the Pig's bristles. One thing I knew from waitressing – most people wanted to be told what they already believed. They had decided on shrimp scampi and wanted to hear that the shrimp scampi was good, and if you suggested something else might be better, they looked at you like you were asking them to relinquish their firstborn.

But tell them the shrimp scampi was delicious, and they never questioned you.

Góngora liked the idea he was fooling people, and I had just presented my boss as a perfect rube, already buying into the whole idea that you could be a kinder, more equal opportunity slave purchaser.

"I see." Góngora smiled at the phone, and it was the smile of someone who had seen a twenty-dollar bill drop out of someone's wallet and had absolutely no intention of returning it. "Well, then, perhaps we can do some business together. As it happens, I am planning a little informal get together of potential clients…" He glanced up at me, sitting in my chair, and then lapsed into Russian.

Well, wasn't that a fly landing straight in my peach cobbler? I had a moment of hope, thinking maybe Lloyd knew some Russian, but no luck.

"Blabbity blabbity," Góngora went on. "Choroshoh?"

Come on, con woman. Think of somethin', and fast. I searched my memories and Lloyd's for some kind of a Hail Mary pass. Wait, wait, that was perfect. Thank you, Lloyd.

"I am sorry," I said, with a slight air of affront. "I do not speak Russian."

"But your accent…"

"It is the language of my oppressors," I improvised. "From when we were part of the former Soviet Union. Ptui! I only speak my own country's language now."

"Which is?" Góngora looked like he was buying this, but how the heck did I know how many languages the man spoke?

"Krgyzzzhhhh." I made a crackling sound like the connection was breaking up.

"Kyrgyz?"

Oh, hell, was that an actual language? "A dialect. It is not well known." I was flyin' by the seat of my pants, now. Also, I had a tickle in my throat that made me think Lloyd's powers might be wearing off.

"Southern, eh? I only speak Northern." Another quick look

at me in my chair. "It is all right, then, I will use English. Can you and your employer come to visit us in three days' time? It is short notice, I know, but it is never wise to keep merchandise in one place for too long." He rattled off the address and a few more details, while I tried to judge just how much juice I had left. "I am afraid we cannot offer overnight accommodations, so you will have to leave with your new purchases. Is that acceptable?"

"Absolutely," I said, but now it was definitely just my voice, with a bad Russian accent. I was out of time.

Góngora frowned. "Wonderful. Tell me your name again?"

Time for a distraction. Jumping out of my chair and knocking it over, I screamed and pointed at the opposite side of the room.

Góngora, startled, dropped the phone and recoiled. "What? What is it?"

"A rat! I saw a rat peek its nose out of the corner there." I manufactured a shudder. "Filthy animals." Please be such a germophobe that you can't think of anything else, I prayed.

For once, my prayers were answered.

"I am afraid I must go," said Góngora, pressing a button on his phone and then pressing another. "Mortimer! Rita! Come at once! We have vermin in my room!"

After that, things moved very quickly. I was pressed into duty, helping Tessa clean the house to prepare the prisoners for what Góngora kept calling "the dinner party." As a lowly human servant, my job was to scrub and mop and dust, while Tessa used her powers to clear the area of bugs. After six hours, we had cleared the downstairs and were both exhausted, although only I was filthy and covered in cobwebs. I had been fantasizing about getting back to my room and soaking in my bath when

Rita informed us that only Tessa was allowed a break. I was drafted to help Sherwood distribute a pile of new clothes to replace the prisoners' banana-colored suits. Sherwood was in a sulky, distracted mood, and kept rubbing at the flaking skin around his ear slits and then distractedly chewing on the dead skin. The moment we arrived at the barn, he barked an order and sloped off to scratch himself and brood.

I had to admit, I wasn't exactly feeling chipper myself. I had been given a moment to wash my hands and face, but I still smelled of sweat and dust, my eyes were stinging from bleach fumes, and my knees ached.

On the one hand, I was happy to have the chance to see Remy and go over our plan, but I was also fretting about what I was missing by not being at the big house. Presumably, Góngora and his minions were conferring in private about last-minute details for tomorrow's event while I passed clothes through the bars of each stall. Of course, they could also be putting the finishing touches on whatever was in the cellar.

"You have got to be kidding me," said Lin, holding up a triangular green felt cap. "Am I Peter Pan here, or Robin Hood?"

"A cape! I've always wanted to wear a cape," said Lloyd, twirling so that the brightly colored fabric fluttered. The bright bands of yellow, aqua, green, magenta and blue reminded me of an old television test pattern.

Axel's new outfit was bright neon green. "I hope there's a jockstrap in here somewhere. What did you get, Remy?"

Remy went very quiet as he shook out the buttery soft brown leather trenchcoat. "My old clothes." There was also a red leather vest and something black. For some reason, Remy did not look thrilled to see any of it.

I resisted the urge to put my hand on his arm. "What's wrong?"

Remy rubbed at a stain on the brown leather that looked suspiciously like blood. "The last time I wore these was not a good day. And there's only one way Góngora could have gotten my coat and vest." He looked up, smiling his crooked smile. "Guess you're going to meet some of my childhood friends, chère."

I frowned. There was so much I didn't know, about Remy, and about what was going to happen when the potential buyers showed up. I felt the uncertainty twisting in my stomach. When the mysterious Kyrgyz woman's employer never arrived, would Góngora be suspicious? How long would we have to set our plan into action?

"Marie." Remy reached through the bars on the top of the horse stall door. "It will be all right."

"Unless I screw up. And there are so many ways for me to screw up."

"You won't." His fingers reached for mine. "You're going to do great, you." His Cajun accent grew more pronounced when he was anxious, and the knot in my stomach twisted tighter. I was so used to being the outcast, the black sheep, the pariah. It had never occurred to me that having people pin their hopes on me might be worse. "I haven't been able to practice. What if I just freeze?"

"You won't. Take my hand."

I pressed my forehead against the door. Underneath the smell of horse and hay, I could smell my own sweat, laced with fear. "I can't touch you. You know I can't."

"Just for a moment."

"You'll need your strength." But I passed my fingers through as well and closed my eyes when I felt the warmth of his skin, touching mine.

When had he come to mean so much to me? Stupid, stupid. One way or the other, I was going to lose him. Even if our plan worked...

His hand tugged me closer, and suddenly our faces were scant inches apart. "What are you doin'? You know this isn't a good–"

"For luck," he said, and then his mouth was touching mine, through the bars. For a moment, the world fell away, and a jolt of pure desire went through me. When Remy pulled back, it took me a moment to regain my balance. "Have faith in yourself." His voice sounded a little hoarse. "And remember – I have faith in you."

The door banged open and Sherwood called out, "Rogue! Come on, I'm needed back at the big house."

As I was leaving, a flock of starlings flew into the barn, calling out in whistles and chirps as they settled on one of the ceiling beams.

"Storm is coming," said Lin, almost to herself. Still in a just-kissed daze, I didn't register it fully at first. My whole body was thrumming like a plucked guitar string, tense as an unexploded grenade. It was only as I stepped into the coolness of the October night, hearing the frantic whirring and clicking of insects who know their time is drawing to a close, that I realized that a big storm might complicate our escape plans. Tornado season in the Dixie alley was usually in the spring and late fall, but there have been October tornadoes. Wouldn't it be just our luck to have one now?

Then something broke free and drifted to the surface of my mind, distracting me from the gathering wind.

A memory. Not mine, this time. Remy's.

Who the hell was that pretty, sharp-faced blonde, and why had Remy been thinking of her while he was kissing me?

TWENTY-ONE

My new uniform was too damn tight.

Góngora had dressed me up in a little black cocktail dress and white apron, with white gloves to match, and high heels that I was leaving off till the last possible moment. I had pinned my cowlick back with a jeweled pin, in a nod to Nineties fashion, and, all in all, I felt I looked pretty good. Rita had even given Tessa and myself some makeup to wear, which was reassuring. If I had to go into battle this evening, I preferred to do it armored with a touch of eyeliner and nicely arched eyebrows.

Still, the dress was too tight. And too short. How was I supposed to fight bad guys if I was worried about ripping my side seams and flashing my old cotton undies?

Tessa waved my concerns away. "You can't worry about how you look in a fight, Rogue." She had studied Para Jiu-Jitsu for years, and had been telling me some key principles as I fixed her hair. "You also can't worry too much about getting hurt. And most importantly, you have to be willing to cause some damage."

"I get that." I combed the back of Tessa's slippery blonde hair into a chignon and began applying bobby pins. "So how come you get a normal dress and I look like a French maid?" I bit my lip, realizing that this might have come off as insensitive. Her dress covered her legs, which were nowhere near as muscular as the rest of her.

Tessa shrugged, unperturbed. "We're both dressed like staff because G thinks we won't fetch much of a price – you, because he thinks you're human. Me, because I use a chair."

"Nah." I added another bobby pin to keep her chignon in place. "He knows you're valuable. He just wants to keep you around to get rid of any pesky germs."

I had meant it to be a light, jokey comment, but Tessa flinched as if I'd struck her, pulling her hair loose. "But why? Rita can do what I can do with magic. Or he could buy himself a damn operating room. Or encase his mansion in a bubble!" A large ant, which had been crawling on the arm of her chair, stood on its hind legs, clearly agitated.

I didn't know if my answer would make her feel better or worse, but I knew that Tessa was the kind of person who preferred knowledge, even if it came with a side order of pain. "You may be right about it having something to do with using a chair. Góngora likes feelin' powerful, and I suspect that whatever he looks like when he's not covered in pig illusion, he's not exactly powerful."

Tessa scowled. "So instead of a shiny red sportscar, he runs around disguised as a monster pig. And instead of keeping a trophy girlfriend or boyfriend, he surrounds himself with slaves."

Gingerly, I began repairing her updo. "I think that's the size of it." The window rattled, and I realized it was raining outside. I wondered how drafty it was in the barn.

"But there's so much more I can do. So much more I want to do." Tessa looked up from her chair. "I can't live like this, Rogue."

I felt a tickle on my arm. The ant was running in circles, discombobulated. I picked it up and set it in a corner, far enough from Tessa so that it could hear the signals of its fellow ants and find its way home. "You and me both," I said, and then spritzed her hair with hairspray as I glanced at the clock. It was 5 pm, and already mostly dark. "And we're going to do them." Of course, everything depended on my being able to perform under pressure, and using my power in a way I never had before. Piece of cake. What could possibly go wrong?

"It's raining hard now," said Tessa. I followed her gaze and saw the rain was coming in the open window, dampening the floor and rug. I walked over and closed the pane. Down below, the trees were bending and swaying. At first, I thought it was because of the storm, and then the helicopter dropped into view, buffeted by the wind and struggling to touch down. Mortimer was bent double as he ran toward it, carrying an umbrella that immediately blew inside out.

The first of the buyers must be arriving, along with the storm.

As the helicopter hopped before landing on our front lawn, Mortimer ducked his head clear of the propeller blades, which had slowed but not stopped. The passenger emerged, tall and dark haired, wearing a gray suit which instantly darkened in the downpour. The pilot climbed out as well, and I must have made a sound, because Tessa asked me what was wrong.

"Nothin'," I lied. No point in telling her that I recognized both the goateed and suited gentleman and the blonde helicopter pilot from Remy's memories.

I didn't know who they were by name, but I did know that

these were definitely players for the opposite team and at some point in the past, Remy had loved them both – and perhaps loved them still.

The lights flickered and then abruptly went out – somewhere, a tree must have fallen on a power line. While Tessa and I looked at each other, wondering how long the outage would last, the door to Tessa's room slammed open. Rita walked in carrying a camping lantern, and I could see that her dyed blonde hair was slicked back, and her tanned face was wet from rain and taut with nerves.

"You need to get downstairs."

Rita was worried enough to confide that there was a weather emergency alert. The storm, which had not been predicted for our area, had changed course, buffeting our county with strong winds and flooding some of the lower lying areas. Hearing the heavy drumming of rain on the walls and windows, I felt my old childhood excitement, that feeling of being charged up when the skies turn turbulent and you know that trees that have been standing for a hundred years could come toppling down, changing the landscape forever. No one knew when power would be restored, and Mortimer, who had been a mechanic, was down in the basement, trying to figure out what was wrong with the backup generator.

It seemed that Góngora had made a lot of cosmetic changes to the old horse farm – terracotta tiles in the kitchen area, the electric stairlift, central air and the opening of a skylight in the cathedral ceiling – but had not thought to check that the backup generator was operational. This meant that the stair chair lift wasn't an option and Rita had to wave three of her arms to levitate Tessa down the stairs in her wheelchair. My job was holding the red hurricane lantern, which smelled of kerosene and didn't cast much light. In the moments when Rita's face was illuminated, she was showing the strain.

Looking over the stairway bannister, I saw that the main floor was illuminated by thick, white storm candles that had been placed all around the room, making the Spanish tiled room look like the setting for a seduction. Well, I supposed a sales deal was a kind of seduction, but I always wondered about the wisdom of lighting a zillion candles. Presumably, the idea of a seduction was to focus all your attention on the person you were trying to seduce, and not to fret about the potential dangers of open flames. Your Hallmark movie of the week romance could easily turn the channel and become a Raging House Fires docudrama.

There were, I realized, so many ways this night could go wrong. I just couldn't figure out if any of them were to my advantage or not.

Góngora flung his cellphone at the wall. It seemed that another guest was missing, this one the good doctor Lorenzo. The pigman was not handling these setbacks with equanimity.

"*Cosa de mala leche!*" Gongora stared at where his broken phone had landed as though it had failed him. He had traded his customary purple silk robes for a three-piece white suit, which made him look even more ridiculous, like an anthropomorphized pig in a children's picture book. I was surprised to find him out of bed and standing with the aid of a handsome wood cane carved in the shape of a pig's head.

There was a flicker from the electric candles in the chandelier and a whirring sound as the ceiling fans started to turn again. The rhythmic strains of flamenco guitar filled the room from hidden speakers, and there was a chirp from something – an alarm system or the phone, presumably.

The power was back on. Rita waved her hands, extinguishing the candles but not removing them. Either she was conserving her own magical power, or she wasn't overly confident about the electricity staying on. As she gave Tessa her instructions – stay close to Góngora and use her microbe-dispersing powers to establish a cordon sanitaire around him – I pretended to be listening to her while I was really attending to Góngora.

"Boss? I'm sorry to disturb you," said the Toad, entering the room from a small wooden door in the hall between the living room and the kitchen. "Just wanted to let you know I fixed the backup generator in the main house." He brushed aside a cobweb that had attached itself to his bowl haircut. "But the one in the barn is missing pieces. We're going to need to bring the others in from there."

The boss responded in rapid Spanish, and his henchman's mottled green skin darkened with embarrassment. "I did! I even licked the hose clamp so it would stay in place." He stuck out his tongue, which was black. "See?"

Góngora's response was short and sharp.

The Toad bobbed his head and opened the front door, letting in a gust of wind and rain. He slammed the door shut behind him, leaving a puddle on the floor.

"No point cursing Lady Luck, my friend," said a voice that reminded me of Remy's. I looked up the stairs and saw the man from the helicopter. From where I stood, he appeared to be a well-seasoned forty-something, rakishly handsome in a gray suit that looked like it had been cut and sewn specifically for his measurements. "Like most ladies, she requires a bit of courting to get the best results." He descended the stairs without holding onto the bannister.

For a fleeting moment, Góngora's snout wrinkled in distaste. This micro-expression was almost instantly replaced by a smile that did not reach his pale-lashed eyes. "Courting the ladies is more your specialty than mine, Jean Luc. Welcome, welcome." Góngora used his cane to walk over to his guest, giving no sign that a moment before he had been melting down like an overgrown porcine toddler. "I am just concerned for my other guests, who have not yet arrived."

"Ah, yes." From the bottom of the stairs, Jean Luc had looked every inch the mature hottie, still fit and flat stomached, with a splash of distinguished white at his temples and a little goatee that made him look like a gentleman pirate. Up close, I noticed the slightly masklike look of a face plumped with filler and tautened by a surgeon's knife, and revised my estimate of his age upwards by ten years.

"Rogue!" Rita sounded exasperated, as though she had been saying my name a few times. "You said you were a waitress, right? Well, get your keister over here and help me serve." Rita handed me a tray of champagne glasses – the narrow kind that keep the bubbles going longer – while two of her other hands uncorked a bottle. As she poured, I thought about how much money a six-armed waitperson could make. One of Rita's hands brushed my wrist, and this time I felt a little tingle of power. Maybe she was too tired to keep her magical wards up.

As Rita waited for the bubbles to subside before filling the rest of the glasses, I noticed that Jean Luc was still talking to Góngora, but his hard, dark gaze kept sweeping around the room, taking in the lovingly restored wood beam ceilings, the gleaming earth-toned tiles surrounding the fireplace, the Persian rugs, and all the possible avenues of escape. "This is a lovely house," he said, turning back to his host. "Who else, besides ourselves, is coming tonight, Góngora? Anyone I know?"

"There have been some last-minute cancellations, due to the inclement weather," admitted Góngora. "Still, what can one do about an act of God?" He shrugged. Apparently, the thought of God throwing monkey wrenches into his plans for an elegant little slave auction did not trouble the pigman overmuch. "Besides your party, we are expecting Doctor Lorenzo, as soon as his driver finds a route around a fallen tree." Góngora side-eyed me, and I realized he was wanting some of his good champagne down his guest's throat, and quick. I gave my head a little tilt and Rita stopped pouring so I could bring the filled glasses over to Jean Luc. "We will also be joined by a charming businesswoman from Tennessee." Yes, of course, slave auctions always attracted the most charming clientele. "There will also be a Kyrgyz colleague, and one other guest that shall be a most pleasant surprise to you."

Of course, I knew the Kyrgyz colleague wasn't going to be showing up, tonight or any other night. The storm was a blessing in one respect – Góngora would assume that any guest who didn't arrive had been delayed by bad weather.

I proffered the tray of drinks. "Would you like an aperitif, sir?"

"Yes, thank you." The way that Jean Luc reached for his glass, however, contradicted his words. He picked up the glass as if it might contain some lethal substance, the way customers with severe nut or wheat allergies acted when I served them food at the diner. When he lifted the glass to his lips, I noticed that he only pretended to drink. Oh, I get it, I thought. You think someone might have spiked your drink with something far stronger and more lethal than vermouth. He couldn't afford to look nervous, however, or lacking in confidence. So, Jean Luc pretended to enjoy his host's expensive champagne, an uneasy pirate visiting another pirate's ship.

"Don't tell me everyone is starting to drink without me." The two men turned at the low female voice, and watched as the pretty, sharp-faced blonde descended the staircase. She had changed for dinner, and was now wearing a white halter-topped pantsuit and false eyelashes. It was a late Sixties, retro look, and I might not have hated it if I hadn't suddenly plucked her name from Remy's memories.

I was about to meet Bella Donna Boudreaux, the Assassins' Guild's version of a mafia princess, and the other woman in Remy's life.

TWENTY-TWO

Bella Donna Boudreaux took a champagne glass from my tray without actually registering my existence, which told me all I needed to know about her. She was a woman who only noticed those who could be of some use to her. "What are we toasting here? The return of your prodigal son?"

This was directed at Jean Luc.

"Remy was never my son by blood or law, and now he has lost the right to claim that title by affection or loyalty."

Bella Donna raised her glass, as if this had been a toast. "Yes, Remy does have quite the talent for betrayal. Let's just make sure that you feel no last-minute pangs. The Thieves' Guild is subject to a certain, shall we say, sentimentality." No wonder her parents had named her after a deadly species of nightshade. This woman oozed poison.

Jean Luc bristled visibly. "My dear Bella, I believe the only source of that particular rumor is the Assassins' Guild. Perhaps your cohort mistakes loyalty for sentimentality? As far as I can tell, the only thing that keeps your members from all killing one another is the threat of mutually assured destruction."

Bella shrugged, unperturbed. "As I said, your guild tends to be sentimental. Mutually assured destruction is a fine deterrent to violence in the ranks."

"Perhaps. Though this did not seem to be the case with Julien."

The cold fury in Bella's pale eyes was unsettling. "Do not," she said, "speak of my brother. His name should not belong in your mouth."

The name Julien triggered a frisson of regret and sadness. Not my emotions, I realized – Remy's. Whatever had happened between this sharp-faced blonde, her brother and Remy, had left at least two of them with lasting scars. Preoccupied with this little soap opera, I was unprepared for the sudden banging of the front door, and nearly upset my tray of champagne glasses. Luckily, waitressing reflexes helped me save them before they spilled and shattered.

"Dr Lorenzo! You made it." Góngora beamed at the short, bald, middle-aged man in a black fedora and trenchcoat. He was accompanied by a younger man, also soaked, wearing a brimmed cap and jacket. The driver, I assumed.

"Why did no one inform me of this storm? I am lucky I escaped with my life." The unhappy doctor lapsed into Spanish, presumably to continue his litany of complaints, as he removed his hat and overcoat. Across the room, I met Tessa's eyes, and she wheeled herself forward and took the doctor's coat. See, look at us and then forget all about us, model prisoner employees, useful and unobtrusive. As safe as those candles.

I offered the doctor champagne from the tray when the door banged open again. Sherwood barreled in, followed by Lloyd, who stumbled over the rug because his dark glasses were fogged up and his hands cuffed together. He regained his composure almost immediately, looking bemused by this strange gathering, and by his own tight, caped outfit, which revealed his barrel chest and slightly rounded tummy. Axel followed close behind, thin as a dancer in his bright green lycra, his pale face mottled with blushes. Lin was next, slouching as if her Robin Hood tunic and tights were her own ironic choice. She had perched the little feathered cap between her antlers. They were all still wearing their inhibitor collars, but then Tessa and I had been expecting that. I wondered where the Toad had gone. Was he still in the barn, trying to get the generator working? I didn't want to forget about him, only to have him turning up at the wrong moment, tipping the delicate balance of power.

Remy came in last. In his battered brown leather trenchcoat and high boots, he looked like a movie star action hero. For a moment, his eyes met mine, and I felt my heart give a nervous flip. Then he registered Jean Luc's expensively tanned face and Bella Donna's teased blonde head, and took a step in their direction, tautening the chain that connected him to Axel and making Lin lose her balance. This earned Remy a cuff from Sherwood's meaty arm.

"Back in line, leather boy," said Sherwood, clearly relishing this moment of power.

"Tsk tsk," said Góngora, shaking his head. "We do not damage the merchandise, my friend. Besides, we want them to mingle. Let the buyers see what they could be getting."

Sherwood rubbed his nose where the scalelike plating began, clearly disconcerted. "Meaning no disrespect, but letting the prisoners wander freely adds an unnecessary level of risk." He glanced at Remy. "Wouldn't it be better to have the buyers–"

"No." Góngora had gone very still. His small, piggy eyes had become mean and hard, and he suddenly seemed even larger and more powerful than he had a moment before. "Unless you feel you are incapable of guarding the door?"

"No, boss. Sorry, boss." Sherwood ducked his head.

As Góngora stomped away, his cane adding a percussive accent, the young guard unlocked the prisoners' chains. At first, Lin and Lloyd remained together in one corner of the room where some interior designer had created the kind of unprivate but slightly antisocial space you see in hotel lobbies. Axel made a beeline for me, grabbing a flute of champagne and downing it before Rita could stop him. He was reaching for another, his hand brushing mine, when Rita intercepted him.

"That's enough," she said sharply. "Go mingle."

Axel gave me an apologetic glance and allowed himself to be shepherded away. I became aware that Remy had come closer to me with studied casualness, his red-on-black gaze roving from one end of the room to the other, as if looking for a familiar face but not finding one. All the while, he was moving toward me.

I started walking, angling my face away from his but watching him out of the corner of my eye. Like any good waitress, I kept one eye focused on what was going on around me. To my right, Jean Luc surreptitiously poured a bit of his champagne into a potted palm and then made a show of sipping at what remained of his drink. Over to my left, Bella Donna was looking intently at Remy. It wasn't a "where have you been, my love, and how did you come to be sold at a slave auction?" sort of look. In fact, unless my face-reading skills had gotten rusty, her look translated to "I can't wait to tear strips of flesh from your hide with my bare hands, and then feed your innards to my pet vulture."

What the heck was the story there? The rush of feeling I had picked up from Remy told me that, at one point, the two of them had been friends. Okay, maybe more than friends. Scratch that, definitely more than friends, because no one hates on a purely platonic friend with that much vinegar.

"No, it's not here," said Dr Lorenzo, drawing my attention. He was holding an old-fashioned black leather medical satchel, which he snapped shut. "Eduardo," he said to his driver, "go fetch the case from the car."

The driver said something in Spanish, removing his cap to wipe the damp hair off his forehead. In the moment before he replaced the cap, I saw that the young man had a third eye right in the center of his forehead.

"Yes, I want you to do it now!" The doctor's pale, doughy face flushed an angry shade of red. "Are you afraid of a little rain?"

The driver turned toward the door, his face set and unhappy.

"So hard to get good help," said Dr Lorenzo. "I fear it is time to replace Eduardo."

Góngora snapped his fingers without looking at me, and I brought the tray of champagne glasses over. "You never keep your drivers long, do you? As I recall, the previous fellow had an eye in the *back* of his head."

"Yes, well, I am always trying something new. The eye in the back turned out to be too much for the visual cortex to process. Now Eduardo is complaining of headaches. Perhaps I shall find my replacement tonight." Dr Lorenzo downed his champagne in a gulp, replacing the glass and taking another full one as his eyes roamed over me. "What's the story with this one? Any modifications in mind for her?"

Góngora gave a great boom of a laugh. "Always looking for a

way to gild the lily! But this one is merely a human. Not worth wasting your time and skills on her."

Time and skills? Additions, as in extra eyes? Without thinking, my eyes rested on Rita, who was carrying six different trays of finger foods.

Had Rita's extra arms been a modification rather than a mutation? And if so, had she undergone the procedure willingly?

"But there's nothing wrong with modifying a human. An enhanced human can be as valuable as a mutant, no?" Dr Lorenzo's eyes moved past me and found something else to capture their interest. "And who is that lovely young woman?"

Góngora followed his gaze and saw that he was looking at Tessa, who had been ordered to remain close by the pigman. "Ah, that is the lovely Entomona – Queen of the Crawlies. I intend to keep her as well, but we will find you someone perfect for your needs. And wait till you see the new… but no, let me not spoil the surprise."

In general, I tried not to make snap judgments about people, but I was beginning to form a definite dislike for Doctor Lorenzo. His attention was diverted by his driver, who returned, soaking wet, carrying a heavy hard-shell suitcase.

Rita gave me a nudge with one of her elbows. "Take this. And careful, it's hot."

I took the sizzling platter of shrimp, their heads and tails still intact. There were little forks arranged around the tray, each with a different color handle. I contemplated throwing the hot oil in Góngora's face and making a run for it. Then I felt a little sting, and saw that an ant was crawling on my left hand. I glanced over at Tessa, who gave a brief shake of her head. *The plan. Remember the plan.* I forced a bland serving person smile onto my face and brought the platter of shrimp over to Jean Luc and Bella Donna, who were clearly disagreeing about something.

"No, Jean Luc, that is not what we agreed!" Bella Donna's eyes narrowed, making her look even more foxlike. "You said you would give him to me. Do not think the Assassins' Guild will just roll over and permit this to go unanswered."

"Of course not," said Jean Luc, with a flash of white teeth that was more challenge than smile. "But I did not tell you that you could have Remy. I told you that you would have your revenge, n'est-ce pas? And what could be a more fitting revenge than handing him over to the Benefactress?"

"It is not my revenge if I am not the one who takes it!" Bella's eyes slid sideways to me.

Damn it. I needed to hear more about this Benefactress. I gave Remy's ex my blandest waitress expression and held out the tray. "Care for a shrimp?"

"No, I do not care for a shrimp. Jean Luc, do not walk away from me!"

Jean Luc sighed and half turned back to Bella. "What do you suggest we do, Bella? Tell the Benefactress to accept a substitute? She has as much reason to want his blood as you do, and a lot more clout."

"Do not underestimate *my* power or the strength of the–" Bella Donna began, and then whirled on me, making a growly noise deep in her throat and thrust her hand under my chin. I could feel her fingers pressed against my windpipe, and the jab of something sharp. A shock of cold went down my spine. "What are you doing? Eavesdropping?"

Out of the corner of my eye, I saw Remy move. I wasn't sure, but I thought he might have thrown something. With the inhibitor collar dampening his powers, though, the object didn't travel very far – and did not explode.

"Cut that out," said Sherwood, doing something that made Remy grunt in pain. I couldn't see his face, but I could tell he was having a rare moment of job satisfaction.

"Góngora," said Bella Donna, bringing my attention back to my own predicament. "I apologize in advance for staining your carpets with this girl's blood."

"And shrimp." My hands were shaking, and I had spilled more than half the contents of the tray I was holding.

Bella Donna cursed and released me. "You've splattered oil on my suit!"

"I'll grab napkins," I offered, but she was already stalking off, probably to find the ladies' room. As I knelt to clean up the spilled shrimp, I fought the urge to grin. For the first time, I had managed to absorb a bit of someone's energy without shocking them into alertness or sending them into a coma. Bella Donna Boudreaux might not have a mutant power, but she was an assassin, and suddenly I felt infused with calm and steely with purpose.

After I had cleaned up the oil and shrimp as best I could, I started heading in the direction of the kitchen, passing Góngora and the doctor, who was inspecting the contents of a black leather box. I wasn't sure, but I thought I caught a glimpse of something metallic and sharp before the case was closed.

"So, no word yet from the Benefactress? Unfortunate." Dr Lorenzo scowled, and despite his bald head and jowls, I could easily see him as a truculent middle schooler, forced to wash the dishes by hand. "I suppose we'll have to do everything the old-fashioned way. So slow and messy."

"She will be here shortly, have no fear," Góngora said, his easy tone contradicted by anxious glances at the front door. "The weather has simply delayed her."

With an assassin's calm, I pretended to slip and lose control of my tray, bumping into Góngora. "Oh, lordy, I am so sorry! Shoot me now, I think some oil got on you… please forgive me, I'll just get that right off." I continued babbling apologies as I dabbed at Góngora's white suit. "Did it get on your hand, too? I am so clumsy. I can't believe I did that."

"*Basta!* Cease your touching of me." Góngora nervously touched his massive platinum watch. I guess he was worried I might have been trying to steal it. "Clumsy fool. I shall need to go to my chamber to change." As he turned to leave, the front door opened and the Toad came in, holding an umbrella over a woman's head.

"Lordy, what a downpour! Is my hair a mess? I bet my hair's a mess." The woman was pulling a rainscarf off her elaborately teased and curled hair, which was now fire engine red instead of strawberry blonde. The color might have changed, but I didn't need to see her face to know who had just arrived a little late for the slave auction. I would have known that husky voice anywhere.

Lucretia Borger was Góngora's special guest.

TWENTY-THREE

Lucretia Borger had dressed for the slave auction as if it were a Vegas wedding, and after greeting Góngora with what appeared to be unfeigned enthusiasm, she sashayed over to the bar trolley, the ruffles on her bright blue dress swaying hypnotically. Ignoring Rita, Lucretia poured herself a glass of champagne. I felt as if the room had tilted on its axis for a moment, and there was a rushing in my ears. Even with Bella Donna's icy calm running through my veins, I was having trouble processing the awfulness of this development. It wasn't just the shock of betrayal, as sharp and unexpected as a slap in the face – or a knife in the back. All those promises of helping young mutants realize their potential – of helping me – were lies. She was no different than Góngora.

Okay. She's your enemy. Get over it. The voice in my head sounded disconcertingly like Bella Donna, but it galvanized me into action. Turning on my heel, I headed toward the kitchen, nodding at Rita and miming the need to get more shrimp as I passed her. I was halfway down the hallway, breathing a little more deeply when I realized that the sharp tap-tap-tap I was hearing wasn't part of the flamenco soundtrack. I glanced over my shoulder and saw Lucretia walking toward me as quickly as her four-inch heels could carry her.

There went my cover, there went the plan. I searched my brain for another way out. I had managed to touch Góngora. If I had succeeded in absorbing his power, I might be able to cast the illusion I was an urn or a lamp.

Unfortunately, Lucretia was looking straight at me. "Wait up, I'm a comin'!" Her girlish, breathless voice filled me with rage, but I composed my face as she drew closer, one hand dramatically pressed to the generous shelf of her bosom.

Lucretia smiled, her lipstick bright as arterial blood. "Hey there! Bet you weren't expectin' me."

"Or you me." As a comeback, it wasn't much, but the fury and hurt I was feeling were not conducive to coming up with clever retorts.

Lucretia shook her head. "Not hardly. Why d'you think I'm here?" When I didn't answer right away, she dimpled and said, "I'm here to rescue you, silly."

I hesitated. Clearly, she wasn't about to out me immediately. Was she sympathetic to me because we had met before I was taken prisoner? Perhaps she didn't realize that I was here against my will. Or was she just another bad guy, looking to fill her own stable of powerful young mutants, and everything she said was just a part of her act, along with the hooker-with-a-heart-of-gold hair and makeup and the old-timey country singer wardrobe?

My poker face must have needed some work, because Lucretia tilted her head, skewing her enormous red hairdo sideways, where it defied gravity by not falling. "I knew you were here, Marie," she said, gazing at me with maternal concern. "My friend Irene saw it coming – but not soon enough to prevent it."

Was she telling the truth? What reason might she have for lying? "So, you're here to rescue me?"

"You bet I am." Lucretia clasped my wrist and squeezed. The jolt that went up my arm felt like I had slammed my funny bone into a rock. "Here's a little something for you to play with. Just you hang on and wait for my signal, OK? Now, I'd better get back in there before the Pig notices I'm gone."

She walked back to the party, her heels clicking with determination. I shook my arm, wondering why her touch had felt so strong – almost painful. *A little something for you to play with.* I suddenly recalled that Lucretia's power was to enhance her appearance. Did the woman really think that a little more mascara and brighter hair color would help my current situation?

Taking a deep breath, I walked into the kitchen, where two women in white chefs' aprons and hairnets were busy taking things out of the Viking range. I exchanged my old tray for a fresh platter of shrimp, then rejoined the others in the main room.

No one seemed to have noticed my absence. Lucretia was flirting with Jean Luc, while Rita was mixing drinks from a bar cart trolley. Bella Donna was having a deeply tense conversation with Remy. At the other end of the room, Doctor Lorenzo was examining Góngora's leg while Tessa sat nearby, hands spread out, squinting with the effort of dispersing microbes. The Toad was watching Tessa from under his bowl cut as though she were his rival for Góngora's affections.

Okay, I had to assume that Lucretia wasn't going to rat on me and just forge ahead with the plan before we ran out of time.

Tessa and I were banking on the idea that I could layer more than one power at once. So next on my list was Sherwood, since he wasn't wearing an inhibitor collar. I figured that underneath his pangolin scales and stern attitude, Sherwood couldn't be all that much older than eighteen, and emotionally he was even younger. Since he hadn't levitated or turned all brown things orange or shown any kind of unusual ability, we figured he was probably your run-of-the-mill strong dude with a side order of enhanced endurance – and the thick scales probably served as a bit of protection, which meant he didn't instantly hurt his paws when he punched an opponent. So all I had to do was get close enough to absorb enough strength to disable the inhibitor collars. We figured Axel had to go first – his ability to projectile vomit acid might be bad news on a date, but made him a definite asset in a prison break.

I wished I had a moment to freshen my lipgloss, but I took a breath and licked my lips. "Hey, Sherwood," I said, walking over to the young guard, who was slouched with one hand on some kind of electronic device, the other thumb looped into his belt. "Can I offer you a shrimp?" I deliberately kept my gaze from straying to Remy, but I was aware of him. For once, he did not appear to be looking at me.

Sherwood, on the other hand, was staring at me as though I'd grown a second head. "Huh?"

I held out the platter. "Shrimp?"

"Um, sure." His eyes were disconcertingly human in his scaly face as he took a shrimp, still staring at me. "Aren't you supposed to just mingle and enjoy yourself?"

I stared back at him. "I don't think so. I'm supposed to be working."

It was hard to tell with the impassive face, but I was pretty sure Sherwood seemed confused. "Okay," he said. "I guess it's a kind of work? Like, shmoozing?"

I was about to say something about his work being harder when I caught a glimpse of my own hand with its long, bright blue fingernails. Taken by surprise, I took an involuntary step back and stumbled, which was how I discovered I was wearing sky-high heels. "What the hell?"

Lucretia. Somehow, I had turned into Lucretia.

"You OK, ma'am?" Sherwood reached out a hand to steady me, then jumped back as my power gave him a jolt. Just over his shoulder, I saw Lin and Remy watching me. Lin's sullen face was impossible to read, but Remy looked confused, with a generous side order of suspicion. Okay, great, I probably had super strength, but none of my friends was going to let me close enough to touch their inhibitor collars because I didn't look like me.

"I'm fine," I said. "Just a little dizzy for a sec. Probably low blood sugar." Shoot, that sounded like me, and not like Lucretia at all. I pitched my voice higher and girlier. "Will you excuse me for a moment? Thanks, you're a doll." Sherwood looked a bit dazed himself as I shoved the tray into his hands and started walking, my heels clicking on the tile floor as I hurried out of the main room and down the hallway where I had run into Lucretia. Putting a hand on the wall, I tried to think. I didn't want to go into the kitchen – that would raise too many questions from the catering folks.

Bathroom. I needed a moment alone to get my bearings.

I opened the first door I found – closet – and then closed it before trying another. Bingo. Downstairs guest bathroom, decorated in luxe rustic, with lots of knotty pine and brass pinecone accents.

I turned on the light, closed the door behind me and stared in the big, raw-pine framed mirror at Lucretia Borger's reflection. My left eye twitched, and so did the false eyelash in the mirror.

Okay. I took a deep breath and tried to go over what had happened. I had touched the Pig, and then Lucretia had touched me. Góngora had the power of illusion, and Lucretia could enhance her appearance – maybe the two powers had combined in some way, one layering on top of the other. My heartbeat slowed. That made sense. I smiled at Lucretia's reflection in the mirror. This was actually kind of cool. I could use this.

There was a sharp knock, and my heart stuttered a beat as the door opened. I wasn't sure who I had been expecting, but it certainly wasn't the face that appeared in the doorway.

"Thank God I found you," said the woman who looked exactly like me.

TWENTY-FOUR

For a moment, I felt pure confusion as I stared at what appeared to be my identical twin. She was wearing the embarrassing French maid's uniform I had been wearing before I had transformed into Lucretia, and reflexively, I put my hand to my mouth. My mirror image did not follow suit. Instead, she walked into the bathroom, closed the door behind her, and regarded me with her hands on her hips.

"What on earth were you thinking? Were you even thinking? Sorry if I'm not pulling my punches here," said my double. For an awful moment, I thought it might be Góngora himself, glamoured to look like me, but then I recognized the girlish voice. Lucretia. For some reason, Lucretia now looked like me. I was so confused that it took me a moment to make sense of what she was saying. "I told you to wait for my signal. And why did you go and turn into me? There was already one of me out there. Didn't you think someone would notice?"

"I didn't know. I didn't mean to." I was completely confused now. "You-you said your power was to enhance your appearance.

But you just... how did you..." I gestured at her transformation into my own perfect double.

Lucretia shrugged, and it was like looking in a mirror. No – not quite. Her part with its streak of white was on the wrong side. Then it hit me – I was used to seeing myself in the mirror, which reversed my image. Looking at Lucretia was like looking at a photo. "I may have been a little modest about the extent of my abilities."

I could feel a tightening in my right temple – the beginnings of a doozy of a headache. "What does that even mean?"

"It means I can change my appearance."

"Like Góngora?"

My own face looked surprised. "Oooh, so that's not his true appearance?"

I explained about touching his leg and figuring out that he was not a six-foot-something anthropomorphized pig.

"Clever girl," she said. "But my power is to change appearance, not cast illusion."

My headache was getting worse. "That seems much of a muchness."

My own face looked back at me, clearly disappointed. "Oh, I keep forgettin' how new you are to all of this."

Now I was beginning to get mad. "Spare me the condescension and let's figure out how to get the hell out of here."

Lucretia tapped one finger against her cheek. "I think maybe we keep it simple. Just slip on out while I cover for you."

I shook my head, appalled. "I can't leave," I said. "I'm the only one on the outside, besides Tessa. We're supposed to free everyone else."

"I'll my best to help the others." My double held up a gloved hand, stopping me before I could protest. "And I know you want to help, but really, it's best you stay out of the way. I'm better equipped to handle this. You barely know how to use your powers, and even if I give you instructions, you'll probably do more harm than good."

Fear's a funny thing. You can't just turn it off like a light switch, but you sure can flip it into fury. "You know, lady, I have heard how ignorant and unprepared I am for the past ten years, and I am sorry I have not had time to train, but I am not about to turn tail and run. So even if I am not all that much, I'm going to give it all I got."

Lucretia sighed at me, with my own face, and then, lightning quick, pulled back a hand and smacked me in the face. I stared at her, shocked. "Now, did you see that coming? No, you did not. Because you are not used to fighting. It's a shockin' thing, someone actually tryin' to hurt you. It discombobulates. And that's just a plain ol' physical fight." Removing a paper towel from the dispenser, Lucretia ran cold water on it before pressing it to my cheek. "But we're not just talkin' a physical fight. Powers, now they take some gettin' used to – and you're a babe in the woods. You start mixing it up with the likes of Rita and Mortimer, and you're just going to get yourself in a mess of trouble."

I pushed her hand away, sucking in a surprised breath as the cool, wet towel was removed. In the mirror, there was no white handprint on red, and the sting of pain was gone, too. Was I losing my mind, or was that strange? I hadn't been slapped in a while – not since that last big fight with Aunt Carrie – but it seemed to me that the handprint had lasted longer. "You heal fast," I said. And then I slapped my double in the face. "Hmph," I said, watching that print fade as well. "Very fast."

"Marie, I am a trained martial artist. There is no way on earth that you can fight me without–"

Before she could finish the sentence, I had my arm around her neck. "I do believe this hold is frowned upon in official circles, but then, you never follow the rules, do you?"

"Of course. You absorbed some of my muscle memory along with my power." Lucretia twisted, but I held her in place.

"Not just yours, sugar." I could still feel Sherwood's easy strength coursing through my muscles, along with a dose of young male testosterone-fueled confidence. That's right, I thought, I can mix and match powers. Then it hit me – this was my chance. I imagined Góngora, first the broad outline of his huge porcine head and misshapen body, then the details – the furrowed pink of his snout, his tiny beady eyes, the bristles on his chin – the white suit. When I looked in the mirror, I saw Góngora holding my double in a chokehold.

"With a little training, you're going to be amazing." With a smile, Lucretia turned boneless and slipped out of my arms. In a blink, she reformed, this time as her red-haired self, and now she had torqued my arm up behind my back at a painful angle. "You're just not there yet."

"You don't get it. The longer you fight me, the more you touch me. The more you touch me, the stronger I get." I pulled free of her grip, scraping myself on one of her large diamond rings in the process.

Distracted, I glanced down to see a few drops of blood on the back of my right hand, and was startled to see Góngora's strangely attenuated fingers. Hard to believe you can forget that you've cast a giant pig illusion, but in my defense, there was a lot going on. I grabbed a paper towel out of the dispenser and dabbed at the bloody spot – and that's when the penny dropped.

My fingers didn't just look like disgusting, spidery long digits. They felt that way, too. I rubbed my hands together, and then touched my snout.

"What's wrong, you can't stand the sight of blood?" Lucretia shook her head. "See, this is another reason why–"

"It's not an illusion."

"What?"

"Your power. It's not an illusion. I really just did turn myself into a giant pig." I looked at the scratch, but where there had been a few drops of blood a moment before, there was nothing. No blood, no scratch – just completely healed skin. "You can manipulate skin and bone and… you heal up in no time."

Lucretia nodded. "Yep. That's what I was trying to tell you. Sounds like Góngora projects illusions, but I can change my appearance."

It took a moment for the full implication to sink in. "You can actually turn yourself into other people. No, more than that – you can recreate their clothing and jewelry as well." That was some serious matter manipulation. "Wait – do you even look like this? Is this a disguise?"

She raised her eyebrows. "I'll give you this – you're no dummy." Which was tantamount to saying, Yes, this is a disguise. Lucretia glanced at her watch. "But we can't stay in here much longer, or someone might notice." She took a deep breath. "So you win. We'll do this together."

I paused. "How do I know I can trust you?"

"What's the alternative?"

Good point. As Lucretia rearranged her bodice, I had the disorienting sense that I was no longer myself. I closed my eyes, and pictured myself as clearly as I could – the shape of my eyebrows, the cowlick on my bangs, the zit on my dang forehead. Was it weird that when I tried to see myself in my mind's eye, some of the details were blurry? I breathed a sigh of relief when I opened my eyes and checked in the mirror, and there I was, looking back at me. "Who's a quick study?"

Lucretia shook her head. "You forgot the little rhinestone bobby pin in your hair. Don't roll your eyes, girl. My power's not worth much if I'm tryin' to pass as someone and I put a beauty mark on the wrong side."

"Your power's not worth much the minute you open your mouth," I pointed out.

"You are green as spring lettuce, ain't you?" Lucretia took a deep breath, and this time, when she spoke, she sounded just like Góngora. "I can do ten different dialects of Spanish," now she switched to a Parisian accent, "and ten of French. I can also do twenty distinct American regional accents," this last was said in an accent that reminded me of the rich guy on Gilligan's Island, "as well as more than thirty-seven different British accents." Here she sounded like a tough Cockney girl. "Oh, and I'm also fluent in twelve languages." That was her own accent. At least, it was the accent I was used to hearing her use.

Out of my depth, I just nodded. It hadn't escaped my notice that, unlike Remy, she didn't seem in the least drained, even though I had absorbed some of her power. She must be incredibly strong – and, unlike me, in complete control of her abilities.

"Now," said Lucretia, "fill me in on how you got here in the first place. I'm assuming you're not waitressing for a notorious mutant slave trader just to make a little side cash. Not sure why he's not keeping you with the others…?"

"He was after my friend, Remy. I'm just collateral damage."

Lucretia raised her eyebrows. "I see."

"He doesn't know I'm a mutant."

"Then he's an idiot." She smiled at me, and I got a glimpse of the woman I could be if I were in command of my powers and confident in my abilities. "I'm here because of you, you know."

"You – how did you even know about…" I waved my hand. "All of this?"

"Because I have sources. And the Pig goes for some of the same candidates I do. His methods of recruitment are a bit different, as you have seen." Lucretia checked herself out in the mirror before turning back to me. "Now. You want help getting your friends out of here?"

Did I? She had deliberately given me her power to take on someone else's form – down to the clothes and nails, which meant she could produce inorganic as well as organic materials. That was a double scoop of mutant power, all right, with a dang cherry on top. No reason for me to think she wasn't being on the level – except that every time I met the woman, I seemed to learn a new and completely contradictory fact about her.

Still, as they say, beggars can't ask for an ID check before accepting your help. "If you're offering, I'm accepting."

"Then wait for my signal."

Lucretia put her hand on mine, and I felt a second jolt, along with a flash of memory – a city in late fall, the smell of coal smoke and chicory coffee, the old fashioned "ooga" of an air horn as a rounded, low-slung vintage car veered around a horse and cart. Lucretia's memories? Then it hit me. Maybe she was not who she appeared to be. Maybe her whole look was a facade. Maybe she was someone else entirely – someone older, if the memories of the 1930s were anything to go by. Her healing powers might keep her youthful for far longer than ordinary folks.

I shook my head, trying to clear it. The mystery of Lucretia Borger would have to wait, however. I had more pressing concerns.

"You OK?" Lucretia was frowning at me, and I felt a dizzying moment of disorientation, because she looked like herself again, and I was back in my face and body, with my maid's uniform. I had never been so relieved to see myself. "Just hold on to you. You got this, Marie."

I sure hoped she was right. I left the bathroom first, the tingle of Lucretia's second touch still racing up and down my arms – and ran straight into Rita, who was carrying three platters of food and another hot skillet.

"Where have you been, Rogue?" Rita didn't wait for a reply. "Góngora's freaking out because the guest of honor hasn't shown up yet, the phone lines are down, the busty redhead's taken a powder and two of the prisoners are saying they need to use the toilet at once. I don't know what he expects me to do – I can't be in the kitchen preparing the food and serve at the same time!"

Ah, the challenges of holding a high-class slave auction during a major storm. "Why don't you go on back to the food prep," I suggested, "while I serve?"

Whatever Rita was about to say was cut short when the lights in the room flickered and then went out, leaving us all in pitch darkness for a moment. The unobtrusive flamenco soundtrack, which had been playing in the background this whole time, ceased abruptly, and there was long beat of silence, broken by murmurs of concern, accompanied by the rustling of nervous movement. Then, with a quick scratch, all the candles flickered to life and began to rise in the air, accompanied by the sinuous melody of a Middle Eastern flute.

Then the overhead chandelier flared into life before breaking apart, so each electric taper moved to a different wall and attached itself.

"That's better," said a gravely female voice, and suddenly a disembodied head appeared, hovering in the center of the room. I had the sinking feeling in the pit of my stomach that I got when rollercoasters gathered speed, and from the look on everyone's face, I wasn't the only one feeling the subtle, unmistakable hum of a huge power source right nearby.

The guest of honor had just arrived.

TWENTY-FIVE

The disembodied woman's head bobbed along, taking in the Southwestern decor and the other guests with a jaundiced eye. Her white hair floated around her as though she were moving through water. "I can't abide overhead lighting. So unflattering to anyone over forty." Now the head descended until it was about five and a half feet above the ground, and the hair settled into a neat pageboy as the speaker's body appeared beneath it. "I think that was Edith Wharton who said that. Or the other one – Henry James? Oh, what's the use – I doubt any of you has read a book since fourth grade."

"Welcome, welcome!" Góngora struggled to lift himself out of his leather chair without putting pressure on his injured foot. Mortimer gave his boss a hand, hauling him upward. "We have been so worried about you, Madame Candra!"

"How absurd you are. Worrying about me because of some piddling storm!" Candra waited for the big man to approach her, the red sequins on her dress glittering like flames. The woman might have been a hard living sixty-five or a well-preserved seventy-five, and it didn't take much imagination to see that she had once been a stunning beauty. As a kid, I used to watch old reruns of *The Love Boat* with my Aunt Carrie, and I was always fascinated by the episodes where the guest star was an ancient celebrity, stiff with age and hairspray and girdled by the hauteur that came from knowing you were an immortal star of stage and screen, and the people around you were lesser mortals.

Candra was clearly a star who had condescended to slum it with lesser beings. "Well? What are you all gaping for? Is this the way you treat all your guests, Godzilla?"

I caught a fresh wave of sweat stink off Góngora. "My dear lady, we are beyond honored by your estimable presence!"

Candra made a moue of distaste. "Don't fawn over me, Gorgonzola. I loathe fawning. Bring me a chair that doesn't stink of your flop sweat."

"Tessa!" Góngora clapped his hands. "Clear the good chair of any offensive microbial matter."

Tessa wheeled over and frowned at the leather chair while Candra impatiently tapped her foot. "Enough, enough!" She sank down into the chair, fussily rearranging the folds of her gown. "Really, I'm not even sure why I bothered. Am I even going to be offered something to drink? Honestly."

If there was one thing I knew from my time helping Aunt Carrie's church friends, it was crotchety old ladies. As Góngora relinquished his leather chair to the elderly guest of honor, I pushed the drinks trolley over. "How are you doing tonight, ma'am?"

Her eyes narrowed. "What do you think? The power lines were down. I had to telekinetically transport myself over six miles, while keeping the rain off. Do you have any idea how much energy that requires?"

"You must be a powerful telekinetic."

She was not going to be mollified that easily. "I don't enjoy it, you know." Her eyes drifted to the drink cart. "Aren't you going to offer me a drink?"

"I'm sorry. What can I make you tonight? Martini? Manhattan? Old fashioned?" I took in the mulish set of her jaw. Not a vodka or whiskey drinker, then. "Gin rickey?"

This perked the old girl up. "Hmm. I was going to ask for blood from a living victim, but I have always had a fondness for the old mother's ruin."

I smiled, assuming this was a joke. Hoping it was a joke. "Don't you worry," I said, cutting the lime. "I make a mean cocktail."

Candra sniffed.

"Benefactress," said Góngora, seizing his opening. "Once you have your drink, would you like something to eat?" He snapped his fingers. "Rita! Appetizers!"

Candra shuddered. "I haven't eaten solid food since 1879."

"Intermittent fasting," Jean Luc said approvingly. "I've been trying it myself. And may I say that you look amazing."

"I look like crap," snapped Candra. Then, turning to me as I crushed the ice, she added, "Do you know how old I am?"

"Fifty-four," I hazarded, lopping a good ten years off my most generous estimate. As I poured out the gin, Bella Donna maneuvered through the tight circle surrounding Candra and sidled up beside me. Of course she would be one of those people who can't bear to wait her turn for anything. I gave her a pointed look as I cut the lime and she gave me a brief, insincere smile before slinking off.

"Fifty-four!" Candra bristled visibly before conjuring a small hand mirror out of the air. "Good lord, I stopped aging at twenty-nine. I can't possibly look that old."

"My dear lady, you are still as beautiful as ever," said Góngora, investing each word with absolute conviction.

"Am I?"

I added a small paper umbrella to the drink and handed it over. "Unfamiliar mirrors," I said. "My aunt always said she looked older when she caught a glimpse of herself in an unfamiliar mirror."

"Easy for you to say. Look at that subcutaneous fat layer!" She poked my sleeve with one crooked finger. "I want your fat."

Ordinarily, I would have made a joke, like "take it, it's yours," but one glance at Lucretia told me to keep my quips to myself. Lucretia had gone very still and quiet, which was so out of character that I realized she was a little frightened of Candra herself. Lucretia might be powerful, but Candra was a different order of mutant. If I offered her my excess fat, she was the sort who might just take my offer at face value and suction all the fat out of my body so she could pad out her hollow cheeks. I forced myself to tamp down on the panic I felt welling up and tried to think of her as a washed-up movie star. "Tell me how that drink is, sugar."

Candra sniffed the glass, then tossed the whole drink back in two swigs. "Needs to be stronger," she decided, holding out her empty glass. As I mixed her a second gin rickey, Candra looked beadily around. "Well? Is this all the greeting I get?"

"Indeed, no–" began Góngora, but Jean Luc cut him off.

"Benefactress, the Thieves' Guild would like to present you with an offering." Jean Luc's overly white and unnaturally even teeth flashed in his charming pirate's smile. "Our regular tithe was delivered to you, but, malheureusement, due to an unfortunate set of circumstances, you did not receive the intended package." There was a quick sidelong glance at Remy here, and I understood that somehow, my favorite Cajun had been involved. "Tonight, we have an even better specimen for you to enjoy."

Bella Donna made a little sound of displeasure. It reminded me of the noise a cat makes when you take away the chipmunk it has been torturing.

"Well?" Candra snapped her fingers. "Don't keep me in suspense. I loathe waiting for anything." She glanced at me. "And I do mean anything." Shoot, I had forgotten about her drink. I handed Candra the fresh gin rickey and waited as she took a sip. No complaints, so I could only assume she liked it well enough.

"Then you shall not have to wait another second for your surprise." Jean Luc grabbed Remy by his bound hands and dragged him forward, knocking him into other prisoners, this made Lloyd and Axel stumble so they knocked into Lin's antlers.

"Ow! Watch it," she said, rubbing her forehead.

Candra was unimpressed. "Is this the comedy section of the evening?"

"No, Benefactress." Jean Luc glared at his son before turning to Góngora. "Can we please release Remy LeBeau so he can be presented?"

Góngora snapped his fingers, and Sherwood unlocked Remy's handcuffs. Things were looking better and better, but my stomach kept twisting. Would I be able to make full use of every advantage that was presenting itself? I couldn't help but wonder if Remy, with all his swagger and bounce, would be better at this than I was.

Candra had beckoned Remy forward, and was looking him over as if he were a suspect piece of beef. "Isn't this one your heir? As I recall, his cousin was meant to be the tithe."

"He *was* my heir," said Jean Luc. "Now he is yours, to do with as you will, so that you and your loyal servants may benefit from the Elixir of Life."

"How very Abrahamian of you," said Candra in a dry tone. Her bony fingers prodded at Remy's midsection. "So, this one is to be the sacrifice. He's a handsome hunk of flesh, I'll grant you, but it is what's inside that counts with me. Remind me of his talents?"

"The ability to release the latent energy of objects," said Remy, going down on one knee so that he was looking up at Candra, like a supplicant – or a suitor about to propose. Of course, he was trying to charm her. While everyone was watching Remy, I sidled up behind Mortimer, as if I were trying to get a better view.

"Energetic – I like that. Take off your coat, young man," Candra was saying. "Let me see you properly."

Remy removed his coat and handed it to Rita. "Your turn to remove something," he said, with a wink. It was hard to read Rita, but I got the vibe that she did not look entirely comfortable with the proceedings. I wasn't sure exactly how she and Remy knew each other from the past, but he did seem to have the Georgie Porgie talent for kissing the ladies and then making them cry.

Candra knocked back the last of her gin rickey. "You have what the great Sarah Bernhardt called chutzpah. So, you want me to disrobe? Or, rather, you seek to take back some power by challenging me to do something you think would make me uncomfortable. A classic seduction technique, but often effective." With a twinkle in her eye, Candra shrugged off her red sequined jacket, revealing a white blouse. "Your turn."

Remy seemed unconcerned as he pulled off the tight black shirt, revealing the smooth expanse of his chest. He had lost some weight in the week we had been held prisoner, making the muscled planes of his chest and abdomen even more defined than before. As Candra reached out a hand to trace down the center of his chest, he raised one eyebrow. "How far are we taking this in front of an audience?"

Candra rapped him in the stomach with the backs of her knuckles. "Naughty boy." Then she traced one finger down the center of his chest. I couldn't be certain, but I was pretty sure that Candra wasn't just being a superannuated cougar. Like me, she seemed able to absorb the energies of others. I wondered what would happen if she touched me – would our powers cancel each other out? Or would she, being stronger, consume my power?

"On second thought, maybe I won't use you all up in one night," said Candra, withdrawing her hand. "You're too delicious to consume all at once."

This proved too much for Bella Donna. "I object," she said, stepping forward while Lucretia and Jean Luc, standing beside her, moved away. Bella was undeterred. "Before you remove any more clothing from this man, I challenge Jean Luc's right to offer him. He may be Jean Luc's son, but he's my husband."

TWENTY-SIX

Remy was married. It hurt worse than I would have expected, considering how short a time I had known him. With a rush of guilt, I realized I was mostly to blame. I had known what he was from the start – a charmer and a player. Con artists only con you into believing what you want to believe, and I had wanted to believe I was special.

"He's your husband? Funny." Candra stroked Remy's arm with her long fingernails. "He doesn't act like your husband." For once, she and I were in perfect agreement.

"He killed my brother, and I demand his blood as restitution."

"Julien challenged me!" Remy's voice was rough with suppressed emotion. "I tried not to hurt him, Bel. I only struck out in self-defense, but I didn't mean to kill him. I thought we were friends. We've all been friends since we were–"

Candra raised her hand, stopping him while keeping her attention on Bella Donna. "And if I refuse?"

Bella Donna stepped forward and removed a vial from the mound of her teased blonde hair. "Then I refuse to give you the antidote to the poison I slipped into your drink."

Jean Luc sucked in a breath. So this is what he was fearing – that his son's bride would sidle up to him and spike his drink with something lethal. That should teach you not to marry into a family of assassins.

Candra seemed intrigued rather than alarmed as she tapped one finger against her lips, considering. "You're not going to age well. It's that pointy chin – give it ten or twenty years, and you'll have more wattles than a turkey. Ah, well. Nothing to be done about genetics."

Bella shrugged. "At least I will age. You, on the other hand, have about five minutes left to live."

"And all this is because you want your husband back?"

Bella Donna nodded, holding up the vial. "I want to kill him myself. I'm sure you can appreciate that."

"I can indeed." With lightning quickness, Candra reached out a hand and made a quick turning gesture. Bella Donna gasped and dropped to her knees. As we all watched in horror, her skin turned transparent, changing her pretty face into a monstrous mask of muscle, roped by veins and arteries. Once, in ninth grade, our biology teacher took us on a field trip to Jackson to see the Bodies exhibit. There was a lot of giggling and shrieking as we walked past the preserved human bodies, stripped of their protective layers of epidermis so you could see the bones and muscles and tendons underneath. Those bodies had been repulsive and yet fascinating, especially as they had been placed in action poses.

None of them had moved, though, or looked down at its own hands, flayed face contorting as it registered shock and abhorrence, and then an awful, soul-deep horror. None of them had screamed like Bella Donna was doing now.

I stared at the assassin's disaster of a face, too horrified to look away. Like an actress who knows how to time her delivery to the precise moment the applause dies down, Candra waited to resume speaking until Bella Donna's screams subsided into a low, continuous moan of pain. "Have I mentioned my power, foolish girl? Just as your husband can release latent energy in an object, I can release latent mutant genetics. I can give powers, and I can take them away. I can also unleash unpleasant but essentially benign mutations, such as invisible skin."

Bella Donna had stopped screaming, and even though a muscle near her mouth twitched, she seemed almost composed as she took a breath to speak. "You can't leave me like this."

Candra lifted an eyebrow. "You are a slow learner. If you want to beg me to kill you, you'll have to do better than that."

Bella Donna's eyes were fierce and oddly lovely in her ravaged face. "I'm not begging for my life, but in a moment you will be. The poison should be making its way throughout your nervous system about now. First, you'll feel a tingling in your extremities. Then a choking sensation as your throat begins to close."

Candra opened her mouth, then stopped and grabbed her throat. Her eyes widened as she began to choke with a horrible hacking, gargling sound. Green foam frothed at the corners of her mouth, and a strong smell burned the back of my throat – somewhere between spicy perfume and rotten apples.

The old woman clawed at her throat and then reached out, her eyes beseeching each of us in turn to help her. Then she fell to her knees with an audible crack and began to shiver violently as her head began to make jerking, spasmodic movements. A thick rivulet of foam covered her mouth, and she began to cough violently.

No one made a move toward her. Dr Lorenzo actually took two steps back.

For a moment, I forgot she was a powerful and possibly ancient being and saw only an elderly lady, in desperate need of help. Without thinking, I fell to my knees beside her, trying to roll her onto her side. No one made a move to help me, but no one tried to stop me, either. I looked up for a moment and saw Lucretia whispering something in Lin's ear. The antlered teen looked suspicious. Then Candra moaned and began to retch up more poison, and I angled her head down to keep her from choking. I wasn't sure if that's what you did for poison, but it seemed worth a try. I was trying not to touch the green foam, but there was no avoiding contact with her bare skin.

For once, there was no tingle or shock. Instead, I had a rush of pure, dizzying power. I've never touched any drug stronger than caffeine, so I couldn't compare it to anything like that. I jerked back, stunned by the shimmering sweetness flooding through me. Was I poisoned? Was I dying? If so, it felt… amazing.

As I tried to conceal my reaction, Candra convulsed, giving one long rattling cough and then lying still.

A chill penetrated my euphoria. I had killed her. I had touched her and drained the last of her strength, and now she was…

Sitting up, taking a deep breath, hacking something into her palm. When Candra opened her fist, she revealed a sparkling green gem, lit within by deep purple lights. "Intriguing. What was that, a blend of mustard gas and a nerve agent? It certainly makes for a pretty keepsake."

I fought the urge to laugh, because it was such a self-consciously theatrical moment. Yet I had to admit, I felt more than a little admiration for the old woman as well. There was a sudden babble of voices as everyone seemed to speak at once. Góngora and Jean Luc moved forward, tentatively offering her a hand, but Candra reached out for Remy with an imperious gesture.

"I can't stand brown-nosing sycophants," she said, then paused. "No. I want the… the waitress. There you are. So kind of you to help me before." Very deliberately, she reached out for me. I took her thin, age-spotted hand in mine. As I helped her up, I felt a weird, flipping sensation, as if the air between us was charged. Later, I thought it might be that we were like two magnets touching the wrong side round, so we were repelling each other. Maybe the previous touch had only worked the way it had because of the poison. All I knew was, I was relieved when Candra released my palm. She eyed me steadily for a moment.

"You were kind. That's a dangerous thing to be, young woman. Not everyone repays kindness in kind." She considered me for a moment, and I would have been terrified if not for the euphoric power still shimmering in my blood. "But I think you know that already." She shook back her sleeve from her bony wrist, revealing a charm bracelet sparkling with different colored gems. "Each a poison. This is from the past five years, of course – I have lots of other baubles and bits from previous attempts. This new gem…" she held it up. "…is for you." She handed it over and I stared at it, disgusted and fascinated. "Power is like other people's advice. You have to decide what bits to let in and what to reject."

I knew she was making a good point. I was riding a wave of power so strong that I had to focus on my breathing.

The rounded muscle between Bella Donna's eyes contracted

visibly as she frowned. "That's impossible. This poison was exactly calibrated to your system. There is no way it could have just passed through you."

Candra touched a finger to her lips, then glanced at me briefly. "Perhaps not. Yet it has." I dimly understood that my touch – my power – may have actually been what saved the ancient woman.

Out of the corner of my eyes, I could see Lucretia watching me, and even though she had carefully schooled her expression, I knew she had to be disappointed. Once again, I had acted without thinking. By saving Candra, had I consigned my friends and myself to slavery?

"Now, on to more pleasant pastimes." Candra crooked a finger at Remy. "Come here, beefcake, and sit at my feet. I'd like to take a look at the rest of the chattel."

Remy gave the briefest of glances as he knelt at Candra's feet. I couldn't read him at all. Maybe he was embarrassed because he had neglected to tell me that he was married. Perhaps he was focused on escape, and how we were going to carry this off.

On the other hand, he could have been feeling guilty about his wife, her flayed face made even more horrific by its halo of teased hair. Presumably he had loved her once, and was appalled to see her suffering this way.

"Please," Bella Donna said, the big, curved muscle of her forehead lifting her eyes into a pleading expression. "Kill me. I can't live like this."

Candra waved away the request. "You young people, always confusing *can't* and *won't*. Now stop pestering me." She ran her fingers through Remy's hair, and Bella Donna gave a shriek of frustration and launched herself at the ancient woman.

Candra turned and clapped her hands, and suddenly Bella

Donna was gone. Remy made a muffled sound and I shivered, dimly aware that the storm still raging outside had been steadily dropping the temperature. There was a chill in the room now, literal as well as figurative. "Good lord, she was annoying," said Candra, looking down at Remy. "How did you ever bear it?"

Remy looked like he was trying to swallow something stuck in his throat. "We were friends when we were small." He looked up at Candra. "Where is she now?"

"That is not for you to ask," said Góngora. "We do not question the Benefactress."

"Oh, pish tosh." Candra ruffled Remy's hair with obvious affection. "My little tithe boy can ask me anything. Did you think I sent her to the cornfield? She's about a mile from here. That direction." Candra waved her hand vaguely off to the east. "Now, let's get back to business."

"Yes, indeed," said Góngora, lifting himself with some effort from a stool. "I do believe the moment is right to show you all my little surprise." He waved away the Toad's hand and used his cane to walk across the room. He pressed a small button and a section of the wood paneling slid to one side, revealing a hidden elevator. "If you will all please follow me? There's plenty of room... and an extremely advanced ventilation system."

Candra raised her hand and Remy hesitated before offering his elbow and leading her into the elevator. His expression gave no hint of the turmoil he must be feeling inside. Never mind, I told myself. This was no time for jealousy. I had to stay focused on other, more important things – like not keeling over.

Now that the first rush of power was fading, I was getting vivid flashes of memories of people I had never seen and places I had never visited. My brain was trying to digest the huge dose of

Candra I had just ingested, and, so far, it wasn't handling things all that well. I felt a wave of cold nausea, and a prickling feeling racing up and down my arms.

There was a clap of thunder outside and then a dull thud as another tree fell, some of the branches rattling against an upstairs window.

I felt a hand on my back, pushing me forward. "Come on, Rogue," said Rita. "No way am I leaving you up here on your own."

I nodded, trying not to let on how dizzy and unwell I was feeling. You're a babe in the woods, Lucretia had said, and maybe she was right. I hadn't been thinking of the plan or escape or attempting to absorb anyone's powers when I had pounded the ancient lady on the back.

But that's just what I had done.

TWENTY-SEVEN

I didn't know where I was, or how I had gotten there. I must have lost a chunk of time, though, because we were no longer in the main room, with its elegant Southwestern decor and large windows. Instead, we appeared to be in a cross between a basement and an operating room, with white surgical LED light fixtures hanging down from the ceiling. Taking a deep breath, I tried to slow my racing heart as I took stock of my surroundings. Instead of music playing on a speaker system, there was the soft whoosh of an air purification system. Instead of side tables with trays of finger foods, there were two steel surgical tables, and various kinds of monitors lined up against the freshly painted walls. There was a strong odor of antiseptic in the room that made my nostrils sting.

Bit by bit, things fell into place. I remembered the elevator, though nothing after. This was what Góngora had been building in his basement, I realized. Dr Lorenzo was moving around the room, his dour face breaking into a smile when he saw something he liked.

Candra was holding onto Remy's arm and saying something flirtatious to him. I thought he looked haggard, but maybe it was the stark lighting. Lin and Lloyd and Axel were standing nervously between Rita and Sherwood, while Jean Luc and Lucretia were following Góngora as he pointed out the state-of-the-art equipment.

"I think of this as my little doll hospital," Góngora was saying, leaning on his cane as he walked slowly around the room. "Are any of you familiar with the American Girl Doll store in New York City? A most amusing place."

"Oh," said Lucretia happily. "I didn't know you were a fan. I have quite a collection myself." Now that I knew this girlish enthusiasm was an act, it seemed impossible that Góngora would not see through it.

Góngora, however remained oblivious, nodding appreciatively. "Indeed, it does not seem like my sort of venue. But I went there one day with… well, never mind with whom. But suffice it to say, I was extremely impressed." Candra looked bemused by this unexpected conversational detour while Jean Luc's jaw was clenching with poorly suppressed impatience. "You do not simply purchase a doll, you see – you purchase a story."

I felt a gentle hand on my arm and looked to see that Tessa was right beside me. She looked pale and tired. "You OK, Rogue?"

I nodded. "You?" Belatedly, I realized she must have been working for hours to keep Góngora germ free.

Tessa shrugged. "He's comfortable with the hygienic protocols down here, so I get a break." She looked at me more closely. "What's going on with you?"

I noticed Rita watching us and holding a finger to her lips. "Tell you later."

Góngora was still going on about the dolls. "One doll represents the American pioneer spirit. Another, darker haired doll lives on a ranch in New Mexico with her family. There is also a member of the Nez Perce tribe, a scrappy kid from the Great Depression – even a former slave on a plantation during the Civil War period." Góngora gave no indication that he saw the irony in this. "Another set of dolls can be customized. You may choose the facial features, the skin tone, the hair – and, of course, the personality and interests. This, I admit, intrigued me, but the options were so limited, so – human. But what if a child required something extra?" Góngora walked over to a glass-fronted cabinet and pulled out a doll with long brown hair and a blue silk dress with a full skirt. His long, spidery fingers caressed the doll in his hands, and then he pushed the doll's lustrous brown hair aside, revealing a second face in the back of her head. "And if we are to celebrate our differences, why not enhance them?" Góngora opened the doll's dress, revealing yet another face, this one embedded in her stomach.

Tessa and I exchanged a look of consternation.

"Enough," said Jean Luc. "I am not a child and I have no interest in dolls. If this is the surprise you spoke of, I want no part of it." He turned to leave, then stopped, staring in confusion at the blank wall. "Where is the damn elevator?" I noticed that Jean Luc's eyes never strayed to the part of the room where his son stood at Candra's side, suffering her possessive fingers in his hair.

"So impatient, Jean Luc. And so lacking in insight." With a tight smile that betrayed his irritation, our swinish host handed the mutant doll to Lucretia and walked over to a medical cart with a defibrillator and paddles. "This is my special surprise." He made a showman's gesture. "After you select your purchase, you can have your item modified to your exact specifications, here, on site."

Someone gasped. Out of the corner of my eye, I could see Lloyd putting his arm around Lin and murmuring something in her ear.

"Well?" Góngora was beaming at Lucretia. "What do you think?"

"I'm a little confused, honestly," said Lucretia. "How exactly do you intend to modify these folks?"

"A fine, most excellent question!" Góngora beamed at her as though she were a star student. "Let me demonstrate with – what did we decide to call that one?"

"Zeitgeist, boss." Sherwood pushed Axel forward, as eager as a fourth grader who finally gets to say his line in the school play. I swallowed hard, Candra's power still speeding my heart and making me feel unsteady. On the other side of the room, Lucretia looked as though she were considering purchasing some new item of clothing. That was an act, I knew. I had to be ready, because surely she would give me a signal soon?

"Like many lizards, this fellow can spit or vomit hydrochloric acid," Góngora said, gesturing with his cane as if Axel were a sideshow attraction. "Dr Lorenzo, I was thinking a trunklike nose would be an incredibly useful modification here."

"Yes, yes," said Dr Lorenzo, scribbling something on a little pad. "Perhaps not a full elephantine apparatus, but something more like this?" He held up a sketch.

I blinked, trying to focus, but my eyes kept blurring as memories filled my mental screen.

The narrow stairs leading up into the pyramid were impossible to navigate in a hooped skirt, so I stepped out of the frame. An old Egyptian, his face as creased as the map in my hands, spat at my feet, because I had dared to show my legs.

No. Not my memory. I ran my hand over my face, trying to clear it. I looked over at Candra and Remy. Was it my imagination, or was her hair blonder, her jawline firmer? Remy, on the other hand, looked haggard. He was still handsome, but his skin was weathered, roughened a bit. If he had walked into my diner now, I would have taken him for a man in his mid to late thirties.

I wanted to race over there and rip him out of that old witch's clutches. Could I do it? My head was a little clearer now. At least I thought it was clearer.

Darnique used to say that the first rule of not humiliating yourself at a party was to avoid getting so drunk that you couldn't find the bathroom. The problem was, of course, that you never knew how drunk you were until you got up to find the bathroom.

I wasn't exactly sure how much power I had sucked down, or how hard it had hit me, because I hadn't tried to do anything requiring coordination yet. I was hoping that the longer I waited, the more the power would have a chance to settle down a bit.

Of course, there was the other possibility – that the power would just stay in my system until I expended it. But in order to expend this power, I had to have some control – a classic catch-22.

I squinted, trying to keep my focus on Dr Lorenzo and Axel. Dr Lorenzo was holding up a sketch of Axel with a short, curled trunk, like an elephant seal, and explaining that this would allow for a more controlled release of the hydrochloric acid. "Open your mouth?" Dr Lorenzo tapped Axel's jaw, which was clamped shut. "Ah, no matter." The doctor turned back to Góngora and

Candra. "With the right skin grafting materials, the operation would only differ slightly from my previous attempt to attach tentacles to the face of an amphibious mutant."

"What about the mimic? Are there any improvements to be made there?"

Dr Lorenzo walked over to Lloyd, who gave Lin a reassuring look before facing forward. "The main trick here would be to increase amplification. I always look to the animal kingdom for inspiration – the field of biomimetics is invaluable to my work. Here, a vocal sac of inflatable skin could amplify the vocal sounds by a considerable amount."

"And the girl?" Góngora pointed his pighead cane at a furious Lin, her chin lowered like a stag about to charge. "We believe she has the power to communicate with ungulates, although other mammals may also fall under her purview."

"Oh, this is too easy," said Dr Lorenzo. "A classic goat leg would really make her appearance a bit more special, don't you think?" He scribbled a picture of Lin's lower abdomen replaced by a goatish torso and legs. "It's not necessary, but I do think you'll command a better resale price if the theme is just carried through."

I felt sure my face must be registering my horror, but Lucretia maintained an expression of polite interest. "Very… enterprising."

Góngora was nodding. "Now, unless Miss Borger is interested in buying any of the specimens as is, we need to factor in the cost of surgeries and healing time."

For once, Lucretia wasn't smiling. "I'd like to purchase the lot, as is. No modifications."

"None at all?" Doctor Lorenzo looked crestfallen.

Lucretia had opened her white, fringed leather handbag and was pulling out her checkbook and a pen. "I'm offering one hundred and ninety-five thou per specimen, for a total of five hundred and eighty-five thousand. Check OK? If you need cash, I can have it wired to you by this time tomorrow." She uncapped the pen, which had a lavender feather attached. "If you want to throw in the other two mutants," she gestured at Tessa and Remy, "that brings it up to nine hundred and twenty-five thousand dollars. I'll even take the human girl, for half price – I think that's fair. So if we take ninety-seven thousand, five hundred, and add it to the previous sum, that gets us to…" she did some quick math. "One million and twenty-two thousand, five hundred dollars."

I held my breath. Could it possibly be this simple? Money was a kind of superpower.

"Well!" Góngora snapped his long fingers at me, and said, "Dirty martini, on the rocks." Glad to have something to focus on, I concentrated on locating the vodka and olives. "That is unexpected, Miss Borger – but I can see your point. You wish to take the time to figure out how best to utilize these specimens' skills for your own needs." He stroked his chin, then reached out a hand for the drink. "I am certainly willing to sell you the three which have no other obligations on them – and what the heck, I'll let you buy the human and the bug girl as well. As for Candra's tithe, that is up to her."

"One hundred ninety-five thousand, eh?" Candra looked as though she were considering it.

For a moment, it seemed as though we weren't going to need an escape plan at all. Lucretia Borger was going to use the best magic power of all – the power of her bottomless purse – to free the prisoners. I was going to have time to deal with the heady rush of power and memories from a centuries-old mutant. It was all going to be terribly undramatic, but that was OK by me. If I needed drama, I'd watch a movie.

Then Candra said, "But really, selling a mutant is no different from selling a house. If you take the time to do a little extra work, you really reap the benefits."

Lucretia seemed to take this in stride. "Ah take your point," she said, her accent thick as honey, "but is it really worth waiting for surgery, and weeks of recuperation?"

"No need to wait for that," said Candra. Standing up, she walked over to Axel who looked at her warily as she stroked one finger down the length of his nose. "I can manipulate DNA, remember?" Her grin was almost girlish as she made a quick yanking motion, like someone pretending to play "steal your nose." But this was no game. Axel's first scream was mostly surprise. The ones that followed were pure pain, as the flesh of his nose stretched and stretched into a bulbous trunk.

There was no time to think. I felt something colder and harder than anger settle over me like armor. I had no idea how much longer Candra's power was going to stay in my system, and no real idea how to use it, either. On the bright side, Candra certainly knew how to use her powers – as far as I could tell, she'd been using them for centuries. Since I had sucked up some of her memories and personality, that knowledge was in me as well.

I was going to have to let her take over.

TWENTY-EIGHT

I stared at Axel's inhibitor collar, with its dull brass sheen and bright ruby button, and imagined it going limp as a wet noodle, flaccid and useless, the power button gone dark and flat like the eye of a potato. I imagined the collar slipping down his neck and falling to the floor.

Just like that, the collar fell away, and Axel gave a roar of rage and started spraying bright yellow acid from his trunklike appendage. Lin and Lloyd shrieked and ducked, and I noodled their devices as well. The moment her collar was off, Lin yelled, "I'm calling for reinforcements!" As I aimed my attention at Remy's collar, *limpasanoodle, limpasanoodle,* I heard the drumming of hooves and the angry snorts and grunts of enraged deer outside. There was a smashing sound.

A sudden wail of police sirens added to the mayhem, along with the bullhorn augmented voice of an old-style Irish cop, yelling for us all to come out with our hands up. Another voice, more nasal and slightly Irish, told us that the house was surrounded.

"Screw it," shouted Sherwood, "you ain't payin' me enough for this!"

Góngora slapped Sherwood in the face, stopping him from running out the door. "Stop it, you fool! It's the mimic!"

A spray of something liquid hit my face, and my skin registered cold and then started to tingle, as though I had splashed my skin with astringent. Wait, what? I turned to see Axel in a panic, spraying acid wildly from his trunk. Trying not think about what the acid was doing to my face, I lunged for him, figuring that it was up to me to transform him back and calm him down, since I had Candra's power and, apparently, her rapid healing talent as well. Or maybe that was left over from Lucretia. Either way, I was bulletproof – for a little while, at least.

I grabbed Axel's trunk in my fist and thought, *shrink.*

"What are you doing? Stop!" He twisted away from me, panicked, as I reached for him again. Lin and Lloyd were both grabbing for my hands, saying, "Cut it out it, Rogue," and "It's not his fault." Oh, lord. They thought I was fighting him.

"Stop it, you idiots!" Candra's words, not mine. "I'm trying to put him back the way he was!" Lin and Lloyd exchanged a look, and Lloyd said, "Oh."

It was too late – their bare skin was still in contact with mine. The double jolt of their power sent me flying back. It took me a moment to recover, and when I did, blinking hard, my first thought was that I was hallucinating.

Lin was screaming and flailing, but because she now had a doe's head and forelegs, all that came out was a weird bleating sound, halfway between a kazoo and a wailing infant. The deer outside bellowed even louder, and the smashing sound increased in intensity.

Lloyd stared at his doppleganger head in horror. "Oh, my god, I'm a monster!"

"No, no," replied the second head, "this is fantastic! We can work with this."

It took me a moment to realize that both of these voices were coming from Lloyd. Instead of sprouting a bullfrog's vocal sac, he had sprouted an extra head, and both were talking simultaneously.

"Are you kidding? What's Julie going to say?"

"That we're a thrupple!"

As Lloyd argued with himself, I stared down at my hands. I had done this. My touch, infused with Candra's power to alter genetic code, had mutated them.

There was a loud slap. "Snap out of it," Lloyd told himself.

The other head had a hand pressed to his reddened cheek. "Screw you," he said, and slapped the other face.

Okay, I needed to put this right, and fast. I had barely taken a step when I felt something wrap itself around my arms, immobilizing me. As I struggled against the rope pulling me back, I saw Rita pull a hairband off her wrist. With a flick of one of her six arms, she sent the hairband flying toward me, and now it was a huge black rope wrapping itself around my feet.

"You know what the worst thing about you is, Rita?" With Candra's telekinetic power thrumming through me, I imagined stepping aside in my own mind and letting the old woman take the wheel. It felt as though a missing gear had clicked into place. "You're smart enough to know better, and you still follow this creep around like a demented puppy."

"You're wrong about him," said Rita, waving her arms and guiding the rope as it wound around my legs.

"No, he's an obvious fake. You just like believing in someone, and he took advantage." I looked down at the snakelike rope winding around and around me. "Rope. About face! Attack!" As Rita stared in disbelief, the rope twisted in midair and sidewinded back to her, weaving itself between her six arms until they were all trapped against her body.

As I whirled back to help Lin and Lloyd, I heard a crashing thud and saw a flash of movement. In the moments that I had been battling Rita, chaos had engulfed the rest of the room. Still shirtless, Remy had grabbed the mutant doll and lobbed it at Candra, who laughed at the small explosion. Candra, chuckling with pleasure, had picked up a tray of surgical instruments and was lobbing them back at Remy – and animating them so they swarmed around him like enemy drones. She did not appear to be aiming to harm him, however. I had the sense she was toying with him, like a cat who knows it can finish off a mouse any time it likes.

Tessa was directing an army of termites, who were boring their way out of the walls and marching toward an increasingly frantic Góngora. The Toad was stationed between them, desperately flicking out his long, toadlike tongue and consuming as many of the marauding insects as possible. Axel was using his new trunklike appendage to spray Sherwood with acidic bile, but Sherwood was shrugging it off and slamming his great fists into Axel's narrow gut.

"Quick," said Lucretia. "Someone find the elevator!" I couldn't see where she was standing, but Tessa redirected her termites, and suddenly the insects had outlined the shape of a rectangular door. Lucretia shouted my name, and then Sherwood slammed into me and I lost sight of her as I focused on telekinetically stretching the sleeves and pant legs of his uniform to tie him into a balled-up mound, like an armadillo.

There was a shriek from across the room, where Dr Lorenzo was cowering and pleading with his furious three-eyed driver. "I didn't know about the headaches! I can fix it, Eduardo, I can fix everything!"

In the midst of this chaos came three static-charged blasts, followed by a long, highpitched beep – the sound of a weather alert. "Tornado warning for Western Mississippi, in the following counties." The nasal, computer-generated voice began rattling off locations only a few miles from us. "Coahoma county. Copiah county. Caldecott county." Oh crap, now we were in the path of a tornado. In my head, Candra cooly told me we had enough power to raise a forcefield that would keep us – keep me – safe. But I had no intention of leaving here on my own. "If you are outside," the weather alert droned on in a monotone, "seek shelter immediately. Large hail reported, along with funnel-shaped winds, traveling in a southwesterly direction."

Wait a minute, where was this alert coming from – a radio? No, wait – Lloyd! Or one of the Lloyds.

What we needed was a way out. I turned to the termites. "Grow stronger." I imagined them swelling in size, growing until they were almost a foot long, their mandibles growing to scale. "Tessa," I said, directing my voice so it bypassed the crowd and whispered in her ear. "Tell your friends to find us a way out."

Eyes widening, Tessa directed the swarm, and within moments the enhanced superbugs were drilling through the steel-reinforced drywall as though it were paper.

The Toad, seeing this, shot out his tongue, but the termite was too large and fierce to surrender without a fight. As it bit at his face with its giant pincer-like mandibles, I saw Góngora slap Tessa to break her concentration. But she used her powerful arms to throw him off balance. She could use a bit more maneuverability, I thought. I pictured her with a pair of long white termite wings sprouting from her back, and smiled when I heard her startled gasp.

I had thought Remy was still fighting Candra, but suddenly he was beside me, grabbing my arm with his gloved hand. A cut had opened up over one eye, and it was dripping blood down onto the collar of his brown leather trenchcoat. "Come on, chère, no time to waste."

I pulled back. "Wait! We can't leave the others!" I turned to look back, but Remy pushed me forward, toward the rapidly widening hole in the wall. "Tessa! Axel!"

"I'm right behind you!" Tessa was grinning as she hovered in midair, her long wings beating so fast they vibrated, her long black velvet skirt covering her legs down to her toes.

"Lin and Lloyd are already out," said Remy, tugging me along.

"What about Axel? And Tessa?" I craned my head, trying to spot him, but a cloud of plaster and steel dust from the voracious termites made it impossible to see clearly.

"Axel can take care of himself. Rogue, we need to move now!"

Of course. I had Candra's power, but for how much longer? With a last look over my shoulder, I followed Remy through the termites' tunnel and out into the storm.

TWENTY-NINE

Thunder rumbled, followed by a crackling flash of lightning that lit the sky. For a long moment, the tangled vines and sharp branches in front of me were illuminated in stark white, and then everything went dark again. The rain – hail – kept up a steady drumbeat of sound, punctuated by my own labored breathing. Need to do more cardio, I thought as I followed Remy through the thickly wooded property bordering the horse farm, keeping my left arm in front of my face while my right swept branches aside before they took out one of my eyes. Something in the back of my mind was bothering me, but there was no time to focus on anything but running.

I tripped over an exposed root and instinctively clutched at Remy's leather-coated back, and he turned, holding me up for a moment.

"You OK?"

"I am," I said, my teeth chattering. My little maid's outfit was not exactly weatherproof, and the heels were a nightmare. I slipped them off. "I think this country girl will do better barefoot, anyhow."

Remy frowned. "Here. Take this." He handed me his leather coat, and I was instantly enveloped in his warm, masculine smell.

"Thanks." Again, that sense of something not quite right worried at the back of my mind. Then I remembered something. "My face..." I reached a tentative hand up to touch where the acid had sprayed my skin.

"Not a mark on you, chère." he said.

"But I felt the acid..." Then I remembered. I had absorbed a double dose of healing power tonight.

"I know you've been through a lot. Can you keep going?" A flash of lightning made his eyes gleam red.

I moved my hands away from my face. He was right – both Candra and Lucretia had the power to heal, and I had been in contact with both of them. Again, though, I had the sense of dissonance, as though I were missing something. Nothing to do about it now, though. "Lead on," I said, rolling up the sleeves of his leather coat so I could use my hands. The winds were strong enough to make me wonder whether that tornado warning had been real, after all. Still, it wasn't as if we had any choice. There was no way to seek any shelter, so we would just have to hope the worst of the storm passed us by.

Well, I thought, look at the bright side. Lin and Lloyd did get out, and, of course, so did Remy. If I could just get to them in time, I could help them. And if I could reach the police – reach Cody – I could save Tessa and Axel as well.

"Marie," said Remy, "remember how Candra levitated in? Do you think you can do that – get high enough to spot where our friends have gone?"

I swept my rain-drenched hair out of my face and tried to

imagine myself rising up, my feet leaving the ground. Nothing. "I think it's worn off," I said. "Or else I'm doing it wrong."

"That's OK, chère. Keep moving."

I followed his broad-shouldered back through the tangled vines and trees, trying not to think too much about what this meant for Lin and Lloyd. If I couldn't change them back...

No. Stop. Just keep moving. Suddenly, I heard something in the woods behind us. Lin and Lloyd? Could they have gotten turned around? "Hang on a sec." I held up my hand. "I think we might have–"

But Remy was shaking his head. "Someone's pursuing us. Come on, move!"

I could hear them more clearly now – whoever was chasing us was getting closer. I tried running faster, but there was a stitch in my side. Suddenly, I felt an eerie calm descend over me. Whoever was behind us was going to catch up. Somewhere deep inside my mind, it felt as if a switch flicked into a new setting. "Go on without me," I said, and then, before Remy could respond, I felt someone slam into me from behind.

I rolled onto my back and found myself looking up into the skinless face of Bella Donna Boudreaux of the Assassins' Guild – Remy's wife.

"Well," she said, holding a thin knife to my throat, "isn't this cozy? My husband and his new girlfriend. We could go on a reality TV show. I'll call you a tramp and pull your hair." She touched her horror show of a face. "No, maybe not. I don't think anyone in the audience will cheer for me, looking like this. People are so primitive – they like their heroes pretty and their villains ugly." She pulled a razor out – I wasn't sure where she had been concealing it – and held it to the corner of my eye. I felt an animal panic surge in me, and then a primitive, instinctual calm. The muscles of Bella Donna's face twitched uncontrollably, as if she were losing control of them as her rage swelled. "But what if we're both ugly? That would make for some excellent entertainment, don't you think?"

Remy held out a hand, hovering it just above his wife's shoulder. Incongruously, I thought about how wet and dirty her white pantsuit was now. "Let her go," Remy said in a slow, even voice. "I'm the one you want."

Bella Donna increased the pressure on the knife at my throat, but the blade was so sharp I barely felt a sting. "She must still be a bit of a challenge. You always loved the chase, didn't you, Remy? Do you know how tedious it was, listening to you go on and on about some new girl and did she like you and oh, Bella, what's the best way to ask her out?"

"I didn't know he was married." The blade was up against my jugular, and every time I swallowed, I could feel the pressure increase.

"Didn't you?" The rain was pelting down, making it look as though Bella Donna's skinless face was melting. I had been focusing on the knife, willing it to melt like the inhibitor collars, but nothing happened. Or maybe the blade dulled a tiny bit, which, when I thought about it, might not be to my advantage. "Did you ask? Did you say, 'Hey, are you single? Or seeing someone? Or engaged? Or newly married?'" She grimaced. "No. No, you didn't. Because you're just like him. I could see it straight away. You're the kind of woman who breaks hearts and shatters families. You don't fall in love yourself, but the boys sure fall for you."

"I'm nothing special," I said softly. "Remy doesn't feel anything for me. I was just convenient."

Bella Donna looked over at her husband.

Remy knelt down beside his wife, but the angle was wrong and I couldn't see his face. "Bella, I'm so sorry."

It took me a moment to register that it wasn't just rain streaming down Bella Donna's face. The hardened assassin with the knife to my throat was crying hard enough to make her hand tremble. "But it was all right, because the girl would always fall for you in the end, and after two weeks you'd get sick of them. It was never more than two weeks. You've got the attention span of a flea, Remy."

Remy shifted into view. "I know." Okay, fine, I got it, he was trying to win her sympathy, but how about throwing a little bomb and getting me out of here?

"And then it finally happened. That night at the convocation?"

"I remember."

"Do you?" Bella Donna's skinless face revealed every twitch of muscle. "Then say it to me again."

"Bella..."

"Say it!"

There was no hesitation. "I said there would be no one else, ever." Remy looked infinitely sad.

Bella Donna frowned. "That's not..."

Remy looked pained. "And I meant it, Bella. What we have is different. It's stronger than desire. Hell, it's stronger than wedding vows. What we have–"

"Is a lie." We all turned, and there was Remy, shirtless, looking thinner and older than I expected. He must be chilled to the bone, I thought. There were bruises all over his chest and torso, and now I knew what had been bothering me – Remy, the Remy I had followed out of the horse farm, had been wearing his shirt and jacket. And back inside, he had been trading blows with Sherwood, not throwing explosives – because the other Remy had been doing that, shirtless, while fighting Candra. I stared at the fake Remy. "Lucretia." She must have picked up Remy's leather coat before she shapeshifted into his double, I realized. Had she realized that I would be chilled as we made our way through the woods? I was so out of my depth here.

"Remy?" Bella Donna looked from one man to the other, confused. I took the opportunity to throw her off me and onto her back, the knives now pressed to her throat and eye.

The muscles of Bella Donna's furious face twisted into a snarl. "What the hell – how the hell did you do that?"

I shifted my right knife hand an inch closer to her face. "I've absorbed your skills, sugar. So now I can tell you that instead of keepin' my hand over your external jugular, like you were doin' on me, I'm coverin' your internal jugular and carotid artery. That's the no bluff version, am I right?"

Bella Donna's eyes focused on someone behind me. I was partially shielding her from the rain, but the exposed muscles of her face were slick with moisture. "No bluff."

"Rogue. Marie." I felt a hand on my shoulder and whirled around. It was shirtless Remy, his face rougher and more haggard than I recalled. "You're not an assassin."

Wasn't I, though? I could feel the cold calculation in my head – neutralize her, she's too dangerous to leave in the equation. Then Bella Donna moved, her bare skin wet and slippery as an eel's, and my knife hand slipped. The blade barely grazed the surface of her invisible skin, but my bare flesh brushed hers and she flinched, her eyes rolling back as she lost consciousness.

Strong arms hauled me back, and now it was Remy's skin pressed to mine as he held me against his bare chest, lips pressed to my ear, trying to tell me something I could not hear above the roar of the rain and the heart-pounding, stomach-clenching, muscle-tensing rush of power. I tried to push him away, and ran straight into the arms of the other Remy.

"Easy, now. Try to breathe." That voice – not Remy's. Familiar. Lucretia? I pulled away as Remy's red-on-black eyes transformed into Lucretia's blue, heavily made-up eyes. Reeling, unable to catch my breath, I felt like a kid, lost in the dark woods, suddenly catching sight of her mother. With a gasp, I threw my arms around Lucretia's neck – and felt every hair on my head stand on end at the shock of contact. My knees buckled.

"What's happening to her? What's going on?" Remy's voice, alarmed.

"She's absorbed too much from too many." Lucretia – but no. The honeyed Southern accent was gone, replaced by something sharper, lower, stronger. *Fluent in twelve languages.* Was that the only true thing Lucretia had told me?

Kinder und Betrunkene sagen immer die Wahrheit. Children and fools tell the truth. I could hear the voice saying other things in German.

Too many lies, too many lies. Who had said that to me? No. Not to me. To Lucretia. Irene?

Pauve ti bete. Poor little thing. That was Remy's voice in my head – but he wasn't speaking to me. In my mind's eye, I could see him throwing his skinny child's arm around a girl's narrow back. Then the girl looked up, her foxy little face alert and suspicious, and I recognized a very young Bella Donna.

Then the angle shifted, and I saw the boy Remy through Bella Donna's memory.

"How can we help her?"

"I'm not sure we can."

There were other voices, too, speaking in my mind. Don't trust anyone here. You're a valuable commodity, and the one you trust is the one who will get to betray you. The best way to neutralize multiple opponents is to strike decisively. The shapeshifter is the strongest fighter, but don't underestimate Remy.

I couldn't tell which inner voice was mine. On my knees on the wet ground, I pressed the heels of my hands into my ears, shouting "Get out, get them out, get out." Maybe I was going insane. I'd read that drugs could trigger schizophrenia. Maybe my mutant powers were overloading my circuits and now I would never know for certain whether the voice in my head was mine or somebody else's.

Then: the sound of a car, tires crunching over rocks and dirt.

"Damn it." Lucretia's voice – or rather, the harder, deeper voice of a woman who had called herself Lucretia. "They've got an all-terrain vehicle. We have to move!"

I didn't wait. I ran, ignoring the shouts from behind me. I knew that no one was going to come after me. When you are in a small group being pursued, you don't stick together like a school of damn fish – you scatter, because your chances are better on your own.

The rain was still sheeting down, but trees blocked the worst of it. I could hear the crackle of thunder overhead, and the chatter of my teeth loud in my ears. Blundering through the underbrush, I felt thorns catching at my sleeves, and then a branch whipped back, hitting me on the side of the face, scant inches from my right eye. I stumbled, and now my ankles were caught by thorns as well. The sound of a car's motor was growing louder, and my gasp of a curse turned into a strangled sob as I tried to pull myself free.

It's not enough to take the power, girl. You need to know how to use it.

Unsure whether the caustic voice in my head was Lucretia or Candra, I sucked in a shuddering breath and forced myself to think. I was stuck. I imagined the two powerful women looking down at me like opposing lawyers, judging me and my lack of imagination. *This one's a disappointment. Yes, she had some potential, but we got to her too late. Oh, my dear, it's probably in her genes. You know how it is with these poor country kids with no formal education – dirtwater ignorant, and as backward as a hen in a foxhouse. Oh, well, darling, let's go grab a bite at that quaint little cafe in Tangiers.*

Looking down at me.

I thought of Candra's disembodied head, levitating into the Pig's room. How could I have forgotten this aspect of her power? Lifting my chin, I stretched out my fingers and imagined the earth giving me a push. There was a ripping sound as my clothing tore free of the thorny bushes, and a yank as a branch pulled at my hair before releasing its grip. Then I was rising up, higher than the thicket, higher than the bare-limbed maples and birches, and finally higher than the tops of the tallest pines.

Buffeted by wind and rain, it took me a moment to get my bearings. I held my breath when I saw the Pig's van, but the wheels had caught on a rock, and no one was looking up. I pushed myself higher until the van was tiny and I could see the main road snaking along the forest. Now I knew where I was, and where I had to go.

I just had to pray that Candra's telekinetic power would last until I got there.

PART THREE

HOW THE EVIL HALF LIVES

THIRTY

Lucretia Borger's rented mansion was only forty minutes from the Pig's compound. Not if you were traveling by road, mind, but if you could travel as the crow flies, soaring over the Homochitto river without any need for a bridge and rising up over the national forest lands as if the tall, skinny towers of longleaf pine were blades of grass – well, in that case, you could make the journey in less than thirty minutes.

I was traveling as the crow flies, on my own, unprotected over open countryside.

At first, I was terrified, unsure of my power and easily blown off course by every strong gust of wind. It was like a childhood dream of flying turned into a nightmare where no one can reach you and pull you back down to safety.

You can't stay at the white-hot peak of fear forever, though, and as the storm began to subside, I realized I was enjoying myself. All the sweetcorn in the fields had been harvested, leaving a hard stubble behind, and even though I was freezing I felt the rush of adrenaline and accomplishment that comes with completing a hard race. It was only when the mansion came in sight that the power stuttered like a stalled engine, and I fell the last few feet, rolling over and over on the hard ground and then staring up at the front steps. I sat up, a little dazed, with my tailbone hurting like it had when I'd tried to learn how to ride a bike on a rusty old Schwinn that was two sizes too big for me. When the ache subsided, I wiped the dirt and grass off my hands and took stock of myself. I was soaking wet, covered with mud, and my dress was ripped at the shoulder. Now that the adrenaline high was wearing off, I was trembling from the cold.

Suck it up, I told myself. At least you're free. I had no idea where Lin and Lloyd were, or whether Tessa or Axel had managed to escape. I took a deep breath and ran my hands through my tangled hair before walking up to the front door. I knocked, three times, hard. "Hello? Anyone home?"

A barn owl called out from a treetop, *to-whit, to-who*, but other than that, everything was silent. I banged on the door more forcefully, then tried the knob. The door opened with a squeak, revealing the big entrance. There were no lights on. The place smelled empty. "Hello? Lucretia?" I sucked in a breath. "Anyone?"

There were cobwebs on the wall. Weird – this didn't seem like a place that had been uninhabited for a few weeks. There was a flutter of wings in the exposed beams overhead – birds? Bats?

You would think this house had been abandoned for years.

"Cut it out," I said out loud. "I know you guys are there. It's me, Marie – Rogue."

Just like that, the lights came on, the cobwebs disappeared, and the ponytailed girl who had greeted me the last time was standing in front of me. Chieko. She was still wearing a ponytail, but this time she was dressed in gray sweatpants and a slouchy sweater. "Oh, shoot, it's you."

"Am I hallucinating now?" I was swaying a little on my feet. "Are you really there?"

"I am totally here." Chieko reached out a hand, then withdrew it, saying, "Hang on, hang on." She disappeared into the house for a moment, and I heard her shout, "She's here," before returning with a red wool plaid blanket, which she threw around my shoulders. "Sorry, but between your powers and mine, we'd better not take a chance on skin-to-skin contact." Putting her arm around me, she guided me inside. Stumbling barefoot into the entry hall, I realized I was leaving a trail of mud and crushed leaves behind me on the polished wood floor. I would have apologized, but Chieko wasn't pausing long enough to give me a chance. "Sorry about the whole abandoned house thing," she said, guiding me to a large leather couch. There was a fire crackling in the big stone fireplace, and a smell of cinnamon and apples in the room. I sank down into the couch and closed my eyes for a moment. "Sorry again about weirding you out with the false memory," said Chieko. Oh, right, I thought vaguely, recalling Lucretia telling me about this during my interview. "Destiny had a vision," Chieko went on. "She thought it was you, but for some reason your psychic signature's a little messed up and she wasn't sure if you were you."

It took me a moment to make sense of this. "I'm me," I said, opening my eyes. "Mostly." I couldn't think who Destiny was, but I thought I recognized the nickname. Then I allowed my head to fall all the way back and looked blearily up at the chandelier made of antlers. *Lin.* A wave of guilt hit me, thinking of how frightened she must be. I told myself to get up and get back to looking, but my eyes felt weighted and closed of their own accord. This time, I didn't open them again for what seemed like a long time.

I woke to find my mother perched on the edge of the couch, watching me. Her auburn hair was covered by a silk paisley scarf and she was wearing a purple maxi-dress I hadn't thought about in years, but now remembered so sharply it was like a knife in the ribs. "Hey, girlchild." Her voice was filled with a bouquet of subtle meanings.

My eyes teared up. "Momma?"

"My girl. I'm sorry you're going through such a hard time." She reached out and stroked my forehead, pressing the back of her hand to check for fever. "Do you remember how to center yourself?"

"Momma," I said, trying to duck away from her hand. "Don't. It's not safe."

"It is," said my mother, a glint of something fierce in her green eyes. "If you learn control."

"Oh, Momma," I said, feeling a crushing disappointment. "You're not really here." This time, when I opened my eyes, I saw Chieko leaning over me, one hand on my forehead. She drew her hand back as if she had been burned.

"Sorry," she said, sliding into the couch as I drew back my legs. "Mystique said we had a lot of training to do and not a lot of time to do it in."

I rubbed my hands over my face. "Oh, my lord, please stop talking at me. This is a lot to take in before coffee."

Chieko got up. A moment later, she was back with a big mug of coffee. I took a sip – it was perfect, strong, with just a splash of milk. "How did you guess how I take coffee?"

Chieko looked apologetic. I became disconcertingly aware of the contrast between her clean, glowing skin and neat, glossy dark hair and my own unkempt and dirty state. "I tap into memories. Or I can create memories." She held out her hands, which were covered in thin black gloves. "I'm like you, though – my power works by touch. And just like you, I've had to learn not to get lost in other people."

I stared at her. "This is a lot. Even with coffee." I took another sip, and realized she looked genuinely upset. "Plus, you look amazing, and I look like hell."

Chieko chuckled. "You can take a shower and get washed up. Want me to loan you some clothes?"

I looked at her much smaller frame. "In what alternate universe?"

"I have clothes for you," said a familiar voice, accompanied by the clicking of high heels. "But don't take too long. Blindspot here was trying to implant memories for a reason." I looked up at Lucretia, who was dressed down in a plaid cowgirl shirt and jeans, along with a scarf over her hair. I opened my mouth to tell her what I thought about being brainwashed in my sleep.

"You want to get trained while you're awake? Fine. But you're going to have to take the crash course. We have forty-eight hours before Góngora flies your friends to his safe house in Spain."

I was told I had ten minutes to shower and brush my teeth and change into a pair of gray Borger Institute sweats. I had been hoping for a proper breakfast, but instead I was given a protein bar and taken into a large room with wall-to-wall brown and black patterned carpeting and large picture windows. All the furniture had been shoved to the sides of the room, and Chieko and one of the other interns – the blond Australian, Pyro – were practicing what looked like wrestling holds. The stocky Texan, Blob, was wrestling with the dog.

"All right, everyone," said Irene Adler. "Listen up." Everyone snapped to attention and looked expectantly at the German woman, who was dressed in a long green cardigan and plaid skirt. She regarded all of us for a moment, her pale eyes magnified by thick-lensed spectacles. "Do you go by Marie? Or is it Rogue now?"

I thought about it for less than half a second. "Rogue." It sounded tough and capable and I liked the whole idea of embracing a name that had been intended as an insult.

"Ah, so you have embraced your power."

Dimly, I recalled that she had also had a nickname – Destiny. I looked into the German woman's gray eyes, and felt that she was looking through me to a future I could not fathom. I swallowed. I knew that the woman regarding me with an unblinking gaze was weighing me up and assessing my worth.

"I want to get my friends back," I said softly. "I need your help, and maybe you need mine."

"Maybe." She didn't sound happy about it. "Yet allies who cannot be relied on are more dangerous than enemies."

I felt the shame of that. *She knows.* I tamped down the urge to slink away, apologizing for what I'd done trying to help Lin and Lloyd, and for what I hadn't managed to do to help anyone else. "You can rely on me," I said, pulling my chin up.

"That is your hope," said Irene, walking around me as if inspecting me from all angles. "And what we hope to be can certainly influence what we become." She paused, standing just to the left of me. "I am all but blind, you know," she said, as casually as if she were telling me her astrological sign. "All I see are blurred shapes. That's mostly how I see the future, too. I see things out of focus, from far away." I nodded, then realized she probably couldn't see the gesture. "I suppose you could say I sift through possible futures. When one becomes clear, I know it is the future that is likeliest to come to pass." Now Irene turned back and looked directly in my eyes. "Today, I saw you in the thick of battle, surrounded by friends and allies. You were as close as a daughter to me, and we drank Milchkaffee and ate Apfelstrudel on a balcony in the afternoon." Her eyes flickered like a dreamer's.

I had to speak past the lump of fear in my throat. "But you've seen other futures for me?"

Irene nodded. "I have seen you betray us. I have seen the lifeless bodies of your friends lying at awkward angles all around you."

I wanted to argue, but I knew there was no point. This woman's words had the ring of truth to them. Whatever lay in my future, it was not yet settled. "Help me toward the better future."

Irene smiled. "All right. Up until now, you've gone by intuition and improvisation. But now you need to do some preparation. We're going to start by watching how Pyro and Blob use their powers, and then let you have a go."

She nodded at Pyro, who grinned and said, "At your service." The lean, impish Australian produced an old-fashioned flint lighter from his back pocket and flicked it open, igniting a small, flickering flame. Then, with a quick gesture, he directed the flame up and out, so it formed a ring of fire. The ring grew until he divided it, and then there were two rings, and then three, and then five, all hanging in the air. "How's that?"

"Very good. I like how even and stable the rings are now," said Irene. "Now you, Blob." The stocky Texan surprised me by hollering "Yee haa!" and running straight toward the fiery rings. With an agility I had not expected, he jumped up and then dived straight through the rings of fire like a circus acrobat. I was pretty sure he had touched the flame in places, but then he tucked and rolled, landing on his feet with a thud that made the floorboards shake. His sweatsuit had scorch marks on the back, but he appeared unfazed, waggling his eyebrows comically. "C'mon, folks, that was pretty good, right? Where's the applause?"

"I give it a six," said Chieko. "You totally touched the fire."

"Tell me what you saw," said Irene, turning back to me.

"I saw that Pyro can manipulate but not create fire. Blob's athletic and agile, and I'm guessing that his skin doesn't burn easily."

"Pretty damn hard to cut me or shoot me," Blob agreed. "Many have tried."

"You're easy to tickle, mate," said Pyro.

"Enough," said Irene. "We don't have time for banter. Pyro, you and Blob shake hands with our new intern. And then, Rogue, it will be your turn to show what you can do."

I shook hands with each of the boys, trying not to laugh when both made a big deal of yelping at the contact. "Don't spill all my secrets, now," Blob added with a wink, and I laughed, before I felt his power settle into me and realized he wasn't joking. Frederick Dukes might look like a reckless good ole boy, but he had a very fraught relationship with food.

"Here," said Pyro. "You're going to need this." He handed over his lighter, and at the second touch of his hand I realized that Sinjin Allerdyce struggled with depression and anger. I suddenly realized that both guys knew full well that by touching me they were revealing their vulnerabilities. Yet they were doing it anyway. I looked at them with new respect. Would I be as brave if using my powers meant revealing all my hidden weaknesses and doubts?

I swallowed, trying not to show my nervousness. "All right, fellas," I flicked the lighter open. "Here goes nothin'." For a moment, my words seemed prophetic. I couldn't figure out which power to reach for, and the lighter's small flame began to burn my hand. I closed it, feeling embarrassed. "Sorry."

"Help her, Chieko," said Irene.

"I like to cook," said Chieko. "But I don't use cookbooks. So I think of signature flavors, like, butter and lemon for a French inspired dish, or coconut milk and lemongrass if I'm going in a different direction."

"Stop," said Blob. "You're making me hungry."

"Everything makes you hungry," said Pyro.

"Every person has a signature blend of emotions and thoughts, too," said Chieko. "Focus in on that."

Closing my eyes, I found Pyro's blend of irritability and moroseness, mixed with a genuine undercurrent of kindness and a sense of humor that blended perfectly with his friend Blob's. Opening my eyes again, I grinned as I flicked the lighter open and directed the flame into a ring. I was just trying to figure out what to do with the lighter before making an attempt at Blob's gymnastic maneuver when I caught a blur of movement out of the corner of my eye, and then I was tumbling backwards as something solid slammed into me.

THIRTY-ONE

The deer reared up, pawing the air near my head. I rolled to one side, ducking under the deer's hooves, then rolled and sprang up. At Góngora's house, I hadn't done anything more strenuous than clean, but the adrenaline pouring through my system was giving me enough speed to dodge a direct hoof to the head.

The deer gave an enraged bleat, and then I heard Lloyd saying, "Stop it, Lin, you'll hurt her!"

"Like that's a bad thing," said Lloyd's second head.

Distracted, I turned *my* head in his direction, which gave Lin the opening she needed to charge me again. I dodged just in time to avoid being impaled on one of her antlers. Even though she was on the attack, I felt a surge of relief at the sight of her. Lin and Lloyd were here and safe! I forgot to defend myself, and then I saw the hooves rearing up over my head.

"Lin, stop," I said. "Can we talk?" I ducked and blocked her hooves with my arm, knowing it was probably going to get broken. I had reckoned without Blob's power, however. I barely felt the impact, but the force of her attack sent me into a backflip, and then I was up on my feet again. That's not adrenaline, I realized. That's Blob's gymnastic training and strength.

Lin made a rattling, snorting noise and I didn't need to be a telepath to know that the top translation was, "the hell you say." In the heat of battle, I barely registered the fact that she was a full deer now, with nothing human left about her. As Lin the deer pawed the ground, preparing to rush me again, I turned to Lloyd, who was looking on with almost parental pride. Well, at least one of his heads was beaming. The other head was all business, his mouth set in stubborn lines.

"Please, Lloyd," I begged. "Tell her to listen to me."

"Sorry, Rogue," said one of Lloyd's heads.

"Stop apologizing," demanded the other. "She needs to focus. Cruel to be kind, remember?"

I felt the twist of guilt again, and for a moment I wished I had never learned about my powers. "I'm so sorry about what I did to you both."

Lin snorted and lowered her head, and in the split second before she charged, I froze, paralyzed by guilt and the feeling that I deserved whatever punishment she was going to dole out. Suddenly, there was a bang and a flash of light as something exploded in the middle of the room. For a moment, I was blinded by the brightness. When I could see again, Remy was standing beside me, poised to do battle on my behalf. "You see? Told you I was reliable."

I fought back the urge to throw my arms around him. "You're reliably unreliable." I couldn't stop smiling, though, a big smile that hurt my face. He looked fit in dark jeans and a long-sleeved gray shirt that hugged every lean muscle of his shoulders and arms, but there were still strands of gray at his temples from where Candra had stolen some of his vitality. "How did you make it over here?"

"I followed Lucretia, and Irene drove out to fetch us in the pickup. We rounded up Lin and Lloyd – you were the one we couldn't find." There was something in his gaze I had never seen before.

"He didn't want to stop searching," said Lloyd's friendly head. "But Irene assured us you were on your way to us."

"Personally," said the second head, "I didn't care what happened to you."

Remy shot the second head a nasty look before turning back to me. "Glad you're all right, chère."

I shrugged, trying to hide my embarrassment – and my pleasure that he had cared so much. "I'm like a stray cat, I guess."

"Fierce until she chooses to come purring onto your lap?"

My cheeks warmed, and then I remembered why it wasn't all right to flirt with this man. "If I did, your wife might scratch my eyes out. Or yours." I wondered where Bella Donna was now.

"Bella was my friend, and our union was arranged to unite our two guilds," said Remy, dropping all pretense of lightness. "We were never really husband and wife. Even if we had remained together, it would not have been a true marriage. She was like a sister to me. That is not the way a man ought to feel about a woman he wants to marry."

My mouth went dry.

There was an appreciative whistle from the side of the room – Blob. "This here's a regular soap opera," he said, beginning to slow clap.

"So much for your chances with the new girl," said Pyro. "You owe me five."

Blob shook his head and held up one hand. "Not so fast, buddy. I'm a rebound kind of guy."

I felt a gentle nudge in my side from Lin's long muzzle. She bleated once, and I looked at Lloyd.

"She's saying she's not mad," said Lloyd's kind head. "This is all part of the accelerated course."

"Which you failed," said the second head. "You never even tried to use your fire power."

The only part I heard clearly was the part that mattered to me most. "Hey, Lin," I said, looking into her long-lashed, dark eyes. "I'm glad you're not mad, but I am so sorry about what I did."

The doe that was Lin seemed to shiver and then shift, and suddenly Lin looked like a fourteen year-old girl again, except for the antlers on her forehead. "Don't be sorry. What you did helped me unlock the rest of my power."

"Oh my lord, that is fantastic!" I looked at Lloyd. "But what about...?"

Lloyd shrugged. "Guess this is what my fully evolved potential looks like. I'm cool with it."

"I'm not," said the second head. "You annoy me."

"You both annoy me," said Lucretia, standing in the doorway. She wore a bedazzled white sweatsuit, her teased red hair tied up in a bun, but she was still wearing her high heels, which made me smile. "We don't have time for this." Then she walked up to me and said, "I think it's time you and I met properly." She blinked, and suddenly her blue eyes turned bright gold, and her pale skin darkened to a deep nightfall blue. "The name's Mystique."

For a moment, I just stared. The woman I had known as Lucretia was someone else entirely. Her indigo skin set off her remarkable gold eyes, and she was tall and lean, with the muscular definition of an athlete in peak condition. She wore a black turtleneck and leggings that fit as closely as a second skin. I took this all in for a moment, then said, "This is what you really look like, isn't it?"

Mystique nodded. "As you can imagine, I get quite a different reaction from most people when I'm not in disguise."

I thought about my old boss, Karl, and considered what his reaction would have been if she had walked into the diner looking like this. "I can imagine."

Mystique nodded, and her expression was so different from Lucretia's that I realized that I didn't really know her at all. It was disorienting, and I suspected she knew that. "Tell me, Rogue," she said, in her bland, newscaster's voice that betrayed no regional accent. "You ever hear of the Navy Seals' hell week?"

I nodded, guessing where this was going. "They push the recruits to their limits."

"Well, we don't have a week, and we can't afford to have any of you drop out. But we need to get you all working like a team."

Irene – Destiny – stepped up beside Mystique. "Having a power is a lot like having a gun – until you train enough to know how to use it under stress, it can cause more problems than it solves."

"Don't I know it." I glanced back at Lin and Lloyd. "Okay, then. Work me hard. Do your worst to make me my best."

Mystique smiled at me, and I smiled back. Her teeth gleamed white against the dark blue of her lips, and for the first time I saw Lucretia in her face. "You're on," she said, and held out her bare hand.

I didn't hesitate. The moment my palm touched hers, I felt

the shock of energy transfer. Then Blob hollered "Yee ha," and I turned bright blue, which didn't help me one iota as he barreled into me and knocked me ass over teakettle.

Game on.

The next two days were a blur. I never knew what was coming next. Sometimes, I would be brought into a room alone with Irene to practice meditation, learning how to slow my breathing and focus my racing thoughts. I had arm-wrestling sessions with Chieko, both of us using her power to mess with the other's mind in small ways. Once, by accident, I made her cry, but she didn't seem to hold it against me afterward. I practiced physical combat with Pyro and Blob, but I barely saw Remy. I didn't need to be told the reason why – clearly, Mystique and Destiny thought he and I knew more than enough about each other.

I tried to tell myself I didn't care.

Lloyd taught me how to mimic people's accents and speech patterns, so that if I absorbed Mystique's power and disguised myself as someone else, I wouldn't give myself away the moment I opened my mouth. Once, I made the mistake of touching Mystique and then petting Rowan and turned into a dog by accident. I spent a full thirty minutes running around the yard and romping with Rowan, and the only reason I stopped after half an hour was because Chieko called me over and patted me behind the ears, restoring my memory of what I was supposed to be doing.

I transformed back into myself while Mystique looked at me, shaking her head. "You better stick close to Chieko," she advised. "She's your failsafe."

We were only allowed one proper meal a day, at suppertime.

Each of us was given different meals, designed specifically for our metabolism and powers. I had no complaints as I tucked into my roast chicken and cheese grits, but Blob complained that his sashimi dinner was not nearly filling enough, and Pyro pronounced his pasta bland and insipid. Remy got a steak and greens, but no potato, and Chieko tucked into a vast bowl of udon noodles in chicken broth.

The first night, I collapsed into bed the moment I went upstairs, and Chieko told me she had removed my shoes without waking me up.

On the second night, we were custom fitted for mission-specific clothes. I felt a little self-conscious in my yellow and green bodysuit, worrying that it was a bit too form-fitting, but Mystique said the material was designed for easy movement, and the fabric reinforced to reduce the possibility of inadvertent power transfer.

"You look wonderful, chère," said Remy. We had all been called to the large, carpeted room where we practiced our physical combat skills. He was wearing his long leather trenchcoat over a hot-pink vest and black tights.

"Wish I could have a coat, too," I said. "What's the deal with the vest, though? Ain't it awfully bright?"

"I chose it," he said, a little defensively.

"Ooh, it's the star-crossed lovers," said Blob, waggling his eyebrows. He was wearing a wrestler's unitard that clung to his barrel-chested, solidly muscled frame, but had thrown a hunter's utility vest over it.

"Is it me," added Pyro, "or is it hot in here?" Pyro was wearing a red and yellow jumpsuit that was so bright it hurt the eyes.

"Who designed these things? Irene?" Lin had opted to wear

jeans and a tee shirt, but I was fairly certain that was not the costume she had been given.

Lloyd's friendly head gave her a warning look, but his second head chuckled maliciously. He, too, was wearing street clothes – in his case, dad jeans and a polo shirt. "Sorry, but no one needs to see me dolled up like Olivia Newton John at the end of *Grease*."

There was a sharp clap of hands, silencing the room. "Okay," said Mystique. "Listen up, everyone." She was wearing a blue turtleneck and leggings, the shade of the fabric almost indistinguishable from her skin. Or maybe she was just wearing her skin disguised as clothes. "You've all done really well, and, by rights, you should have another day to train and another night to rest."

I could hear the "but" coming, and from the looks on everyone's faces, so could they.

"Unfortunately, Irene says there has been a shift, and the clearest future shows that Góngora is going to leave his compound early tomorrow morning. That means we're out of time, boys and girls."

Lin cleared her throat.

"Sorry. You must all remember how old I am. So, listen up, troops." Mystique gave a little nod in Lin's direction, acknowledging that she had been schooled. "We have to make our move tonight." There was a general murmur of surprised excitement, but Mystique held up one hand, and everyone fell silent. There was tension in the air, but for once Blob and Pyro weren't trying to break it with wisecracks. "There's more you need to know. Destiny's visions have sharpened in the past half hour. Tell them what you saw, Irene."

Irene adjusted her glasses, a nervous gesture I had never seen her make before. "Dr. Lorenzo is preparing to operate on your friends. This goes against Góngora's express wishes, so he will wait until the pigman sleeps. If we do not interrupt this timeline's progression, your friends will be ... modified." Irene invested the last word with unpleasant emphasis. "And there is more. Candra is present. This means that Mystique will have to devote most of her attention to one opponent."

Mystique gave Irene's shoulder an encouraging squeeze. "In other words," she said, "you all have a lot of responsibility resting on your shoulders. Especially you, Rogue. If I need to be in two places at once, you will need to be me."

I looked at Remy, unable to hide my concern. Of all of us, I was the least prepared, and yet our plan depended on my performing my part without any slip-ups. Remy smiled reassuringly, and then turned away. It was a good reminder. I had to find the right balance between relying on myself and working with the others. There was no time for silly romantic entanglements.

Heck, I thought, glancing at the clock. There was barely time to go to the bathroom. I had never worn a bodysuit before, but I felt pretty dang sure they took forever to peel off and zip back up.

THIRTY-TWO

We left the van parked by the side of the road and bushwacked our way into the densely wooded forest so we could approach the Pig's horse farm the way we had left it, on foot and in the dark. There were motion detection cameras that had been installed since we had left, but all they would show was three deer. If someone were looking closely, they might have noticed some extra human feet underneath the deer, but really, who looks closely at deer?

Once we were past the camera's range, Lloyd and Remy straightened up and Mystique and I shapeshifted back. I don't know if it was my intense focus on the task at hand or something else, but I didn't have to think too hard about looking like myself. Maybe that little stint turning into a dog had been more helpful than I had realized.

"Just remember," Mystique said, "the more powers you take on, the harder it's going to be to keep centered in yourself." Her voice was deeper than Lucretia's and sounded northern, but the biggest difference was that Mystique lacked Lucretia's bawdy sense of humor. I had to keep reminding myself that this blue woman was the real person, and not the disguise.

"Any advice?"

Mystique's eyes gleamed yellow in the darkness. "Keep talking to yourself like an obtrusive narrator. If you've got a running commentary on everything that's going on, it acts like a strong filter."

What if the running commentary in my head kept reminding me of all the ways I could screw up? I shivered, more from nerves than from any chill. The night had turned colder than expected, but my bodysuit was actually doing a good job of keeping me warm but not overheated.

"They have all turned in for the night," said Irene, who looked surprisingly athletic dressed in a black turtleneck and stretchy slacks. "Do we want to wait for them to enter a deeper sleep cycle?"

Lin made a bleating noise.

"Someone's in pain," said the Lloyd head with the dark-framed glasses. "Lin's picking it up."

The second head, for once, did not disagree.

Mystique frowned, making the faint ridged markings on her forehead more prominent. "Can she tell who is in distress?"

Lloyd's second head made a bleating sound that sounded eerily like a deer. Lin bleated back.

"It's Axel," said Lloyd's first head.

"No, it's not. It's the other one, the insect girl," said the second head.

"Do you need a hearing aid? She said the male."

Lin bleated again.

"Not so loud," I said. "We don't want to wake anyone up."

"Oh," said Lloyd's dominant head. "That explains it."

"Explains what?"

"It's both of them," the two heads said in unison. "The sound is coming from downstairs – the laboratory."

Mystique and I exchanged troubled glances. "Can she tell us where Góngora and the guards are located?"

Irene squinted in the direction of the house, but I knew she was seeing the future. "They're in the laboratory. They're all down there, except for Góngora." She looked at Mystique. "Candra's there."

Her words sent a shiver down my back "What do we do?"

Mystique took me by the shoulders. "Stick with the plan and find Góngora's bedroom." Then she pressed a maternal kiss to my forehead, and even though I knew it was for expediency's sake, I felt steadier. "You've got this."

Before I could respond, Lloyd grasped my hand. Lin was next, butting her head so that her cheek brushed mine. Pyro, Blob and Chieko each slapped their hands against my palm, like members of an opposing sports team. Remy was last. He stood in front of me for a moment, smiling a little. "May I?" I nodded, and he brushed his lips against mine.

I broke the contact between our mouths before he could give me too much of his strength, but just as he was about to draw away I threw my arms around his neck and held him tightly for a fraction of a second, trusting the special fabric of my new costume to keep him safe. "Don't take any stupid chances, Cajun."

"Have a little faith, chère – in me, and in yourself."

No problem there. With some of his gambler's confidence running through my veins, I had plenty of faith. Now all I needed was some luck on my side.

Mystique looked over her shoulder before morphing into Sherwood's thickly scaled form. Pyro located an outside outlet and knelt beside it. With impressive control, he sent a small spark down the wire, knocking out the surveillance system, while Remy made good use of his lock-picking skills. He gave me a cheeky grin when the lock on the back door gave with a satisfying click.

I tried to smile back, but there was still so much that could go wrong. I glanced outside at the sliver of moon visible on this cold, clear night, then followed the others into the house's back entrance.

Once inside, I closed my eyes and tried to locate the strand of Mystique's power among the tangle in my mind. It was so much harder to do here, with so much riding on me, than it had been back in the practice room. Slowing my breathing, I found the indigo glow of Mystique's power, then pictured Rita Wayward's tanned, lightly lined face. Since I didn't know what she was wearing, I dressed myself in a snug, navy colored sweatsuit and sneakers, with a small Army insignia over the right breast. Glancing down at myself, I saw some sort of official looking emblem with Latin words underneath. *Perfect.* I didn't need a mirror to know that I looked like a certain six-armed sorceress.

Time to pay a pig a visit.

Góngora kept a small rose-colored night light in his room, which was convenient for me. He slept on his back, and despite the silk pillows propping up his head and the mentholated humidifier perking away in the corner, he was making an unfortunate, rattling sound in the back of his throat, like a death snore.

After regarding him for a moment, I decided to wake him by

pinching his nose shut while covering his mouth. He flailed for a moment, but I reassured him in Rita's clipped voice. "It's OK, boss. There's been an attempted break-in, but it's under control."

Góngora nodded, sitting up. His eyes were furious as he wiped his mouth, first with the back of his sleeve, then with an antiseptic wipe on the side table beside his bed. "You should have wakened me without giving me your germs." He reached for his purple velvet robe.

"Sorry. But this is a rapidly developing situation. There's a shapeshifter among the intruders, and I need confirmation that it's really you."

Góngora looked astonished. "Are you mad? Who else would be sleeping in my bed?"

"It's Mystique. She's very gifted, and I can't take any chances. Can you verify that this is you by giving me the security code to the laboratory?"

Góngora hesitated. "This sounds absurd, I know, but I seem to have forgotten the exact order of the—"

This was an unexpected setback. Narrowing my eyes, I began chanting while waving my six arms in the air. "Evealray ethay adversaryway inishsway…"

"Rita, what are you doing…?"

"You are concealing something."

"That is slander!" He put one spider-fingered hand on the front of his velvet robe.

"Then you won't object to my casting a spell that removes all concealments." I drew my arms back with a big, dramatic gesture, and Góngora flinched.

"Wait! Listen, Rita, I am Góngora. Ask me to recite the poetry of Lorca. Ask me my favorite food."

I just looked at him. There was a sheen of sweat on his pink, porcine face. Did real pigs sweat? "The code, or the spell."

There were damp spots under the purple silk of his pajamas. "Ask me how we first met! You were so tired of the dead-end jobs you had, remember? And I told you I could give you enhancements that would make you worth your weight in gold, if you just worked for me."

"Yes. Then you neglected to tell me I would never be able to earn enough to be out of your control." This was a lucky guess, but the fear in Góngora's small, mean eyes told me I'd hit paydirt. Of course a slaver wouldn't let his employee earn back what she owed him. Why pay someone when you could just keep an indentured servant?

"You will start earning your money now," he said. "I meant to talk to you about your account earlier, but we have been so busy..." Suddenly, his eyes cut to the left, focusing on something over my shoulder. Shoot. Couldn't just one thing go my way?

Don't think. React. I turned, and by the time I faced Rita, I was a seven-foot tall pigman in silk pajamas. "Rita," I said, summoning Mimic's talents to produce the Castilian accent. "There is an imposter here."

"Boss?" Rita's eyes flicked from the Góngora in the bed to me and back again.

"That's the imposter! Couldn't you see when you walked in the room that she – he – it was impersonating you?" Góngora's voice had risen to a very piglike squeal of outrage.

"I- I'm not sure what I saw." This was what I had been banking on. As an aspiring student of neuroscience, I had spent a fair amount of time watching YouTube videos on the subject. Like most of us, Rita could recognize what she was expecting to see – one porcine boss and possibly one intruder – more readily than her brain could process the unexpected. The fancy name for this was Bayesian inference, but the upshot was so simple Douglas Adams had referenced it in *The Hitchhiker's Guide to the Galaxy*. Rita hadn't been expecting to see her own double, and I had shifted so quickly that she hadn't fully registered it.

Still, I had to convince her that I was the real deal. It was a gamble, but I had enough of Remy in me at the moment to make me feel like taking this bet. "It's very simple, Rita," I said. "I am your boss, and this person in my bed …" I grabbed Góngora's left wrist and yanked off the platinum watch with its blank face and glowing ruby button, "… is an imposter."

"Stop! Don't you dare–" Góngora cringed, bringing his hands up to cover his face as if that could hide the fact that he had transformed from a seven-foot pigman into a short, balding, bespectacled middle-aged man.

I felt a moment of triumph. I hadn't been entirely sure that Góngora had no power of illusion, but it had seemed logical that a man as scared as he was wouldn't hesitate to use his power. That's when a memory came back to me – Góngora's nervous reaction when my hands had brushed near his platinum bracelet. I had taken the chance that Góngora was using tech to conceal his true appearance – tech he barely knew how to use, since he hadn't practiced changing into anything else.

Rita's lip curled as she regarded the unprepossessing little man in the bed. "Hold your hands where I can see them."

"No! No, Rita, you don't understand. It is me, Rita. I'm the real Góngora. That device allows me to project myself the way I truly feel myself to be!"

Rita was shaking her head in disbelief. "You're not even a mutant." She turned to me. "Are you?"

"I am." Time for the second gamble of the evening. I morphed into Mystique, and instantly knew I had chosen right. A strong, mature, blue-skinned woman was someone Rita could relate to, while she had already formed a negative impression of Rogue.

"And ask yourself this – if Góngora was really so eager to be a mutant, then why didn't he have the guts to let his doctor turn him into a mutant? He was perfectly content to let Lorenzo operate on you." I deliberately left out the much more damning issue of a doctor performing surgeries on unconsenting patients, since Rita had been complicit in this. Better to find common ground quickly and get her to feel allied with me. "He tricked you and Mortimer and anyone else he convinced to work for him, Rita. Whatever he told you to convince you that the end justified the means? They're built on lies. He's not like you. He's just a nasty little man who wants wealth and power. He has no loyalty to anyone but himself." I braced myself, because no one likes to admit that they've been suckered, and Rita was as likely to turn on the messenger as she was to turn on the man who had betrayed her. "Now you have to make a choice. Are you going to help me get his prisoners out of here, or are we going to fight?"

Rita hesitated, then looked at the frightened man in the bed. "I did not lie," Góngora said, and he had recovered himself enough so that his words sounded deep and calm and rang with conviction. "I may look different, but inside, I feel I am one of you. Everything I promised, it is all still true! This nasty female does not care for you, she only cares for herself and for–"

"Enough!" Rita raised her six arms, and there was a blast of light, and then the germophobe slaver and his bed were encased in a translucent bubble. He was pounding on it, but no sound came out. "He has enough air for at least an hour, at which point the bubble will dissolve. In the meantime, let's go get your friends."

Was an hour the limit of her power, or had she been lenient with her former boss? I wished I knew the answer, but since I didn't, I set it aside. "Hang on a sec, Rita." I closed my eyes, picturing Góngora's porcine features. When I opened them, Rita was staring up at me. "It's not as good this time," she said. "There's something off about the eyes."

I shrugged. "It will have to do. I was supposed to rendezvous back in fifteen minutes, which means I'm already late."

Rita gave me a considering look, but said nothing. We left the little man in his bubble, wasting his remaining oxygen by railing about the nastiness of powerful women.

THIRTY-THREE

Rita led me down the back stairs to the laboratory instead of taking the elevator. I had some difficulty negotiating the slope with the unfamiliar muscles and bones of my porcine knees. Rita walked in front of me, and even though she seemed on board with the plan of releasing the prisoners, I couldn't lose the feeling that with every passing moment the sorceress was revisiting her decision to help me. I had no idea what to do if Rita changed her mind. I glanced at my watch, which now looked like Góngora's image inducer. Twenty-three minutes had elapsed since I had separated from Mystique and Remy and the others, and I knew we were already onto plan B. If all had gone according to plan, and they had managed to get inside and free Tessa and Axel, then Lloyd would have made the distinctive chirp of a carbon monoxide monitor in need of a new battery. We had figured that was the most carrying noise that would cause no undue panic. Since there had been no sound, I was supposed to make my way down to the lab, prepared to get Mystique's next instructions.

I breathed a sigh of relief when I saw the bottom of the stairway. At least I hadn't tripped and broken any bones, giving away our presence in the most ignominious way possible. There was a faint smell of fresh paint here, along with the sharp, clean odor of disinfectant, and something else that reminded me of the ozone-rich scent you get before a storm. In the back of my head, I tried to quiet a panicky refrain of whatwentwrong, whatwentwrong? Maybe it was just taking them a little longer than anticipated. Hadn't Mystique always said that no mission ever went precisely according to plan?

All at once, I realized something was wrong. Rita had stopped directly in front of me, blocking my view. "What is it?" I asked.

"Guess your friends are already here." Rita stepped to one side and pointed at what remained of the door, which had been blasted in half. "You didn't say that Remy was along for the ride."

"I thought it was obvious."

Whatever she was going to say next was forgotten as someone gave a long, low moan of pain. Pushing past the sorceress, I found myself staring at three hospital beds lining the hallway outside the laboratory. All three of the beds were occupied, but not by anyone I recognized. These patients were old and frail, their skin parchment thin under the unsettling flicker of fluorescent lights. The beds had been adjusted so the patients' heads were raised, and one of them – a woman with Asian features – regarded me blearily. The other two patients were men, both Caucasians. I couldn't guess the exact ages, but if any of them were younger than ninety, I'd eat my gloves.

"H-help." The woman opened her eyes. Her voice was a whispery rasp. Her left arm was hooked up to an intravenous drip. As I came closer, I saw that the plastic tubing was attached by tape to a vein just below the bend in her forearm, where it fed into a ramshackle brass and steel contraption. This didn't look anything like the sterile modern machines I was used to seeing in TV shows about hospitals. Instead, this motley assemblage of gears and pressure gauges resembled something out of an old horror film. With dawning shock, I realized this was not an IV drip at all – the machine was extracting blood from the ancient woman's arm, running it through the steampunkish mechanism, and extracting a glowing amber fluid that was filling a large glass beaker. On a side cabinet, three other beakers were already filled, and they glowed with an uncanny light.

"Goddess." That was Rita, staring at the woman as though she had seen a ghost. "The doctor must be extracting elixir vitae from them."

I looked at the other two patients – they were also hooked up to identical brass and steel machines. "What are you talking about? What is Dr Lorenzo doing to these old people?"

The thinner of the two old men opened his eyes and gave a laugh that sounded more like a wheeze. "Old?" His quavery voice had a distinctly Australian accent. "That's a good one, mate." He made a phlegmy sound. "And why d'ye sound like a girl?"

I had forgotten that I was disguised as a seven-foot pigman, and I was about to explain who I really was when I registered what he had just said. An awful suspicion beginning to form in my mind.

"Because she's Rogue in disguise, Kangaroo brains," said the second man. If I had been in any doubt before, his Texas twang settled it – this was Fred, also known as Blob. Now that I knew who I was looking at, I could see Pyro's lean, sardonic features in the other old man's face, and recognize the contours of Chieko's youthful prettiness hidden by the old woman's wrinkles. How could Lorenzo have drained them of their youth and vitality so quickly?

"Don't worry, we're going to help you," I said with a confidence I didn't feel. I looked at the machines, then at the tubing. "Rita, help me pull out the tubes!"

A nerve jumped near Rita's left eye. "Stop! We don't want to unhook them. We need to reverse the process."

"Right. Of course." I swallowed, feeling clammy with the knowledge that I had almost made things worse. "Do you know how to do that?"

Rita paused, her various sets of fingers twitching at her sides. "I know healing magicks, but what Dr Lorenzo and the Benefactress are doing is a very specialized branch of alchemy." She and I both regarded the three ancient figures, and I tried to make sense of the fact that these were my teammates. My friends.

I turned to the sorceress. "Please, Rita. Can you try?"

"If only I knew the proportions. One formulation grants full immortality. The other concentration extends life. Each would require a different incantation." Rita rubbed her chin with one of her hands while one of her other arms traced shapes in the air, as if drawing equations on an invisible chalkboard. "Okay, I think I know what I'm dealing with here. But you have to keep the doctor and Candra from interrupting."

"They're all in the operating room," said Chieko, in a quavering voice. "They were about to operate on two of the prisoners when we interrupted them. The others must still be fighting." Her eyes met mine. "I've never seen any mutant as strong as the one they call the Benefactress."

For a moment, I felt so overwhelmed with the number of things going wrong all at once that I had to close my eyes. What could be happening on the other side of that steel door that could prevent Mystique from trying to help Chieko and the boys? Then I remembered one of Mystique's first lectures during training: *The first thing to know about battle is that it's disorienting. All the plans you make beforehand will probably be useless. You will be confused and frightened and above all, distracted.*

The only solution? *Stay in the moment.* I opened my eyes and said brusquely, "Okay." I took a deep breath. "Okay, guys. You're going to be all right. Rita knows her stuff." Squaring my shoulders, I turned to go into the operating room. Then, all at once, it struck me – they had all given me some of their powers before setting out. Maybe that was part of the reason why they hadn't been able to fight off Dr Lorenzo.

If only I knew how to give power back. I turned to look at Chieko, and she grinned at me, a young girl's expression on her deeply lined face.

"You've got this," she said.

Pyro tossed me something, and I caught it, surprised. It was his lighter. "Knock 'em dead, kid."

Blob gave me a little salute. "Bring down the house, lady."

I smiled, willing my eyes to stop filling with tears. Then I pushed the last door open.

THIRTY-FOUR

The windowless underground room had become a working operating theater, with a low hanging light illuminating the two patients lying side by side. The coppery smell of blood was thick in the air, and for a moment, I didn't know where to look to make sense of the blur of fighting bodies.

Lloyd and Lin were both occupied with fighting Mortimer and Sherwood, Lin rising up to paw the air with her sharp hooves just as Mortimer's long, prehensile tongue lashed out. There was a dull thud as Sherwood threw Lloyd against a wall, where he lay crumpled. One of his heads, the one without glasses, blinked and looked at the other head in horror. I should help them, I thought, just as something exploded near Mortimer's face.

Remy. As he leaned over the injured Lloyd, something sharp whizzed past my head, missing me by inches.

A second object flew past me, and it took me a moment to realize I was not the target. There was a flash of blue in the corner of my vision as Mystique dodged a steady barrage of hypodermic needles. "Come on, Candra," she said, looking down at one needle that she had not managed to avoid. "You and I have not gotten this old by getting into fights we can avoid." She plucked the hypodermic out of her bare shoulder as if it were nothing more than a burr caught in a sweater.

"Darling, how quaint," said an arresting blonde dressed for death combat in an Eighties music video – molded scarlet corset, matching diadem, and of course, thigh-high boots. "You see yourself as my equal." It was only when she spoke that I recognized the artificial, quasi-British diction of 1930s Hollywood and I was certain this was Candra. This woman appeared decades younger, her skin firm, her hair a natural, lustrous dark gold, her dramatic eyebrows arched somewhere between mirth and contempt. She had drained the youth from my friends, and now she looked as vibrant as a young girl, though with something ancient and corrupt in her blue eyes. "Shapeshifting and accelerated healing factors are such charming little powers, and you've really done your best with them." Pulling a gold chain off her neck, she sent it snaking through the air, where it wrapped around Mystique's neck. "But let's face it – you're just not in my league."

"As I always tell my students, it's better to have limited powers..." Mystique turned into a vividly patterned blue python and slipped out of the gold chain before coiling herself around Candra's midsection. "...if you really know how to exploit them to their fullest." Candra gasped, and python Mystique coiled more tightly around her. "What, no witty rejoinder?"

"Anyone... ever... tell... you..." Candra's face was turning red from the constriction, but she managed a smile. I could see the moment Mystique's strength began to falter as the blonde woman began to absorb her vitality. "You're cute when you're losing?"

In the center of the room, apparently oblivious to all the chaos around him, Dr Lorenzo raised his scalpel hand. To my horror, I saw that it was Tessa and Axel who were lying side by side on operating tables, covered by surgical sheets. They both had breathing tubes taped to their mouths, but they were both clearly conscious and alert.

"*Basta!* Stop," I commanded in Góngora's most stentorian voice. "Dr Lorenzo, put down your scalpel. Your patients are still conscious."

"But of course they are," said the doctor, glancing up over his surgical mask for only a moment. "You know I get better results when the brain remains active."

"Let me put this another way." I picked up a cauterizing tool and pressed a button, making the instrument spark. With a touch of my finger, the spark became a flickering flame. "I said, put the scalpel down."

"You must be mad! You know I can't stop in the middle of the operation. I know you said the buyer in Spain wants to purchase them separately, but just think how valuable these two will be when I combine them into one! We'll find a much better purchaser."

"You just want to experiment on them." If there was a hierarchy of evil, Dr Lorenzo was on top.

"No, no, it's logical. The male can provide close quarters protection. The female will allow me to maintain constant germ control."

Oh, God. If I had arrived just a few moments later – it was too horrible to contemplate. "We're not doing the operation. I order you to release them immediate–"

There was a bang as one of Remy's explosive blasts went off, and then a sizzling sound as one of the electrical monitors began to spark, and a singed smell filled the air.

I froze. Suddenly, it was all too much. The sounds and smells of battle faded to a distant roar, drowned out by the insistent pulse of my own blood pounding in my ears. What to do? I couldn't decide which powers to use. Fire from Pyro, strength and imperviousness to most forms of damage from Blob, the ability to implant a memory from Blindspot. All my training seemed to be deserting me.

For once, there were no other voices in my head, but it wasn't helping me, because I couldn't even hear my own internal guide, telling me what to do next. Should I try to put out the electrical fire edging its way toward the unconscious cloth-draped bodies on the operating tables? Should I help Lin, who was on the floor, eyes rolling in fury and panic as the Toad pinned her down? Where had Remy gone?

There was a crackling sound as the flames arced from the monitor to Doctor Lorenzo's white lab coat. He screamed, throwing himself down on the floor, rolling over and over as Axel and Tessa screamed along with him.

In the movies, no one ever hesitates in the middle of a fight, but I knew from my psychology that fight or flight were not the only reactions to the stress of battle.

Some soldiers froze.

I turned to find Mystique, hoping for help, but to my shock a length of steel pipe ripped through the air like a missile, embedding itself in the blue woman's abdomen. She grasped it where it protruded from her stomach. Across the crowded room, her topaz eyes met mine for a moment, and then clouded over.

Sound returned as I made my way toward Mystique, allowing

me to hear Irene's anguished wail of grief and Remy's startled shout. I knelt beside the woman who could have been my mentor, aware that everyone seemed to have stopped fighting.

"Oh, it's you again." Candra's voice made me look down at myself – without thinking, I had stopped maintaining the guise of Góngora's porcine figure draped in purple silk pajamas and reverted to my true form in its green and gold bodysuit, which seemed specially designed to adapt to whatever powers I absorbed. "I don't usually kill someone who did me a good turn, but in your case, I'll make an exception."

"Wait." I looked up at Candra, as glorious and glamorous as a movie star in her prime, and finally, I knew what to do. "Just for one second, can I touch you again? Before you kill me. I just want one last moment to feel what it's like to be you again."

Candra laughed. "Is this meant to be a trick, little girl? You think a moment of absorbing my power will make you a match for me?" She leaned close. "Well, then. Go ahead." She leaned over and I kissed her cheek. The minty freshness of her breath was tainted by something faintly rotten rising up from her throat, but I didn't pay it any attention. I clung to her neck, my lips glued to her soft cheek as I pulled on her power with all my might, and to my surprise, I felt a second power aligning with my own, and it was flavored with sun and mountain air – Chieko's gift.

Candra made a little sound in her throat as I grabbed hold of her ears, allowing her strength to flow. After a moment, she succeeded in wrenching herself away, one hand touching her lips. "What is that – there's something different about you..."

And that was when I struck, sweeping my legs under hers and knocking her down. Candra bounced back, landing on her heels. "Who the hell are you? I can't remember fighting you before."

Using her own telekinetic power, I rammed the wheeled medical trolley into her knees. "Bet that's not all you can't remember."

Candra shook her head as if trying to clear it. "You little tramp," she countered, but when her right foot lashed out in a flying kick, I was already in motion, rising through the air and hanging there.

"I've been called worse," I said. "Hope it's not too *All About Eve* of me," I added, levitating. "But I'm stealing your act." I slammed down on top of her.

"Sorry, youngling." Candra's power flung me back against the wall, shocking me with pain for a moment. Luckily, I had her rapid healing factor, but when I tried to lift my arm an instant later, I found it pinned by an invisible force. Candra strode over to me in her red thigh-high boots, relishing her moment of center stage villainy. "You might be a power to contend with – in a few decades. Unfortunately, I don't think you'll get that opportunity."

"I think you're wrong," I said.

One imperious blonde eyebrow went up. "What makes you think that?"

"Because I haven't just absorbed your powers, Candra. I've taken your memories."

She narrowed her eyes. "What are you talking about?"

"You friend, Jaroslava, who gave you the ribbon for the harvest festival – can you remember the secret she told you that day? What about that night in Memphis, when you made a deal with one of Napoleon's officers… Dumas, I believe?"

Candra frowned. "It's familiar, but I can't remember." She looked at me, suspecting a trick. "Why can't I remember?"

"Because it's all in my head now. And if you want it back? You have to kiss me again."

"You little–"

There was a muffled blast, and Candra started to turn her head. I thought fast, wanting her attention back on me.

"What's the point of being eight hundred years old if you can't remember any of it? What good is looking young if you're not really you anymore?"

Candra snarled and grabbed the front of my top. "Give it back."

"Make me." The smoke was thicker now, and the air inside the underground room felt uncomfortably hot, making each breath a little painful. The part of my mind that was not busy distracting Candra had registered the moment that Remy blasted through the wall. I wasn't sure how much time he needed to get everyone out, and I hoped he was moving quickly. "Remember the battle of the Kalka River," I said, reverting to her mother tongue. "It took six days for Ryazan to fall. You were so hungry."

Candra's breath smelled like something was rotting inside her. "I was hungry. I can't remember why, but I was hungry."

We are out. It was Irene's voice, in my head.

Candra's eyes looked young, but she seemed querulous and unsteady now, like an ancient spirit in a youthful body. "How do you know all this?"

Arms still pinned, I took a deep breath and summoned all my strength before stomping down with Blob's percussive power, feeling the force reverberating down from my heels, deep into the foundations of the house and lower still.

Candra's eyes widened as she felt the rumbling shifting of the ground beneath us. "What have you done?"

"I'm doing what any good performer does," I said, as the walls began to shake. "I'm bringing down the house."

I felt a flash of fear as the chunks of plaster began to fall. As the floor buckled and a gaping hole grew, the medical trolley slid across the slope, jamming itself in the gap. Then the gap widened, and the trolley plummeted.

"Wait!" Candra began to slide inexorably down into the center of the room, her grip on my top bringing me along with her. I could feel something jagged scraping along my arms, ripping through the specially designed fabric of my suit and through my flesh.

"You idiot." Candra and I were tangled together as we slipped further and further into the hole, the smell of damp earth rising around us. The ceiling lights flickered and then went out, and, above us, the fiery room rippled and undulated. Buried alive beat burnt to a cinder, I supposed, but, to be honest, I wasn't feeling great about either option. Not that there was anything I could do about it now. Something sharp dragged down my thigh, and even though I couldn't see the damage, I could tell something was very wrong. Guess this is how it ends for me, I thought.

Candra was less easily convinced. "Do you think you can kill me like this? I have survived…" She paused, clearly searching for the details of the memory. "Once, I was torn to pieces, and then I… I'm not sure how I recovered. But I did."

"I remember," I said softly. "You guided the pieces of your body together psionically." The longer our bodies were pressed together, skin to skin and blood to blood, the more I could feel Candra's power seeping into me. She was all but immortal, I now knew, one of a rare group of mutants called the Externals who had healing powers so remarkable that they were almost indestructible. Only the loss of her memories was keeping Candra off balance so that it was I absorbing her force, and not her draining me dry as she had so many others.

I wondered if there was a chance that we might both survive this.

Then Candra gasped. "Stop it! Get off me. I need to get out of here… get off." I felt the fierce push of her telekinetic power, thrusting me through solid rock and earth, and now I couldn't breathe, but that was OK, because suddenly I didn't need to breathe. I stared down at my buried body, just visible through the cracks in the cement and plaster and earth, and wondered: Was I dead? Was I a ghost? Or was this another aspect of Candra's immense psychic power?

All at once, I felt myself being pulled as if by a magnet, drawn through the cracks of the mansion as it began to fall in on itself. Free from the smoke and the violent tremors shaking the earth around Góngora's home, free from the constraints of flesh and bone, I flew through the clear, chill October night until I saw them.

Mystique, already healed, was carrying Tessa in her arms, while Remy had slung Axel across his shoulders in a fireman's carry. If only I was in my body and could use Candra's power to restore Axel's original features. Then a thought occurred: perhaps a psychic power did not need a physical body. Tentatively, I floated closer and placed my astral hand on his trunklike appendage, willing it to reabsorb. I heard him gasp, and suddenly the trunk began to shrink until it was a regular nose again. Just in time, too, because I could already feel something tugging me back to the building and my broken body.

Irene looked up. She had lost her glasses, and her milky eyes seemed to look right at me. I brushed a kiss against Remy's cheek, and thought I heard him say my name.

But I was not there. I was back under the rubble, along with Candra. Keep a running commentary in your mind, Mystique had told me. I had hung onto myself for as long as I could, but now I had to let go, of words and everything else.

I let go.

THIRTY-FIVE

It took a long time to come back from being nearly dead. At least, it felt like a long time. I drifted in and out of memories, some my own, some Candra's, and a few that probably belonged to Chieko and her friends. When I finally woke up, I found myself in a soft white room with a slanted ceiling and light streaming in through a skylight. I turned my head and saw that Remy was slumped in an upholstered chair by my bed, sound asleep, his mouth slightly open.

"Hey," I said softly.

"Hey!" Remy sat bolt upright, dropping his phone with a clatter. "How are you feeling?"

"Like I've been chewed up and spit out." I looked down at my body, covered by a pale yellow and blue quilt. My hands were a little swollen, and when I touched my face, I winced. "There's something sticky on my face."

"Antibiotic ointment. We weren't sure how much healing ability you had left, so Mystique's been touching you and letting you absorb some of her power." Remy looked somber. "I won't lie – it was touch and go for a while."

"How long have I been out of it?"

Remy hesitated. "A few days."

"How few?" I reached for a glass of water on a side table by my bedside.

Remy picked up his phone, avoiding my eyes. "Ten."

"Ten days?" I swallowed the cool water, taking this in. I looked down at my body under the French blue duvet. "Do I have all my bits and pieces?"

"Every single one." Remy smiled, and I realized why he looked different. There was a scruff of stubble on his chin nearly long enough to be called a beard, and there were shadows under his eyes. He stifled a yawn and rubbed his eyes with the heels of his hands, and I had the sense that if the whites of his eyes hadn't been black, they would have been visibly bloodshot. "Sorry," he said, straightening up.

"Silly," I said, unable to think of anything else. I wondered if he had been keeping watch over me all ten days, but out loud I asked a different question. "What about Candra?"

"She's gone. We didn't find her anywhere in the area when we dug you out, and Irene says there's an ocean between her and us, but she's not sure which one. We think the Toad and Sherwood hared off together, but we got Góngora. He's currently being questioned by your friend, the cop." Before I could form the words, he added, "Everyone else on our side is OK and safe."

I exhaled a breath I hadn't realized I had been holding. I was reaching for my water again when I noticed that someone had placed a little skunk figure on the bedside table right beside the glass. The skunk was wearing a green dress and riding a tiny tricycle. There was also a little fox boy in black felt suspenders. "Who gave me the skunk?"

Remy looked comically upset. "It's a badger! She's part of the badger family."

"Oh, right."

"Because of the streak in your hair."

"No, I get it. She's adorable." I made a show of picking her up and admiring her, and then my sluggish brain finally produced the most pertinent question. "Remy... where are we?"

Remy walked over to a table and brought back a pitcher of water to refill my glass. "Mystique's mansion."

I sat up, alarmed. "Are you sure it's safe?"

Remy sat down on the side of my bed, which dipped under his weight, rolling me toward him. "I think so. I was worried about Jean Luc and the Assassins' Guild, but Mystique assured me I was safe here. I don't think she would lie about that." I registered that the way he phrased that implied that she might lie about other things.

I settled back down, a little self-conscious with Remy so close. Was my breath OK? No, probably not after ten days. I probably could use a shower as well. As if he could read my mind, he stood. "Maybe I should get Mystique now. She'll want to know that you're awake."

"No – wait." Even though I didn't want him to get too close, I also didn't want him to leave yet, for reasons I wasn't ready to examine. I blurted out the first thought that came to my mind. "Has she offered you a place with her?"

He nodded. Then, very slowly, he turned back and walked over to my bed again. Lifting the sheet so it covered my left hand, he put his hand over mine. Through the thin cotton, I could feel his warmth. "I said no. I'm through working for other people, chère."

I felt a stab of loss, then nodded. "So you're leaving?"

His red-on-black eyes gazed down at me. "I've been waiting for you to wake up."

My mouth was dry. "Thanks."

"No – you don't understand. I've been waiting to ask if you want to come with me."

I felt my lungs inflate. For a moment, despite my bruised and aching face and body, I felt giddy and light. Then I remembered Napoleon's officer, his breath sharpened by cognac, the angle of the sun slanting through the window. Not my memory, but my body tingled with the recollected intimacy.

I couldn't go away with Remy. If we were alone together, I was not going to want a sheet between us. And how could I love anyone, touch anyone, when I kept losing myself?

There was a knock on the door. "Hey," said a gentle female voice. "Irene tells me you're awake?" For a moment, blanking, I thought it was Lucretia.

"Come in," I said, looking up at Remy. He gave my hand a squeeze before releasing it and taking a few steps back away from my bed.

"Thought you might be hungry." Mystique walked through the door wearing a simple, tailored white shirt and dark slacks, her red hair was pulled back in a ponytail. She was carrying a tray with a pot of tea, a mug, and a bowl of mixed fruit.

I realized I was starving. "Thank you." I sat up straighter and Remy arranged the pillows behind my back before Mystique set down the tray.

"I want to thank you – for taking on Candra, and risking your own life to do it." She handed me the bowl of berries, and for the first time I noticed the intricate pattern of scales around her temples. It occurred to me that she was the exact opposite of Góngora, who had never wanted to be seen in his true form. "It was incredibly brave of you not to use Candra's teleportation power to save yourself."

I shoved a spoonful of berries in my mouth without thinking. "That wasn't bravery. I didn't know she had that power, so I didn't think to use it. Shoot, I didn't even think about using her telekinesis to protect either one of us." The berries were actually amazing, perfectly cool and tart and sweet, and I quickly ate spoonful. "Just like I didn't think of using Candra's powers to fix Tessa's legs when I had the chance." So many missed opportunities.

"Maybe you didn't think of her as broken."

I glanced up from my berries, startled.

"You're not used to battle. It's incredibly confusing, and only an experienced fighter knows how to keep track of all her options. When you took away Candra's memories, you brought her down to your level. Neither of you could think straight." Mystique leaned forward and touched the side of my face, and I felt the ache of bruising, followed by a tingle as her healing power penetrated. "Yet somehow, you still managed to figure out how to help Axel. You're nothing short of amazing, Rogue."

For a moment, I sat stunned, savoring the rare sweetness of praise. Mystique pulled her arm back, and I had the sense she was forcing herself not to influence me with touch. "I know Remy wants you to travel with him when you're better. I want you to know you have another choice. Everything I offered you as Lucretia is real. Chieko and Sinjin and Fred are on the mend, thanks to you." It took me a moment to recall that these were

Pyro and Blob's real names. "Tessa and Axel are going to join us. And so is Rita."

I put down my spoonful of berries. Was that supposed to be an incentive? I shook my head. "Thanks for the offer, but the truth is, I don't think I'm up for dealing with my power right now."

Mystique glanced at Remy. "So you're going to hit the road with this gambling man?" Her tone was light, but not mocking – Lucretia's voice.

I shook my head, very conscious of Remy's eyes on me. "Once I'm better, I'm going to make my way to New Orleans and find out how to get accepted at Tulane." I hadn't planned on saying it, but it felt like the only possible answer to all this uncertainty. It was my old dream, solid and heavy from all the years of dreaming.

"Good for you," said Remy. "I can't visit you there, you know – that city is off limits for me. But you will like it."

I fought the urge to ask if he would visit me at some other school, if I went there instead. This way, I would have the illusion that he would have come to see me if he could. At any other school, I might waste time thinking about when he might show up, unannounced, to turn my world upside down again.

Mystique picked up the mug of tea and handed it to me. "Here. Drink."

"Thanks." I took a sip, even though I've never really liked tea. "Aren't you going to tell me I'm making a terrible mistake? That I need your help to control my powers, and that a degree in neuroscience is hardly going to help me the way you can?"

"I'm not going to tell you what's best for you. I'm going to say we need you, and Tulane does not."

I glanced up at her, surprised.

"Góngora's not the only slaver, and slavers aren't the only threat we mutants face." She moved closer, until she was sitting on the foot of my bed. "I know you don't have much confidence in yourself right now. And that's not a bad place to begin. You ask me, confidence is for rubes. Faith is for sheep. But hope? That's something we all need."

I looked from Remy to Mystique. Any choice I made was going to be a gamble. In the end, though, I needed to get more comfortable in my own skin before I could risk getting too close to anyone else.

"I'll stay to see if I can help," I said. "But after that, I'm going to Tulane."

Mystique looked unreasonably happy, considering I hadn't actually agreed to join her. "Just what Irene thought you would say."

That evening, since Remy was going to leave in the morning, everyone decided it was his turn to cook. We decided to eat in the big rustic kitchen, under the exposed ceiling beams, at a long, wooden island surrounded by high stools. I had never eaten in there before, and maybe because it stirred no childhood memories it felt like the happiest room in the house. Outside the window, a new moon was visible, curved like a cradle against the dark sky.

"How much longer? I'm starving," said Lin.

"Invalids first," he said, setting my bowl down. "Et voilá, here you go, Lin." He handed her the bowl with a flourish.

"I don't think jambalaya is supposed to be brown," I said, just to tease him before dipping my spoon in.

"Cajun jambalaya is always brown," he said, looking offended. "Wait, why am I serving? If you're not injured, go help yourselves."

The peppery stew was actually very tasty, although I thought it could have used a few tomatoes. "Delicious," I said, and was instantly rewarded by Remy's relieved grin.

Chieko pulled something out of her teeth and inspected it. "Ugh. Are the shrimp still supposed to have shells on?"

Remy shrugged. "My grandmére always cooked it that way."

"Wait a sec," I said. "You never mentioned a grandmother – you're making this up!"

A heated argument about the proper preparation of shrimp broke out, with Tessa saying that shrimp looked too much like bugs for her to eat and Axel revealing that he was a vegan. This led to Axel and Blob and Tessa getting up to fix themselves peanut butter and banana sandwiches, with Axel loudly proclaiming that he would never eat something that swam around in its own urine.

Lloyd, his eyes dancing behind his black eyeglasses, whispered something in Lin's ear, and she turned, nearly poking Axel with her antlers as he sat back down with his sandwich. It was only when I saw her smirk that I understood she had done it on purpose.

I felt a rush of warmth for them all, coupled with the old, familiar sense of being an outsider. What if the real reason I couldn't keep hold of myself was that there was something lacking in me? Across the table, Remy was charming Chieko. It was probably for the best that he was leaving. The only reason he wanted me was because I was, at the end of the day, the most untouchable woman in the world.

Suddenly, I felt someone pinch me under the table.

I turned to Rita, sitting to my left. She appeared to be focused on unscrewing a bottle top, but she only needed two hands for that. "You did that."

"Maybe."

"Don't you know it's rude to read people's minds?"

Rita snorted. "I can't read minds. I can just read faces, and I know what it's like when that one gets his hooks in you. Nah, don't try to deny it. He seems to have a knack for conning all the best women."

I looked at her closely. "Were you and he…?"

Rita gave a dry bark of laughter. "No, that's not the story. Maybe I'll tell you later, if we wind up as friends. What do you say, Rogue Specimen? Want to be friends?" She poured something fizzy into my empty water glass.

I sniffed it. It smelled like cinnamon and ginger and honey, and something else I could not name. "What is it?"

Rita's smile deepened. "A little concoction I make from the hawthorn of three different continents. There's no alcohol in it, but a bit of fermentation makes magick go straight to the head." She raised her glass. "To the sisterhood of misfits and outcasts!"

I hesitated, not sure how I felt about Rita, but Lin, overhearing, had also raised her glass for Rita to fill. "To the sisterhood!"

"Hang on, hang on," said Lloyd. "Come on, everyone. It's a toast."

"I don't do bubbles," said Blob. "Gives me gas. Anyone got some beer?"

"Australian beer," added Pyro.

"I want a serious cocktail," said Tessa. She still had her wings, but she wasn't used to them yet and kept checking to make sure she wasn't knocking anything over. "One with three kinds of muddled herbs, simple syrup and a kumquat."

Axel leaned in, resting his chin on one hand. "I do like your style."

Tessa looked embarrassed but pleased, and I wondered just what had gone on between the two of them while they had been held prisoner alone. She was wearing her hair down, I noticed. It suited her.

"I'd like to remind you all that some of us are still recuperating," said Chieko, who looked like a woman in her early twenties again, except for a few strands of white in her dark hair. "And some of us are underage."

"Spoilsport," said Lin, sticking out her tongue.

"My potion is perfectly suitable for everyone," said Rita, adopting the tone of a TV announcer and gesturing like a spokesmodel with three of her arms. "It has an effervescent mood-lifting spell on it, and leaves absolutely no hangover."

"Stop that this instant," said Mystique, appearing in the doorway. She was wearing a white sweater that flattered her indigo skin, and white trousers. "Is this supposed to be a celebration?"

We all deflated a bit at this rebuke. Maybe she didn't think we deserved to celebrate, since we had let all our opponents get away.

"You are all – each and every one of you…" Mystique paused a beat, her expression still stern, but her topaz eyes twinkling. "…extremely peculiar…"

A general whoop of laughter greeted this.

"… and astonishingly gifted." Mystique looked at each of us in turn, her eyes shining, and suddenly the mood shifted.

All conversation ceased and all eyes turned to follow the blue-skinned redhead as she walked around the table. "So many people in this world will want to use you for what you can do. They'll say our powers make us dangerous. They'll call us unnatural. They'll call us abominations."

Rita muttered something under her breath.

"They will say that we need to be controlled. You know what I say?" A smile broke out on her face. "Let's make them think twice about messing with us. So let's do this right!" She turned to Irene, who was wearing the same sweater as Mystique, only in a soft shade of pink. Irene was carrying a tray filled with exquisite blue glass goblets. She walked around the table, placing one in front of each of us. When she reached Rita, she poured the contents of Rita's water glass into the goblet. I copied her.

"Excellent," said Mystique. "I was going to use shot glasses, but Irene saw that the goblets would be required, thanks to you, Rita." Before anyone could say anything, she turned to Irene. "The elixir, please." Irene handed her a small vial filled with a palely glowing liquid.

Rita's eyes widened. "Is that what I think it is?"

Mystique's smile was a little smug. "You can call it a parting gift from Candra. I'm saving most of it for an emergency, but I think we can all use a little infusion." She walked around the table until she was standing in front of Rita. "May I?" Rita nodded, her expression softer and younger looking without its usual veneer of cynicism. She had been waiting for this for a long time, I realized. Mystique tipped the vial and a single shimmering drop of the elixir landed in Rita's goblet, mixing with the hawthorn potion. As I watched, the concoction bubbled and sparkled like miniature fireworks.

Rita looked up at Mystique, her eyes shining with unshed tears. "You're sharing the elixir... with all of us?"

"I am. Since this is the birth of the Brotherhood of Mutants, I can't think of a better occasion."

For a moment, I was taken aback. I looked at all the faces around the table, and saw that everyone else seemed to be on board. There was a burble of happy voices as Mystique poured champagne for those who were imbibing. Tessa and Axel were holding up their glasses, and so were Chieko and Pyro. Remy was looking at me, his eyes asking a question I wasn't sure I knew how to answer, and Rita and Blob were thumb-wrestling. Wait, I was wrong – Lin was frowning.

"I object to the term 'brotherhood,'" she said. "It's not even accurate. I mean, look at us. We're hardly a bunch of bros."

"Speak for yourself," said Blob, forgetting that he was still wrestling Rita. Rita immediately pinned his thumb with hers.

"Lin makes a valid point," said Lloyd, in full teacher mode. "How would everyone feel about a Fellowship of Mutants?" A lively argument broke out, with Lloyd's second head acting as the most vocal objector. Was I the only one uncomfortable with pledging loyalty to a leader and a group? I thought about my mother, who had lived in this very house for a time, following a man who claimed to know the path to enlightenment. She had been as mistaken as Aunt Carrie, who had curdled my childhood with her brand of godliness, convinced she was on the side of the angels. According to her view of the world, I was breaking bread with sinners, and yet it felt like I had come home at last. Maybe it was because sinners were allowed to have doubts, and doubts were your last, best defense against getting swept up in someone else's crazy.

I felt something nudge me under the table. Down by my feet, I saw that the dog Rowan was hiding out, clearly hoping for handouts. His tail thumped twice, and he looked up at me, as if eagerly awaiting my decision.

"Rogue?" Mystique had circled the table, saving me for last, and when her eyes met mine I flashed back to the moment in her office, when she had been glamoured as Lucretia Borger. There had been a sense of drinking in celebration then, too, but this felt different – weightier, somehow, more freighted with value, more loaded with complication and risk. This time, I understood what she was offering, with all its ramifications. If I chose to remain here, there would be more dangerous folks like Candra and Góngora in my future.

Heck, what was I playing at here? I had already made up my mind. Standing up, I held out my glass to be filled.

ACKNOWLEDGMENTS

I have been writing books for quite some time now, and some are more challenging than others. I've been longing to write Rogue since I started reading the X-Men in college, but the writing of this book was complicated by the fact that I started work just as the pandemic spring arrived, along with my elderly mother and a host of new caretaking responsibilities.

I owe a great debt of gratitude to my family – Mark, Matthew and Elinor – for helping me so that I could continue writing. In hours of greatest need, Jeremy Fulton, Deborah Coconis and Carol Goodman arrived like masked heroes. At times, my house offered no quiet space for focus, and with no cafes or libraries or writing shared spaces available, I could not have functioned if Nina Fine had not allowed me to use her studio apartment, and Sequoia Neiro had not offered her former massage therapist studio.

As restrictions lifted somewhat, I came to rely on the help of home health care aides Nana Dona and Lili Graves. Anne

Elizabeth and Al Davison inspired me to include a character who uses a wheelchair (and is not Professor X). The Story Whisperers, my writing group, cheered me up and cheered me on when I needed it most. Through it all, my fabulous editor, Charlotte Llewelyn-Wells, was patient, encouraging, and remarkably calm, and the witty, intensely knowledgeable writer Josh Unruh filled in the gaps in my Marvel knowledge. Thank you all.

ABOUT THE AUTHOR

ALISA KWITNEY was an editor at DC Comics/Vertigo and is the Eisner-nominated author of a variety of graphic novels, romantic women's fiction and urban fantasy for adults and teens. She was one of the authors of *A Flight of Angels*, which made YALSA's Top Ten List for Great Graphic Novels for Teens, and the YA graphic novel *Token*, named a highlight of the Minx imprint by PW. Alisa has an MFA from Columbia University, and lives in upstate New York.

alisakwitney.com
twitter.com/akwitney

MARVEL

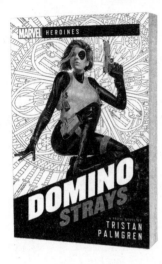

Sharp-witted, luck-wrangling mercenary Domino takes on both a dangerous cult and her own dark past, in this fast-paced and explosive adventure.

Smart-mouthed monster hunter extraordinaire, Elsa Bloodstone isn't easily fazed, but a shocking family revelation sends her down a bloody and action-soaked path.

MARVEL

Two exceptional mutants face their ultimate test and the X-Men's worst enemies when they answer a call for help, in the first thrilling Xavier's Institute novel.

Marvel's X-Men heroes return when a remarkable student rushes to save his family from anti-mutant extremists, but ends up in a whole heap of trouble...

MARVEL

Asgard's mightiest warriors defend the Ten Realms.

MARVEL LEGENDS OF ASGARD

The **HEAD** of **MIMIR**

A PROSE NOVEL BY

RICHARD LEE BYERS

MARVEL LEGENDS OF ASGARD

The **SWORD** of **SURTUR**

A PROSE NOVEL BY

C. L. WERNER

Untold tales of Marvel's greatest heroes & villains.

MARVEL UNTOLD

DOCTOR DOOM IN:

THE HARROWING OF DOOM

A PROSE NOVEL BY **DAVID ANNANDALE**

MARVEL UNTOLD

THE DARK AVENGERS IN:

THE PATRIOT LIST

A PROSE NOVEL BY **DAVID GUYMER**

WORLD EXPANDING FICTION